Agent Devlin Brady didn't move a muscle.

He just stared right at me, his face etched in stone, his eyes penetrating. The man scared me and, unreasonably, that made me feel better. This was a hard man. And a man like this could keep me safe—even if my role in the game was to try to protect *him*.

"Talk to me, Crane," he said. "I need to know what you're doing here."

There was no denying the sharp edge of anger in his voice, and I cringed. "I got a message," I said. "About Play.Survive.Win. I'm . . . I guess I'm playing now." I licked my lips. "And I guess you are, too."

His face never softened, but I saw a flicker of something cross his eyes. Then he shoved his hands into his pockets as he moved out of the foyer and into the living room. Not knowing what else to do, I followed, silently congratulating myself on only looking back toward the door once. There was no place to run, after all. For an hour now I'd been telling myself that this apartment was safety. Now that I was here, I was clinging to that, and nothing was going to make me change my mind.

Not even Devlin Brady.

The Manolo Matrix is also available as an eBook

THE *Manolo* MATRIX

JULIE KENNER

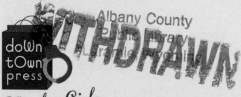

downtown press

Naughty Girls

New York   London   Toronto   Sydney

An *Original* Publication of POCKET BOOKS

 DOWNTOWN PRESS, published by Pocket Books
1230 Avenue of the Americas
New York, NY 10020

Library of Congress Cataloging-in-Publication Data is available

ISBN-13: 978-0-7434-9614-8
ISBN-10:   0-7434-9614-0

First Downtown Press trade paperback edition February 2006

10 9 8 7 6 5 4 3 2 1

DOWNTOWN PRESS and colophon are registered trademarks of Simon & Schuster, Inc.

Manufactured in the United States of America

For information regarding special discounts for bulk purchases, please contact Simon & Schuster Special Sales at 1-800-456-6798 or business@simonandschuster.com

This book is dedicated to Betsy Cornwell and the LBJ Drama Club back in the early '80s, especially the techies and the folks who shied away from the cafeteria to eat lunch in the drama room. I probably would have discovered Broadway musicals on my own, but it wouldn't have been half as much fun!

acknowledgments

Huge thanks are due to the many folks who helped with this book: Hugh Barnett, theater manager, the Broadhurst Theater in New York; Reagan Fletcher, archivist, the Shubert Archives; Special Agent Rene Salines with the FBI; Cornelius Patrick Byrne, owner of Central Park Carriages (and thanks as well to Clancy and Sean); and, especially, the Internet, particularly the totally cool Internet Broadway Database.

1

JENNIFER

Jennifer Crane. That's it. That's my name. Ever heard of me?

I'm guessing not, which, frankly, sums up my entire problem with my life as it currently stands: I'm not famous. And, as far as I can tell, the fame fairy isn't going to be anointing me any time soon.

Sucks, doesn't it?

And what really reeks is that I'm *good*. I've got a voice on me that rivals Julie Andrew's (and that's before she had throat surgery).

Actually, you know what? I take that back. I'm pretty sure it's a grievous sin to compare yourself to Julie Andrews, who is, in my opinion, a goddess of stage and screen. The woman has some serious pipes. But, honestly, I could give Patti LuPone, Joanna Gleason, or Betty Buckley a run for their money any old day.

Which begs the question of why I was currently earning a living (such that it was) as a singing waitress instead of opening on Broadway.

Obviously, the right part hasn't come along. Or agent. Or director. Or producer.

I don't think it's me. Really I don't.

The thing is, I could be wrong. I try not to think about that, though. Someone once said that success is ninety-eight percent attitude, and I'm definitely staying optimistic. (And never mind that the someone who said that was me. It's perfectly sound wisdom and, frankly, I trust myself more than I trust anyone else.)

All of which is little more than a backdrop to the reason why I ended up singing Gloria Gaynor's "I Will Survive" despite the fact that I am not a gay male and hadn't even rehearsed the thing.

It was all Brian's fault.

He's a self-proclaimed screaming tenor, has slept with more producers than I've auditioned for, and is one of my absolute best friends. We worked together at Ellen's Stardust Diner for almost two years, until last week when he was hired to replace an actor who'd tripped down the subway stairs and busted his femur all to hell. No kidding. It was like something out of *All About Eve,* except that Brian hadn't even been an understudy. Apparently he'd auditioned for the show early on, did reasonably well, and the producer remembered him. The other actor's broken leg was, literally, Brian's big break. And he landed himself a minor, but important, role, the bastard. Not that I'm bitter or anything, but talk about luck.

At any rate, the show is called *Puck's Dream,* it's a new musical loosely based on *A Midsummer Night's Dream*. Lots of production numbers, lots of effects. Brian's even featured in two scenes, and in one he actually gets to fly across the stage. From what he tells me, it's pretty cool, and I'm trying very hard, albeit somewhat unsuccessfully, not to be jealous.

The production was scheduled to premiere at the Belasco Theater in about a week, and Brian's cousin Felix—aka Fifi for reasons I'm not even going to bother going into—had come in from Los Angeles to help Bri celebrate. Naturally, Brian brought Fifi to the diner. And, just as naturally, he was giving me a hard time. (Brian, that is. Not his cousin.)

"Sweetie," Brian said, squeezing in beside the condiments, "you're positively maudlin. You need some serious cheer. After work. Drinks. And I won't take no for an answer."

"Are you concerned about me? Or are you just trying to make sure you're not alone with Fifi?"

"Well, he is a little high maintenance, but you know I love him. And don't change the subject, anyway."

I made a face. "You're not even supposed to be back here anymore."

"I go where I'm needed," he said. "And I'm definitely needed here. Look at you! You're going to bring down the crowd if you go out there like that. What are you planning on singing, anyway? 'Memory'?"

I scowled because he'd totally pegged me. "Maybe," I said. I couldn't help it. I *was* morose. I'd auditioned that morning for an off-Broadway revival of *Carousel,* a show I know inside and out, and absolutely love, but I swear I might as well have stood on that stage and farted for all the good my rehearsing did me. I couldn't even see the producer or the director past the stage lights. All I heard was a cough and then a curt, "Thank you. We'll be in touch." And then the stage manager was ushering me off the stage.

Granted, that's often par for the course in the world of open call auditions, but I'd really expected the director to leap to his feet, race to the stage, and sign me on the spot. Or, if not that, then I'd at least expected a good vibe. As it was, I got zilch. No vibe, no job, no nothing.

"Attitude," Brian said, tossing my philosophy back in my face. "Remember?" He pointed toward the main part of the restaurant, where rows of booths were filled with people eating mostly bad-for-you food that really is delicious (I gained ten pounds my first month, then put myself on a strict diet that I've mostly stuck to ever since). Leslie Danziger was strutting her stuff on the railing that ran between two sets of booths. Her microphone was close enough to swallow, her blond wig was slightly askew, and she was belting out "Girls Just Want to Have Fun." She was clearly having a great time. Obviously, *she* hadn't had a crap audition just a few hours before.

"I'm switching you," Brian said. "Michael's on after Leslie. And you, my dear, are taking his place."

"The hell I am." I turned behind me and found Michael, who I like a lot, but who also happens to be a huge wimp with an equally huge crush on Brian. He just shrugged and blew me a kiss. I knew I was sunk. Done in by two gay men with an agenda.

"Attitude, sweetie. Do you want to be consigned to failure? Do you want to sit and mope? Do you want to let your depression fester inside you and give you ulcers and cold sores? One is not fun and the other is *such* a bad look for you."

As a matter of fact, I did want to sulk, but I knew better than to argue with Brian. "Fine. Fine. What is Michael—what am *I*—singing?"

"'I Will Survive.'"

"I don't think so."

"Sweetie, trust me. You need an attitude adjustment."

I *did* need an attitude adjustment, but I wasn't in the habit of utilizing gay male power anthems to make them. Call me crazy, but my best attitude adjustments come when I'm shopping.

Brian, however, was deaf to my protests. He shoved the microphone into my hand, pressed his palm against my back, signaled to Damien (who runs the sound equipment), and pushed.

Suddenly all eyes in the room were on me, and I could either belt out the tune or stand there looking like an idiot. Since I don't do idiot well, I sang.

And you know what? I *did* feel better. Not at first, mind you. At first, I just felt pissed off. At Brian.

But then the words infiltrated my brain. Like Gloria Gaynor, I was strong. I could get along. And, dammit, I was a survivor. Maybe *Carousel* didn't want me, but someone would. I'd find an agent. I'd hit the streets. I'd blow away every producer from 41st to 53rd. And by this time next year, *my* name would splashed across *Playbill,* and the crowds would be lining up around the block, just like they did for *Spamalot.* (Hey, a girl can dream.)

In the end, I nailed that tune. I strutted my stuff, flirted with the men, bonded with the women, and threw a final kiss to Fifi. And when the song was over, I turned on my heel, tossed the microphone to Damien, then launched myself at

Brian. He spun me around, my poodle skirt flaring in a way that probably lacked a certain level of modesty.

"Better?"

"Totally," I admitted. I crushed my palms against his cheeks and planted a huge kiss right on his mouth. "You're a better mood enhancer than Xanax."

So what if I'd flubbed an audition? There would be others. It wasn't as if I was dead. The sun would come out tomorrow. I was going to put on a happy face. Nothing was gonna get me down. And a bucket full of other sunshiney clichés.

Bottom line? I was coming out of this a winner.

And nothing—not bad agents or tasteless producers or even rude customers—was going to change that.

Chapter

2

BIRDIE

"Hey, babe. You look thirsty. Can I buy you a drink?" The man sidles closer, the smell of bourbon on his breath and the fire of lust in his eyes. I smile and preen, the skills that had faded during my long years in prison returning swiftly. Just like riding a bicycle, I think, my confidence increasing as his gaze roams over my body, taking in my long legs, bare under my short skirt. Since the three-inch heels of my newly acquired Jimmy Choo sandals shape my calves and raise my ass, I know he likes what he sees. His inspection continues, honing in on my nipples, hard under the soft silk of my Joie tank top. My panties dampen and I squirm a little in surprise. Years ago, this man would have bored me. He, with his blatant lust and unoriginal approach.

My body's reaction is testament to my need. Five years without a man. Five long years in which I'd gotten myself off to fantasies of freedom, not of a cock.

Freedom. I used to reach for it through steel bars only to have it escape from my grip, a slight brush of air against my fingertips the only hint that there was, in fact, a freedom to find. And now here I am. Destiny achieved.

I crook my finger and urge the man in closer. He comes quickly, like an eager puppy, and I press my mouth to his, my hand sliding down to cup his cock and his balls. I squeeze, not too hard, but not gentle either. I nip at his lower lip with my teeth. He makes a low sound in his throat, pain mixed with pleasure, and I know I can have him if I want him.

I do. But at the same time, I don't. As the saying goes, there are many fish in the sea, and the one I catch tonight is the one I intend to fry. "Go," I say. "You don't want to fuck with fire."

He pulls back, the lust in his eyes now cool. I wait a beat, another, then mouth the word again: "Go."

He leaves, his tail between his legs and his dick limp. I've ruined him for the evening, and for that, at least, I feel a tug of proprietary pleasure. I may not have fucked him, but tonight he's still mine.

Other members of the happy hour cattle call surge around me. The men stare, they lean in, they try to make eye contact. I grant them each a smile. Even after living in a goddamn box, I've still got it going on. And now, in the clothes I was born to wear, a drink in my hand and my hair freshly cut, I know I'm hot. More, I know I'm going to get laid tonight. I just have to find the man I'm looking for.

As I survey the room, I notice the women. They're watching me, their heads bent together, something in their eyes that I assume is jealousy. What else could it be? Certainly, I'm worthy of their envy. But as I watch, I wonder. One of them whispers and the other snickers. One of them sits up straighter, thrusts her breasts out, then does a little shimmy motion. Are they talking about me? I don't know, but something tells me they are. Fucking bitches. Fucking whores.

I wonder if they'd be so cavalier if they knew who I am? Probably.

If I've learned one thing throughout my professional life, it's that people are stupid. They believe what they want to believe, ignoring what's right in front of them if it doesn't fit neatly into their imagined little world.

Like me, for example.

"You look like a lady with a lot on her mind."

I turn and look at the stockbroker face that's talking to me, and I wonder if this man has ever had an interesting thought in his life. Has he ever had a moment of excitement, ever felt a pure sensual rush?

Has he, for example, ever felt the thrill of the kill?

His eyes widen, and I'm sure he has read my thoughts. I smile coldly, and he turns, then pushes through the crowd to get as far away from me as possible.

I watch him go, using the moment to scan the crowd, looking for my quarry. No luck, but it's early yet, and the profile I have indicates that he comes later, after the men and women looking to hook up have left. He comes to forget, it says, and I have to wonder if he's forgotten me.

I smile a little at the thought, because the truth is we've never met, he and I. But he knew me, so many years ago. Knew my name, knew about my jobs, my network. Even though he'd never once laid eyes on me, he knew enough to help bring me down.

I hate him for that. I'll hate him until the day he dies. A day that, thanks to a twist of fate and an unknown benefactor, promises to be sooner rather than later.

"Another round?" The bartender stops in front of me, his eye on my now-empty martini glass.

I shake my head. "Water." I need to stay sharp. Clear.

As the bartender fills a wine glass with sparkling water, I place my handbag on the bar. It holds four things: my gun, my lipstick, a large syringe, and a neatly folded computer printout. It's the paper I'm interested in right now.

Of all my possessions, it is the only one that matters to me, for this piece of paper holds the key to my rebirth. Only a week ago, I had no prospects upon my release. No plans other than to reenter my profession and hope that the authorities didn't again track me down. This time around, though, the odds would not be in my favor. I'd already been caught once. I was in the system. I was damaged goods.

Which meant that my client list would be significantly shorter. More important, the eye of the law would be on me for any crime with a similar m.o. A serious detriment to my ability to earn a living, and I'd spent many hours pondering the conundrum.

And then I received the email. As a model prisoner only days away from parole, I'd been blessed with certain perks, including access to the Internet. Of course, certain websites were off-limits, and I had no formal email account, but all those things were only minor inconveniences. Not true obstacles.

By the time the gates opened and I was free to step out onto the street wearing my thrift store jeans and shirt, clutching my shopping bag full of possessions, I had been contacted, had responded, and knew the game that was in play.

A game that would allow me to shine. And would pay me handsomely for doing something I so very much love to do.

I sniff a little, suddenly overwhelmed by the nostalgia. This will be my last job. After my mission is achieved, I'll be relocating to Switzerland. Not permanently, you understand. Just until I arrange for a waterfront cabana on a remote island. A staff of three, I think. A cook. A housekeeper. And a well-oiled and buff cabana boy to keep me . . . limber.

I smooth the paper and scan the information that I've already committed to memory: Information about the other players in this wonderful little game. I look around again and—suddenly—there he is. Unshaven, rumpled, but with a feral look in his eyes. A man come to drown his sorrows. He's come for the bourbon, but I intend to convince him to try another remedy—the low, hot pulse of a woman.

I slide off my stool and grab my glass. And then I move across the room, every movement an invitation.

He sees me, and his eyes flash with a heat born of alcohol and lust. I smile, and I know it's a done deal. First a fuck. And then, later, death.

That's the point of the game, after all.

Winner take all. And I don't intend to lose.

Chapter

3

JENNIFER

I spent Sunday afternoon sitting in Starbucks reading the *Times,* the *Post,* and *Backstage* while I sipped a venti mocha and munched on a blueberry scone. I'm tall, a size six or eight depending on the designer, and I maintain my relatively thin thighs and reasonably tight ass through deprivation coupled with binging.

Here's my rule: I go the entire week on salads and fruit, with a can of tuna (packed in spring water, of course) to give me a little protein. My standard drink is water or black coffee, with one grande skim latte tossed into the mix every morning. Just for the calcium, you understand. Alcohol I don't worry about (though I should), and if I do binge with a friend or on a date, then a day or two of nothing but Diet Coke, rice cakes, and sugar-free gum puts me back in full diet equilibrium.

With a routine like that, is it any wonder that on Sundays, I go a little wild? A pastry at Starbies and a mocha. With *whole* milk. It's just decadent enough to hold me over for an entire week. And I like my system a hell of a lot better than Atkins or Weight Watchers or whatever fad is currently in fashion. My way is tried and true; it's kept me thin since high school. It may be boring, but it works. And I'm not inclined to meddle with success. Not entirely true, actually. I used to be a size *four.* But that was back during my pack-a-day years. And while my size four jeans still hang in the back of my closet for nostalgia's sake, I don't expect to ever return to those heady days. The ciggies may have kept me thin, but they also did a number on my voice. Plus, there's that whole cancer thing to worry about.

At any rate, the scones at Starbies are one of my guilty pleasures, and I look forward to my two hours of heaven every Sunday. (Since I don't bother with the international or financial sections, about two hours is all it takes to plow through my various bits of reading material.)

I'd awakened at my usual time, showered, and arrived at Starbucks shortly before noon. By two I was heading back home, which these days is a tiny studio apartment in midtown Manhattan, walking distance to both my job and the theater district.

My new studio is way smaller than my old place, but what it lacks in square footage it makes up with fresh paint, new carpet, and plumbing that actually transports water in the appropriate direction. It also has decent security—a keyed entrance to the foyer and then another keyed entrance from the foyer to the stairs. Not as ka-ching as having a doorman, but still pretty safe. After what happened to my roommate last year, I'm all about safety.

Which explains why I totally freaked when I stepped onto the sixth-floor landing and saw that my door was cracked open.

Now, I am *not* one of those idiot girls in horror films who hears the scary noise in the creepy house and decides to run toward it while everyone in the audience is yelling "No! No! Go back! Go back! He's in there with an ax!!"

So instead of taking a step forward, I spun around and headed back down to the lobby to calmly and rationally dial 911. *After* the cops were on the way I'd have my little paranoid breakdown, thank you very much. Until then, I was playing the role of the coolheaded diva. Totally calm. Totally in charge of my surroundings.

I use an oversized Marc Jacobs tote bag (a gift from the parental units) in lieu of a purse, since I'm always schlepping scripts, paperbacks, and flat-heeled shoes (Manhattan is hell on your feet). I adore the soft leather and classic lines of the bag, but I hate the way my stuff just falls to the bottom. And now, as I trotted down the stairs toward the lobby, I pawed through the detritus, trying to find my phone. My fingers found it about the time I hit the second-floor landing, and I whipped it out triumphantly, unlocked the keypad, and started to dial.

I'd hit the 9 and the 1 and then the phone rang. I stared at it, totally befuddled. I swear, it took me a full minute to realize I had an incoming call. Not the brightest of moments, but there you go.

Since I have no clue how to work my phone, I didn't know how to get rid of the call so that I could finish dialing the cops. So I answered. It wasn't like a masked gunman was barreling down on me. In fact, I fully anticipated that the police would find no one in my apartment. They'd also find no stereo, no laptop, no television, no cash. Oh, wait. I didn't have any cash in the first place . . .

"I can't talk," I snapped. "I need to call—"

"Jenn! Where the hell did you go?"

"Mel?" Now, Melanie Prescott is my best friend and former roommate, and I'm thrilled to talk to her pretty much any time. But not now. Especially when she was talking nonsense.

I pushed through the final door, emerging near the mail-boxes. "Listen, I gotta call you back. I think someone broke into my apartment. I need to—"

"*I'm* in your apartment."

I stood stupidly for a moment as her words oozed along my cognitive paths.

"Jenn? Did you hear me?"

One synapse fired. "What do you mean, you're in my apartment?"

"It's not a difficult concept. I was watching the street from the window and saw you coming. I'm making appletinis for us, so I opened the door for you and went back to the kitchen. But now I'm drinking an appletini all by myself. Which totally begs the question of where the hell are you?"

"Oh." I felt a little bit foolish. I cast about for an excuse, then noticed Terrence Underhill from 5B coming in through the front door. "I, um, bumped into a neighbor. We started chatting. You know."

"Cute?"

I gave Mr. Underhill's octogenarian frame a once-over. "Oh, yeah. A real hottie. Definitely worthy of lobby flirtation."

"In that case, I forgive you and I won't drink your 'tini. But get up here, already."

"On my way."

I slunk back upstairs feeling like an idiot for totally overreacting. By the time I reached the sixth floor, however, I'd completely changed my attitude. What could Mel have possibly been thinking? This is *New York*. A kindler and gentler New York, perhaps, but I've watched enough *Law & Order* episodes to know that we're not safe even in these post-Giuliani kick-a-little-criminal-butt days.

By the time I got inside the apartment, I was in a full-blown snit. "What the heck were you doing leaving the door open like that? I was just about to dial 911. Did you *want* to spend the afternoon with the cops?"

Mel pressed a drink into my hand. Since I know her well, I could tell she was trying really hard not to laugh.

"What?" I demanded.

"I thought you got held up in the lobby."

"I did. I—oh," I finished lamely. So much for my career as a professional liar. "It's your fault, you know. I come home to an open apartment, and what am I supposed to think?"

"I'm sorry I scared you."

"It's my own fault for giving you a key. Why didn't you call and let me know you were coming?"

"I wanted to surprise you."

"It worked," I said dryly. "My pulse is still pounding triple time." Not entirely true, but I like being in the limelight. It's a curse.

She nodded at the drink. "Go ahead. You'll feel better."

I scowled at the translucent green drink, then took a sip. Okay. She was right. I did feel better. "Have you got more of these?"

"I filled your martini pitcher."

Back during the days when women stayed home and greeted their men at the door with a cocktail (like Samantha in *Bewitched,* though why Darrin bothered to hold down a job, I'll never know), my mom and dad bought a fabulously sleek glass martini pitcher. Tall and skinny, with a long glass stick for stirring, the thing managed to survive not only me and my siblings' rampages through the living room of our youth, but it also survived a trip to New York (albeit well-packed in bubble wrap and Styrofoam peanuts). That was my mom's idea. "You're moving to Manhattan, sweetheart," she'd said. "I've seen *Sex and the City.* You *need* the pitcher." My mom is very cool.

Which has nothing to with anything, really. But the fact that Mel had filled the entire pitcher (which holds about eight drinks total) told me that she was serious about getting shitfaced. I put my diet on hold, mentally planned to eat nothing but water and aspirin tomorrow, and finished my drink.

"So why are you here?" I asked, then immediately got worried. "You and Matthew aren't—?"

"Stryker's great," she assured me, referring to her live-in boyfriend, Matthew Stryker. I think it's more than a little bizarre that she calls him by his last name, but Mel says she can't break the habit. Me, I think I'd try a little harder. "*We're* great," she added, a hint of self-satisfaction coloring her voice.

"Yeah?" I glanced at her left hand, then found myself gaping at the solitaire that winked at me, sparkling brilliantly even in my apartment's crappy lighting.

Mel saw me looking and held her hand out proudly. "He picked it out himself. Awesome, isn't it?"

"It's fabulous." I realized I was standing there like some

slackjawed yokel, so I threw my arms around her and gave her a hug, managing to spill her drink in the process. She laughed, we both filled our glasses again, then toasted ourselves, Matthew, men, sex, and alcohol. In that order.

"How'd he do it?"

"The traditional way," she said, her cheeks flushing pink. "Dinner. Flowers. Down on one knee."

Mel is a really pretty woman, but she's also a geek (and I say that in the most loving way possible). Seriously, the woman has a computer for a brain. And although she's got as much fashion sense (or more) as I do, she's always approached life from a purely analytical perspective. So to now see her blushing—*blushing*—about this guy was not only disconcerting, it was absolutely thrilling.

"This is so cool!" I said with genuine enthusiasm. "And your job. You still love your your job, don't you?"

"Totally." Mel now works for the NSA—the National Security Agency for idiots like me who originally thought it was a new television network—doing something. I'm not entirely sure what, but I know it has to do with codes and spy-type stuff. Very hush hush. Very John le Carré. And very, very Mel.

I gave her a quick hug. "I'm proud of you. Everything you wanted, you're totally getting."

"Thanks." Her eyes darkened. "Sometimes I think about the price, though . . ."

I shuddered, then nodded sympathetically. The thing is, Mel probably would never have met Matthew, never gotten the job at the NSA, never have gotten her life off the fast-track to Dullsville, if the unthinkable hadn't happened. Honestly, I still can't get my head around the freak show that was her life last summer. I'd been visiting my sister and my new niece, and I'd returned to find that my roommate had been at the center of some maniac's scheme to kill her.

She'd survived (well, obviously), and she'd even profited—not only had she gotten Matthew out of the deal, but her bank account had been nicely enriched as a result. But the cost had been high.

"*Are* you doing okay?"

She nodded, and I saw a shadow cross her face before she chased it off with a smile. "I'm doing great. And I'm not here to talk about last year or my personal life or anything else. I'm here to visit you."

"You came all the way up to New York to visit me?"

"Actually, I came all the way up here to go to a conference and meet with a colleague."

"NSA stuff?"

Mel shook her head. "No. This one is off the clock." She avoided my eyes and displayed a rampant fascination with the signed poster from *The Producers* I have hanging over my sofa.

"PSW," I said, making it a statement, not a question. PSW is shorthand for Play.Survive.Win, an incredibly popular online game that Mel had played for a while. The game was also the centerpiece of the nightmare that had been Mel's life—and near death—last summer. And because I'm cast as the overprotective best friend, it bothers me more than a little that, now that she's safe and the horror is over, Mel can't seem to just let it go.

PSW (the real game, not the freak show Mel got stuck in) takes place in an elaborate cyberworld with three players: a target, an assassin, and a protector. The players—and there can be an infinite number of games going on at any one time—run around an online version of Manhattan, with the target solving a series of clues. Pretty basic stuff, except that the clues are specifically generated for each target based on the profile that player submitted when he'd first signed up to play the game. So a player who was a nuclear physicist would have a totally different set of clues than a player who was a biker dude. Pretty cool stuff. And I'm not the only one who thinks so. Basically, once PSW went live, everything else out there in the online gaming world looked like sloppy seconds.

The way the game works is that as the target interprets each clue, he gets that much closer to the final prize. All well and good, except that while the target's busy solving clues, the assassin is busy hunting the target. And the protector's job is to stand up for the target.

The nature of the clues got PSW noticed, but it was the final prize that really put PSW on the map. Real cash money for the winner, whether that was the assassin or the target. So much money that a lot of folks who would never have played an online game signed up to take a shot. I even tried to play once, but got killed right off. I gave it up then, prize or no prize. I'm not big on computer games, much preferring the real-life drama of a shoe sale over a cyber-fight. But even with my limited experience, I could see why the game was so popular. And the inventor—a geek named Archibald Grimaldi—soon found himself up there in the financial stratosphere, along with Bill Gates and Donald Trump and all those other financial guru guys.

Unfortunately for Grimaldi, he's not around to spend his money. He died a while back, but his game lives on. It's still hugely popular. So popular, apparently, that some psycho decided to mimic it in the real world, sending my best friend racing for her life.

Just thinking about it made me antsy, so I got up and topped off my martini. I realized Mel had kept quiet, and I debated whether I should press my point. It wasn't a long debate; I have a tendency to say whatever's on my mind. "I'm right, aren't I? You came up here because you're still trying to figure out who's behind the whole thing."

"It was an online gamers convention. I thought I might—"

"—find someone else who got sucked into your version of the game?"

"Trust me," she said with a definite edge to her voice, "it wasn't *my* version of anything."

I nodded, immediately guilty for sounding heartless. Chalk it up to the vodka and schnapps. "So, how did it go?" I asked, hesitating just a little over my words.

She glanced sideways at me. "You really want to know?"

Had she nailed me, or what? "It's just that I think you're wasting your time and your money. Have you found even one other person who's gotten sucked into a real-life version of the game?" I didn't think she had. "You've got a great job. A great boyfriend. Maybe it's time you let it go. You won the game. It's over."

She met my eyes dead-on, and I could tell right off that I wasn't going to like what she had to say.

"We did find another one. The colleague I said I came up here to meet? He's been helping us for about three months now."

"Shit. Really?"

"Andrew Garrison," Mel said. "He's got a loft over in

Tribeca. Nice guy. Got sucked into the game as a protector."

"His target?"

"Dead."

I licked my lips.

"Andy took a bullet for him—went right through his abdomen, too. Andy was lucky. The target wasn't. The second bullet nailed him."

"How'd this guy find you?"

"One of the feelers we put out. We sent the information to the FBI, but the trail's gone cold again."

"Shit." I was repeating myself, but my brain wasn't clear enough to find vocabulary words, and *shit* summed up the situation nicely. "So he's working with you now?"

"Pretty much," she said. "He's a freelance programmer, so his schedule is pretty flexible. When he's got a big chunk of time, he comes down to D.C. and stays in my guesthouse." Mel bought a *huge* place in Maryland after she took the job at the NSA. It's got a house, a pool, a guesthouse, and an office. The office is where she obsesses about PSW.

"So is he much help?" I asked, trying to sound interested.

"Yeah, I think so. We haven't uncovered much, but he's got a good head and he's good with computers."

"A geek."

"Not totally. He can carry on a conversation, he's cute, and he always starts coffee in the morning." She cocked her head. "Actually, you should give him a call. He's nice. You'd like him."

That point was debatable, but she was already scribbling his number on the back of her business card. She handed it to me, and I tried to look grateful. Ever since Mel hooked up with Matthew, she's been trying to fix me up, too. Not that I couldn't use the help, but Andy the Geek didn't sound like my type.

I took the card, though, then put it on my coffee table. "I'm sorry somebody else got sucked into the game, but I guess it's good he found you."

"That's my point. If Andy found us, others will, too. Enough information from enough sources, and we can shut this game down."

I nodded. I couldn't argue with her. And, honestly, I didn't want to. I hated that she was still living the nightmare every day, but I understood why. "So was the conference any help?"

"Who knows? I go to these things, put the word out. We'll see if something comes up." She got up, paced the length of the apartment. "But I'm off the clock now. The conference ended a couple of hours ago, and I'm catching the last shuttle back to D.C. In the meantime, I'm all yours. And I promise I didn't come here to talk about this stuff. I have another agenda entirely."

"Excellent." I moved to the kitchen and got a 'tini refill. "So what do you want to do? Get drunk and talk about men?"

"Appealing, but no." She snatched up her purse from the coffee table, then dangled it from her finger. "How about get drunk and go shopping?"

See? That's why Mel and I are such good friends. The woman knows the way to my soul.

Chapter

4

>>http://www.playsurvivewin.com<<

PLAY.SURVIVE.WIN

>>>WELCOME TO REPORTING CENTER<<<

PLAYER REPORT:
REPORT NO. A-0001
Filed By: Birdie
Subject: Status update.
Report:

- Primary subject located and contacted.
- Interaction successful. Subject expressed no knowledge or suspicions relating to mission objective or steps undertaken to achieve same.

- Phase One completed. Microchip in place.
- Game currently proceeding on schedule.
- Rendezvous with secondary subject and implementation of Phase Two scheduled to commence momentarily.

>>>End Report<<

Send Report to Opponent? >>Yes<< >>No<<

Chapter

5

JENNIFER

"The blonde," I said to Brian, talking out of the side of my mouth. "The one by the Shu Uemura counter." Then, "No, no! Don't look. That's too obvious!"

"Well, then, sweetie pie, how the hell am I supposed to see her if I can't look?" No one can pull off a put-upon tone like Brian can, and beside him, Mel laughed. After a second, I laughed too.

"Come on, you guys," I said, trying to pull myself together. I ran my finger over some eyeliner at the Chanel counter, trying to look like I was focused on shopping. "I'm serious. I think that blonde is scoping me out."

We were in the basement Beauty Level at Bergdorf's, checking out the various samples and trying to decide which counter had the best free gift with purchase. Of course, we'd arrived fully loaded, Mel and I having polished off two martinis each before we'd headed out, armed with credit cards.

I'd called Brian from the street, and he'd agreed to join us. He's always adored Mel and hadn't seen her since she'd defected from Manhattan to the hurly-burly of Washington. (His words, not mine.) More important, he'd agreed to join us because Fifi was in a snit, and Brian wanted to get out of his apartment. Fifi's a lot of fun. But, as Brian will be the first to say, he's best enjoyed in small doses.

He met us in front of Givenchy at 63rd and Madison, where Mel bought two dresses, a pair of shoes, a skirt, and a pair of sunglasses. I'd drooled so much that Mel offered to take pity on me and purchase the haute couture item of my choosing, but I'm lousy at taking charity. That's one of the reasons I'm making a go of it in New York on my own, with no help from my parents. (Or, very little help. I'm more than willing to accept pricey Christmas and birthday gifts.) My parents may have bucks, but my dad's stock options can't buy me a starring role in a musical. And even if he could write a check and get me on Broadway, I'd turn it down. I want to do it myself. And I will. It's just taking me a while.

Once Brian joined the party, we'd traipsed to Bergdorf's and headed straight down to the makeup. I never buy makeup without having Brian around. The man can be a pushy little queen, but he's got more taste in his little finger than most of the women I know. (Case in point: You know those women with pale foundation topped by two inch slashes of cream rouge on their cheeks? Brian once started a petition that would have them all charged with some sort of anti-beautification misdemeanor. It didn't pass, but his heart was in the right place.)

We'd been discussing the pros and cons of crème versus powder eyeshadow when I'd noticed the blonde. I didn't think anything of it at first, but there was just something about the way she was watching me from across the room. And when I caught her gaze, she didn't look away. Just kept her eyes locked on mine.

I was starting to get creeped out enough to leave when she broke eye contact and turned her back to me, apparently fascinated with the display of oil-free moisturizers. She wore a D&G camisole and tight Diesel jeans that looked like she'd purchased them five minutes before. She had the grace and bearing of a model, tall and thin and totally perfect. But that wasn't what I noticed about her (there are a lot of model types in New York, and they often cluster in the Bergdorf basement). No, it was the tattoo on her left shoulder blade that really caught my eye. A tropical bird, resplendent in a rainbow of colors, his tail feathers trailing down her back and head turned so that one eye seemed to be keeping a lookout.

I stared longer than I should have, something about the woman oddly fascinating to me. But then she turned and aimed a slow smile in my direction, before dividing her attention between me and a display of lipstick samples.

Busted.

I snagged Brian's sleeve, earning a contemptuous look before I explained the sitch in hushed tones. After reasonably pointing out that he couldn't analyze the situation without looking at the girl, he managed to shift around until he found a position from which he could take a look at her without being too obvious.

He watched her watching me for a full minute, then turned back to me with a shrug. "So she's checking you out. She probably thinks you're hot." He lifted a brow. "Or are you interested, too?"

"No!" I've had my share of girl-crushes, but never like that.

I'm totally and completely open-minded when it comes to other people. But as for me, sharing of bodily fluids is strictly limited to the male of the species. Just call it one of my quirks. "Do you really think that's it?" I whispered.

"Probably. Why?"

I shook my head, something about the woman making me nervous. I guess it was her eyes. Piercing blue and very intense. If this woman was on the prowl, I felt sorry for all the lesbians in the neighborhood. One glance, and I could tell this was a take-no-prisoners kind of lover.

"What's up?" Mel had been testing lipsticks on the back of her hand, and now she joined us, rubbing a tissue over skin that looked like it had been decorated with war paint.

Brian gave her the Cliffs Notes version of my dilemma, and Mel turned to inspect the woman, whose back was now to us. After a second, Mel shrugged. "I can't get a good look, but if she's giving you the creeps, let's get out of here."

Since I thought that idea was just nifty, I led the way, with Mel and Brian following. We circled around, then headed up the escalator to the main level. Along the way, we passed the dozens of Swarovski crystals suspended from the ceiling and twinkling in the store's lighting scheme. That piece is the epitome of Bergdorf's, all class and light and elegance. It's supposed to be the northern lights or something, but to me, it's just fabulous whatever it is.

I turned back once, ostensibly to give one last glance to the crystal sculpture, but really to see if Bird Girl was following. Since I didn't see her, I led my troops up the escalator, which opened right in front of one little corner of heaven—the Manolo Blahnik shoe display.

I glanced around again, and was pleased to see that my new best friend was still nowhere to be found. Probably testing lip gloss a few floors down. I took five steps forward and paused right in front of the center display. Then I just stood there for a bit and drooled.

I've had a thing for Manolo shoes ever since a friend gave me a print of one of his sketches ("him" being Manolo Blahnik, not my friend). The sketch was of this totally off-the-wall shoe that he designed for Madonna. I hung it on my bathroom wall, along with some others I managed to snag on eBay.

Once I had a sketch, I had to own a shoe, too, and let me tell you, if the goal of a fine shoe is to make a woman's foot look sexy and her leg look stunning, then these shoes do the job in spades. I own three pairs, but only one was bought new. (I got a hundred-dollar tip one night and decided that was a sign. Two days and half my savings account later, and the shoes were mine.) The other two were also eBay finds, and amazing bargains at that. All told, I've spent over a grand on those three pairs of shoes. But they were worth every penny, because I wasn't just buying shoes; I was buying a life change. They're the best things that ever happened to my legs. Really. Tons better than Pilates or kick-boxing. (Slight exaggeration, but I'm trying to make a point.) And I really do get more attention from the male of the species when I'm wearing them. Trust me. I've kept a log.

I've been a Manolo fiend since long before Carrie Bradshaw sang their praises on *Sex and the City*. I haven't, however, bought a new pair in over eight months. Finances too tight, and I can't justify asking my mom and dad for money to buy shoes. And although I love each and every shoe in my current footwear collection, the truth is, it's hopelessly out of season. And even though I'd never completely abandon the precious pairs I'd stored lovingly in my closet, I'd be lying if I didn't admit that I was sorely tempted to break out my credit card. Especially for the little aquamarine kitten-heeled thong decorated with flowers on each leather strap.

"Go ahead," a little devil whispered in my ear. "You know you want to."

I turned to scowl at the devil—her name was Mel. "I *do* want to. But I don't want to turn to a life of crime, and that's what I'd have to do in order to pay the bill." For the record, Bergdorf's isn't exactly a discount venue for Manolo's. And as much as I wished it wasn't, $495 was a little rich for my blood. (Of course, I could be lusting after the $2500 pair of alligator pumps. By comparison, the sandals were practically a steal!)

"You could work a double shift for a couple of weeks and eat at the restaurant. Make extra money, save on food."

This time, I scowled at Brian. "If I work doubles, I won't have time to audition."

"True," he conceded. "So don't work extra shifts. Just put it on your Visa and deal with it later. Consider it an installment plan investment."

"AT&T stock is an investment," I countered, channeling my father. "And you're a terrible influence."

"If you really want them, I could spot you for them," Mel said.

I licked my lips, sorely tempted. Why not? Mel had started out just as broke as me. But now she could probably buy and sell Mr. Blahnik if she wanted to. (Okay, maybe not. But she could certainly buy out his warehouse.) Buying *me* a single pair of pumps really wouldn't be any big deal.

I nearly said yes—I really did—but I couldn't quite get the word out. I wanted the shoes—a lot more than I'd wanted the Givenchy fix she'd offered up an hour earlier—but I didn't want the charity. If Mel just happened to wrap up a pair of Manolos for me at Christmas, well, then I'd be rude to complain. But right now, in the middle of March, I just couldn't bring myself to say yes.

"I'm just looking," I said.

Mel and Brian exchanged a look.

"Really," I insisted. "I've got my eye on an amazing pair on eBay. By this time next week, I'll be the proud owner of a brand-new pair of Manolos. Just wait and see." That was a big fat lie, but at least I was keeping my pride.

Since I was still holding the shoe, I gave it one final stroke, then resisted the temptation to kiss it good-bye before putting it back on the display.

I was just about to move away when I heard the husky voice behind me. "Fabulous, isn't it?"

I turned, then jumped a little when I found myself face to face with Bird Girl who, apparently, had moved from makeup to shoes the same as me. Close up, she was even more exquisite, and I felt like a total schlub, even though I'd been pretty proud of the outfit I'd pulled together under the influence of apple-tinis. Still, you couldn't argue with the facts: I might have the clothes, but Bird Girl owned the attitude.

"Um," I said, displaying my rapier wit. "It's a really great shoe."

Bird Girl held up a finger, immediately commanding the attention of a harried clerk. "I'll take these," she said. "Size nine." No caveat for "if it fits." No hesitation. Just "I'll take these."

I swear, I hated her. Even more when she smiled at me. An icy smile that gave me chills, and seemed to hold more malice than the snooty rich smile I'd come to expect whenever I decided to pose among the fabulously wealthy.

Immediately, I turned away, irritated with myself for being jealous of her looks and her money, and telling myself that at least I had smaller feet. But despite that little bit of bling for my ego, I was still unable to stop the one word that flashed like neon in my head: *bitch*.

Chapter

6

BIRDIE

I watch the girl for a few more minutes, but it's not really necessary. I already know all that I need to know. She is weak, untrained, and certainly not up to the task before her.

Most important, she's no match for me.

Jennifer is already dead, and she doesn't even know it.

The sales girl returns on that happy thought, and I pay cash for the shoes, ignoring the look of surprise that flashes in the clerk's eyes. In a world of credit and debit, currency is going out of style. There are those of us who utilize it exclusively, though. Hard cash is the currency of the hidden. And I have lived my entire life in the warm comfort of shadows.

The girl puts the shoebox into the shopping bag, and I take it, allowing myself to enjoy the purely feminine rush that comes from the purchase of footwear. I must admit that I am practically tingling with excitement. For years, I made no purchase that didn't involve the bartered exchange of cigarettes or sex. I open the box and enjoy a quick moment breathing in that new shoe scent. And then, without any further hesitation, I put them on and discover that, yes, they fit perfectly.

I step back, doing a small pirouette in front of a nearby mirror.

Brilliant.

I'm free, recently fucked, and I'm on the hunt.

Really, what more could a girl want?

The question is rhetorical, and I don't ponder it. Fashion is all fine and dandy, but I have a schedule to meet.

I check my watch and see that it is almost four. My deadline approaches.

I extend my hand and examine the ring I wear, the one I retrieved that morning. I'd left my nighttime companion snoring softly in a drunken haze, then headed for the private PO box referenced in the message. The ring was inside, tucked in a padded envelope addressed to me. With a thick band and cheap gemstones, the ring is wholly unremarkable. Tacky, even. And yet I'm wearing it as instructed. Also as instructed, I turn my hand over, then run my thumbnail along the band until I find the tiny indention. I pry, using my nail as I might use a screwdriver on a battery casing.

With very little effort, the metal backing pops off, revealing a series of tiny needlepoints, a dozen in all. I keep my hand open and stiff, close enough to my body that I don't risk touching anyone else, yet far enough away that I don't accidentally scrape myself. I don't know exactly what the needles are coated with, but I know that if an antidote isn't administered within a certain amount of time, the toxin is deadly.

Then I pause beside a Jimmy Choo display, letting my gaze scan the floor as I reacquire my quarry. *There.*

My heart pounds with a thrill I haven't experienced in over five years. And with a nonchalance learned from years of practice and training, I ease toward my prey.

Chapter

7

JENNIFER

"Are you sure you can't stay overnight?" I asked Mel, as we crammed onto the already full elevator. "You could catch the first flight out in the morning."

The doors started to shut, but then a bag shot forward into the gap. My gaze followed the line from bag to arm to woman, and I gasped a little when I realized the bag was being held by Bird Girl. She mouthed an apology to everyone on the lift, then squeezed inside, easing around a pencil-thin woman with a severe expression until she was in the far back of the elevator. The other passengers jostled to make room for her, and I held out a hand, steadying myself against Brian's shoulder. He glanced at me, his narrow expression telegraphing exactly what I felt: she couldn't have waited for the next car?

Mel watched the whole thing impassively, and when the car was moving again, she returned seamlessly to our conversation.

"I wish I could, but I have a 7 A.M. meeting. If I don't make my flight, I'm screwed."

I debated trying to talk her into staying anyway, but Mel is devoted to her job in a way that borders on obsessive. More, I knew she wanted to get back to Matthew. "Fair enough. At least we got to hang out for a few hours."

We kept on, chatting about nothing much, when the elevator stopped and we all moved forward. I felt a surge of people from behind me, and I stifled the urge to shout out a curse and tell them to wait their turn. And then suddenly I was pushed roughly forward. I fell against Brian, then felt someone grab my arm and pull me back upright. I looked down at the hand clutching my arm, wincing as I saw the gaudy ring smashing into my flesh. The hand belonged to Bird Girl, who now stood me up and steadied me.

"I'm so sorry!" she said. "I completely lost my balance."

"It's okay," I said, as I followed Brian and Mel out of the elevator. "I'm fine."

"You're sure?" She was out now, too, her eyes looking me up and down as if she'd caused me some grievous injury.

I smiled brightly, just wanting to get away. The woman might be a beauty with great fashion sense, but she gave me the creeps.

"It's these damn shoes," she said. "The heel caught on something."

My eyes moved automatically to her feet. Not only was she now *wearing* my shoes, but she was bad-mouthing them. *Hello?* If she can't figure out how to walk in thong sandals, she has no business buying them.

And then she did something that completely blew me away.

She bent down, slipped the shoes off her feet, and shoved them in a nearby trash can. As I gaped, I heard the solid thump of the shoes hitting the bottom of the can.

I swallowed, my fingers itching to rescue the shoes. I managed to hold myself back. I might have a thing for Manolos, but I couldn't bring myself to stick my arm through a trash can slot and feel around for a pair of shoes. Especially when I don't wear a size nine.

Instead, I just stared as the girl pranced barefoot across the sales floor, the bird on her shoulder swaying with the rhythm of her walk.

"That's one fucked-up female," Brian whispered.

And that, I thought, pretty much said it all.

Chapter

8

JENNIFER

Sometimes, the stars align in your favor. Not always. But sometimes. And after I parted ways with Mel and Brian, I was the happy recipient of some serious celestial line-dancing.

No, I didn't get a callback for *Carousel.*

No, I didn't win the lottery. I didn't even win a shopping spree at Bloomie's.

But I *did* find that very pair of Manolos on eBay. And the truly stellar part? They were listed at well under a hundred dollars!

(Take *that*, Bird Bitch!)

What happened was this: I'd come home still suffering from Manolo-lust, and feeling a tinge of regret that I hadn't dug Bird Girl's pumps out of the trash. So I logged onto the auction site, punched in "Manolo," filtered out everything but the shoes, and honed in on those auctions that were ending soonest.

And there they were. Right in the center of the list. Complete with a slightly out-of-focus picture. Those very same shoes. True, they were in lime green—and gently used—but Manolos are Manolos, and after squealing and staring at the computer screen for a good two minutes, I finally realized that the only way these reasonably priced Manolos would be mine is if I bid on them. Which I promptly did. And—yes!—I came up as the high bidder!

Was life good, or what?

I checked the computer twice before I went to bed (no one bid against me), and again after I woke up (someone else had bid, but the price was only up to one-hundred-twenty-eight, and I was still in the lead).

I managed to put the shoes out of my mind long enough to go forth into the world to be both productive and social. In other words, I sang my way through my shift then hit Starbucks with Brian, where he worried and preened and raved about his upcoming debut.

"You're making that face," Brian said, during a pause in his spiel.

I carefully erased any and all emotion. "What face?"

"The one that says you're never going to make it, never going to amount to anything, and you might as well move back to California and pass out baskets at Wal-Mart. Personally, I think you should work the Clinique counter at Bloomingdale's, but when you get that face, there's no reasoning with you."

"You're an ass," I said. "I don't have a face, and I'm not wallowing in self-pity." Not much, anyway.

"Here," Brian said, pressing a business card into my hand. "Nicolae is taking new students."

"Brian . . ." I'm sure he heard the exasperation in my voice because I sure as heck didn't try to hide it. "I told you. I've taken voice lessons my whole life. I'm thoroughly schooled."

"Then why aren't you thoroughly employed?" He held up a hand. "No, don't look at me like that. This is my moment to say serious shit. You're good, Jenn. But you can be better."

"I practice. I train." Okay, even as I said it, I knew I sounded lame. "When am I supposed to squeeze in classes? When I'm not working, I'm auditioning."

"Or shopping . . ."

"Now you're just being mean."

"Seriously, sugar, you've got a voice that can make me cry like a baby, but you're raw, you know? You've been here, what? Two, three years now?"

"Getting on that," I admitted.

"Well, news flash for you. No one is going to swoop down and discover you. You need to make your own luck. Bust your own ass."

"I audition!"

He leaned back, then sucked down the rest of his caramel machiatto. "I'm not interested in excuses. I'm interested in seeing your name in *Playbill.*"

"So am I," I said, because that was the truth. And then, because the whole conversation was skirting a little too close to my reality, I steered us off on a tangent that I knew would interest Brian: him.

The ploy worked, and we spent the next hour analyzing the various *Puck's Dream* cast members and fantasizing about where he'd be five years from now. He was gunning for a Tony, and I think he just might make it. Of course, that didn't change the fact that I wanted to make it first. And *that* thought brought me full circle to his implied suggestion that I wasn't working hard enough at my craft. Since that wasn't a road I wanted to go down again, I gave him a quick kiss good-bye, then made my exit.

I was tired and I really wanted to just call a taxi, but it's only a ten-block walk, and I couldn't justify the cost. Fortunately, I was still in my practical (and practically hideous) waitress shoes. Ugly but comfortable. That's *so* not my motto. But you know what they say: pride goeth before painful feet.

Which got me thinking about eBay and the Manolos all over again.

I hurried through the series of locks designed to keep me in and bad guys out, tossed my bag on the floor, then headed for the desk and my laptop. I'd left the screen up, so all I had to do was hit the refresh key and . . . *Yes!* I was still the man! (Or the woman, as the case might be.)

I did a little jig as I clicked over to check my email (all spam) then expanded my happy dance to cover my entire apartment. The dance turned into a striptease as I tugged off my clothes on the way to the shower. In the steam, I lathered up and soaped down, breathing deep of Aveda and Dove as the clingy scent of french fries and hamburgers coiled down the drain.

Half an hour and half a bottle of shampoo later, I sat in front of my computer, ready for a laid-back evening in my favorite pair of jeans and a faded black t-shirt. I curled my legs under me, then got ready to count down the minutes until the shoes were mine.

Five seconds . . . three . . . and then . . . YES! THE MANO-LOS WERE MINE, MINE, ALL MINE!!!!!

My computer dinged and a little envelope appeared at the bottom of my screen, signaling that I had new mail. I clicked over right away, expecting to find an invoice generated by eBay for the seller. Instead, I found an email from a sender I didn't recognize. Curious, I opened the message . . . then immediately wished I hadn't. My stomach roiled, and I realized my hand had gone to my mouth and I'd quit breathing. I hadn't ever seen a message like this before, but I'd heard about it. Mel had told me all about the emails, and I never, ever wanted to get one.

Apparently, though, what I wanted really wasn't the issue.

FROM: MessageCenter@playsurvivewin.com
TO: Jenn_Crane@Broadwayjenn.com
SUBJECT: Message Waiting
MESSAGE:
You have ONE message in your inbox at the PSW Message Center. Click >>>here<<< to Login to the Message Center and immediately retrieve your message.

I didn't want to . . . dear God, I really didn't want to. But I did. I had to know. And so I clicked. Then just about threw up when I saw the message that filled my screen:

>>http://www.playsurvivewin.com<<

PLAY.SURVIVE.WIN

PLEASE LOGIN
PLAYER USERNAME: *BroadwayBaby*
PLAYER PASSWORD:********

. . . please wait
. . . please wait
. . . please wait
Password approved
>>>Read New Messages<<< >>>Create New Message<<<
. . . please wait

WELCOME TO MESSAGE CENTER

You have one new message.

New Message:

To: BroadwayBaby

From: Identity Blocked

Subject: Funding

Advance payment deposited your account.

Amount: $20,000.

Client name: Devlin Brady.

Additional funds to be delivered upon successful completion of protection mission.

Rule Refresher: Involvement by police or other authorities is expressly forbidden.

Good luck.

>>>Player Profile Attached: DB_Profile.doc<<<

I read the thing twice, somehow managing not to be sick. I'm not entirely sure how. I wanted to throw up. I wanted to crawl under the covers and go to sleep. I wanted to scream. This game was a death warrant. Hadn't Mel just told me about the protector who'd ended up with a bullet in his gut? And the other guy dead on the floor?

Hell, Mel and Matthew had both almost died trying to win

this game. A game they hadn't even wanted to play in the first place. They'd lived, but there was no guarantee I'd be so lucky.

I thought about that—thought about how much I didn't want to play. How much I'd rather curl up under my covers and hide.

But I didn't. Instead, I reached for the phone, grateful for speed-dial since my hand was shaking so badly. Miles away, in Washington, D.C., Mel's cell phone rang. I prayed that she'd answer. I needed to talk to her. Dear God, there wasn't anyone else in the whole world I needed to talk to more.

And this time, we sure as hell weren't going to be talking about shoes.

No answer.

I stared at the phone, not quite comprehending that Mel couldn't be there, and when it kicked over to voice mail, I left a frantic message for her to call me. Then I rummaged through my desk for my address book. I'd only programmed her cell number into my phone. Maybe the battery had run down. Surely if I called her house . . .

I found the book and pounced on it, then immediately started flipping pages. The second I found the number, I dialed, then did the finger-tapping routine until the machine clicked on. A regular answering machine, I assumed, and I went through the whole "Mel? Are you there? Mel, goddamn it, pick up!" routine. Nothing. I sighed, then added, "Call me the second you get in. It's urgent. It's about this fucking game! Mel! It's about PSW, and you have got to call and help me!"

Then I hung up the phone and stood in front of my computer. My chin was thrust forward and my hands were fisted, as if I was afraid it would attack. Actually, I realized, that was exactly what I was afraid of.

I took three deep breaths and forced myself to relax. Just as if I were backstage and had to calm down and get into character before stepping out on that stage.

Right. Okay. Right.

Calm.

That was me, the leading lady who's the total spine of the show. Calm and collected and not the least bit hysterical.

Three more breaths and I'd pulled myself together. I glanced toward the door, saw that I had locked it, just like I always did. Good. My heart was still pounding, but I played my role with aplomb, searching every nook and cranny, just to make absolutely certain I was alone. I was. And the window was locked. For the moment, at least, I was safe.

I dropped back into my desk chair. In front of me, the PSW message screen seemed to leer, and suddenly my little Manolo victory seemed entirely pyrrhic.

Fuck.

Fuck, fuck, fuck.

And, just for the hell of it . . . Fuck.

I didn't know what to do. I might be the calm leading lady, but the fact was that I didn't have a script. I didn't know if I should be terrified (I was), proactive (how?), or if I should go hide under my bed (appealing). All I knew was that this message signaled the start of a deadly game. And somehow, someway, I was now right smack dab in the center of it.

Unless it was a hoax!

The possibility gave me something to cling to, and I started spinning scenarios in my head: Mel was irritated that I wasn't supporting her attempts to figure out who was behind her ordeal last year. And so she'd sent this email to give me a taste of her medicine. That's why she wasn't answering her phone. And when she *did* answer, I'd be pissed, but I'd have to agree that I sort of understood now.

It was a wonderful scenario, but I knew it was only fiction. And since Mel still wasn't answering her phone, there was only one way to find out. I picked up the phone again, then called the automated system at my bank. If the money wasn't there, I was fine. It was just a stupid trick.

I waited, drumming my fingers on the table as the voice went through the entire intro message, then punched in my account number, then 1 to retrieve my balance: $20,157.43.

The one-hundred fifty-seven I'd been expecting. The twenty thou meant I was screwed. Even Mel wouldn't transfer huge sums just to prove a point. This wasn't a hoax, and I grabbed my cell phone once again and dialed 911.

"911 operator. What is your emergency?"

I stared at the phone, thinking about the message. "Expressly forbidden," it said. And I also remembered something Mel had told me about how she and Matthew hadn't called in the cops to help them, not until it was all over. Breaking the rules, Mel had said, would have been bad, bad, bad.

"Please state your emergency."

"I . . . I'm sorry. I accidentally punched a speed-dial number. I'm fine. Everything's fine."

"Miss? What is your location?"

"I'm fine, really. I'm sorry. I'm okay. Bye." I snapped my

phone shut, then looked around frantically, half-expecting armed assassins to descend from ropes from my roof, machine guns ready to take me out. I'd broken a rule. I'd called the authorities. I didn't remember exactly what the consequences were, and I wondered if I'd just fucked myself over royally.

There was something perverse about convincing myself that I didn't want the police riding to my rescue, but I told myself I'd done the right thing. Someone had just sucked me into a game that was played to the death. I didn't know enough yet to risk disobeying the message.

Mel had survived, but Mel is smart. Hell, Mel is a Mensa-certified genius.

I couldn't even get a callback audition.

My mom had always told me that the odds of making it on Broadway were slim. But right then, I'd be more than happy to take those odds. Because I had a terrible feeling in the pit of my stomach that the odds of surviving this game were even slimmer. Plus, now I wanted my mom. I didn't call her, though. What could I say that wouldn't make her call the cops?

Without a plan or the police, and fueled only by adrenaline, I got up, sat down, got up, sat down, then got up again. Something familiar had tickled my brain, but I couldn't remember what.

Out of frustration, I grabbed my phone and dialed Mel again. Not too surprisingly, I still got no answer.

Okay. Fine. Obviously I was in this on my own. I could handle that. I might not be a genius, but I wasn't an idiot either. I sat myself back down in the seat, looked at the screen, and tried to think what to do.

First thing, what did I know?

Well, just from the message, I knew that even though I'd definitely been sucked into a terrifying situation, I wasn't the one whose ass was on the line. At least, not directly. Because I wasn't the target in the game. Instead, I was the protector. (Which, frankly, made me feel a little sorry for Mr. Devlin Brady. I mean, I'm qualified to do a lot of jobs, from waitress to receptionist to makeup consultant. Bodyguard, however, is not on the list.)

And that's when I remembered: That little tickle in my brain was because of Devlin Brady.

Devlin Brady was the FBI agent who'd investigated Mel's case.

And now *I* supposed to protect *him?*

This was not computing in a big way. How the hell was I supposed to protect an FBI agent?

But then I realized that I was looking at this all the wrong way. Maybe this was a good thing. The man had a gun and a badge, right? If he couldn't watch his own back—and mine, too—then who could?

Chapter

10

DEVLIN

Devlin only remembered because of the panties.

He'd dropped his goddamn beer, and he was bent over sopping up the mess when his fingers had brushed a bit of satin under the sofa. He'd tugged it out with two fingers, the light from the television illuminating the pale pink panties. Panties that brought back a rush of memory highlighted by a wash of self-loathing.

God, he'd been a fool. When was that? Yesterday? The day before? He couldn't remember; it was too much of a blur. All he remembered was picking up the girl. Fucking the girl. Forgetting the girl. And all in the hopes of forgetting his own damn problems.

Hadn't worked.

Now he sat on the couch, the panties in his hands, feeling lost and disgusted.

And, once again, alone.

Frustrated, he shoved the balled-up panties down into the couch cushions to rot with the loose change and old Cheetos. Then he just sat on the couch in the dark and tried to lose himself once again.

Didn't work.

The shades were drawn in the apartment, the black-out kind, designed for people who worked at night and slept during the day. Devlin didn't care about that. All he'd wanted when he'd pulled the shades weeks ago was darkness. All he'd wanted was to forget. Forget his partner, dead and buried. Forget the investigation that was either going to clear him or crucify him.

Forget every goddamn thing.

Lately, though, that was getting harder and harder.

Had he really nailed the girl just so he'd have a reason to escape from his thoughts? From the fucking mess his life had become?

He sat there like a slug, miserable and drained, as colors flashed from the television, illuminating the room with images from *Gilligan's Island*. Or maybe it was *Bewitched*. He hadn't bothered to look up once, and even now, with the television right in front of him, he didn't care enough to look at the screen. It was just television. He didn't give a fuck about television. He told himself he didn't give a fuck about anything.

Disgusted, he shoved himself up off the couch, kicking the take-out containers that littered the floor in front of him out of the way. He stumbled to the kitchen, then turned the water on in the sink. He leaned forward, staring down at the Indian food stuck to his cheap plastic plates, glasses half-filled with watered-down scotch, apple cores, pizza crusts, and half a dozen other unrecognizable food products. In short, a disgusting mess. If anything, the mess gave him some minor degree of satisfaction. He wasn't a complete basket case. Not yet, anyway. Because at the very least, he was still remembering to eat.

Idly, he wondered if he'd bought the girl dinner. He doubted it. Somehow, he didn't think that chivalry had been on his mind.

Devlin shoved his hands under the running water, then splashed his face. The back of his neck ached, and he rubbed his wet hand along his hairline, trying to ease the tension.

Three sharp raps sounded at the door. Automatically, Devlin's hand went for his hip . . . and the gun that was no longer there. *Fuck.*

The pounding sounded again. Who the hell was that? Had to be a resident. No way for an outsider to get past Evan. The building's concierge wasn't tipped better than a starlight whore at Christmas for nothing. The man had some serious cajones on him. If Evan didn't want someone in the building, then that someone wasn't coming into the building. Simple as that.

Again the sound. Devlin considered ignoring it, but the truth was he was craving distraction. He'd either answer the door now or crawl down to a pub at midnight looking for another woman who could make him forget.

He eased down the hallway silently, avoiding the one parquet tile that squeaked when you stepped on it just so. He settled in next to the door, reconsidered whether he really wanted to do this, then finally called out, "Who's there?"

"Oh, Agent Brady! Thank goodness. I could hear the television, and then when you didn't answer the door I thought— Well, let's just say I was worried."

Devlin rubbed the bridge of his nose and considered going

back to the couch. But then Annabel rapped again. "Agent Brady! Now you open this up right this second. I want to take a look at you."

The television he could tune out, but not his neighbor, and so he unlocked the door and tugged it open. And as he leaned against the door frame, he looked down from his two-foot advantage into the cloudy gray eyes of Annabel Carson, resident, apartment 12B.

She took a step back, shaking her head and making the kind of *tsk-tsk* noises his grandmother used to make. When it came right down to it, that's probably why he let her in. It wasn't like he could slam the door on Grandma.

In the hallway, she looked Devlin up and down, this inspection even more intense than the last. "Agent Brady, you look terrible."

He shrugged. This was hardly breaking news. "Then I guess there's some justice in the world, Annabel, because I feel terrible, too."

"And what are you doing about it?"

Sitting in the dark, feeling sorry for himself, screwing around, eating only when he had to. To Annabel, he just said, "I'm coping. I'll be fine."

"Will you? When? It's been two weeks since the shooting."

He flinched at her bluntness. Even his buddies at the field office had danced around it, calling the shooting "the incident." OPR had been more bold, of course, especially when they'd confiscated his weapon and sent him off into exile. That had raised some eyebrows. Time off after a shooting was par for the course. But the suits in the Office of Professional Responsibility only confiscated your weapon and badge if they thought the shooting was dirty. If they thought *he* was dirty. Bastards. Wasn't it enough that he had to live with killing his partner? If you could call what he was doing living. . . .

As for Annabel, she didn't seem to expect an answer, and she just barreled on. "You need to get out, young man. You need fresh air. Friends and family."

"I'll keep that in mind."

"Mmmm." Her appraising look peeled over him one more time, and this time he shifted uncomfortably, fearing that maybe old Annabel Carson, with her tea cozy décor and Lawrence Welk sensibilities, might be seeing more in him than he wanted her to. "What were you doing when I knocked?"

"Mrs. Carson . . ." He left the question unanswered, but managed to infuse his voice with a hint of warning. It was a tone that had silenced numerous unfriendly witnesses.

It wasn't silencing Annabel. "Don't you 'Mrs. Carson' me, young man. You were sitting in here in the dark watching television, weren't you?"

"There's a lot of quality programming on cable these days."

That almost earned him a smile, and Devlin was amazed to realize how much lighter his heart felt.

"All right, Devlin. Have you got a hammer and nails?"

Although he had a feeling that any answer would be the wrong one, Devlin answered that, yes, he had those particular tools.

"Good. Go get them. I'll wait here."

He opened his mouth to ask why—no, to tell Mrs. Carson that she could purchase her own hammer and nails for under twenty bucks at the hardware store on the corner—but some gremlin ordered him to keep his mouth shut. He left her standing in the doorway, then headed to the kitchen where he rummaged around under the sink until he found the small plastic tool chest. Dutifully, he lugged it back to the door, feeling a little like a prized puppy when she nodded approval and said, "Good."

He started to hand it to her, but she didn't take the thing. Instead, she pointed to the hook just inside the door, and the key ring hanging there. "You might want to lock up."

"I might?"

"You can never be too careful, can you?"

He agreed that you couldn't, and grabbed his keys, now fully aware that he was being handled. "Want to tell me what we're doing?"

"Does it matter?"

"I'm curious," he admitted.

"Good. Means you're alive." She took her own key out—apparently she'd locked up even though she'd never been out of sight of her own door not ten feet away. "Spring cleaning. I've got stacks of boxes with things that need sorting, old bills to be filed, and at least a dozen pictures I need to hang. You're helping me."

He honestly meant to protest, to tell his well-meaning but interfering neighbor that he'd be going back to his couch and *Gilligan's Island* or whatever it was. And good luck getting those pictures straight. But when he opened his mouth, all he said was, "It's March."

"I'm starting early." She reached out and squeezed his hand, her wrinkled skin soft and cool in his palm.

He didn't argue. Didn't have any reason to. Because even though he might not want to admit it to her or to himself, the truth was that he knew this was about more than helping Annabel Carson. It was about helping himself.

Chapter

11

JENNIFER

I knew from Mel that the real-life game was played almost exactly like the Internet version. And even though I'd disliked the online version intensely, I'd played it a couple of times, so I knew the basic rules. Knowing the rules, however, didn't mean that I knew strategy, and, in fact, the few times I'd played I'd lost badly.

On that encouraging note, I scooted my chair closer to the desk. Now was not the time for negative thinking. Success is ninety-eight percent attitude, right? And I'd beaten the pants off my brothers in Nintendo dozens of times. *That* was a victory I could focus on.

The bottom line was that I knew how the game was played. Three roles: a target, an assassin, and a protector. The target is the one who, like the title sounds, is the "target." The one the assassin is after. The game starts when the target receives the first clue, also called the qualifying clue. Until the target solves that first clue, the assassin has to just sit tight. But once the clue is solved, all bets are off. And then the target has to follow clue after clue until—finally—the last clue is solved and the assassin is called off. (Or the target dies, but we won't go there.)

But what, you might ask, is there to keep the target from just ignoring the clue altogether? If the first clue is never solved, then the assassin can never hunt.

Yeah, you'd think that would be a good plan, wouldn't you? So would I. But I know it's not. I just can't remember *why* not.

Clearly, the first order of business was to get in touch with this Devlin Brady guy. My initial instinct was to call the FBI and just ask for the man. They'd know how to find him, wouldn't they?

But about the same time, I realized that I probably had Agent Brady's phone number right there on my computer—DB_Profile.doc. The file that the game had sent to me. I wasn't crazy about going back to my computer—at the moment I blamed it for my predicament—but I didn't have a choice.

I opened the file and saw that I was right. Everything was there: Devlin Brady's name, address, phone number, occupation, hobbies, previous employment. Even a photo. A candid shot, with Brady turned slightly from the camera.

We'd met once, and I remember thinking that he was pretty hot, which the picture reflected quite well. He had dark, unruly hair and a firm jaw. But what really got me was his eyes. Clear and blue. Very sexy.

At the moment, though, I wasn't particularly interested in sex appeal. I was much more focused on the fact that Agent Brady had a solid, capable face. And, from what I could tell, he had a decently muscled body under that suit. He looked like a man who could watch his back and mine. And under the circumstances, that was more appealing than a kissable mouth and a sultry grin.

I snatched up the phone and dialed the number listed for his home. The phone rang three times, and as it did, I drummed my fingers on the table, waiting for him to pick up. He didn't, and I found myself faced with his answering machine and absolutely no idea what to say. In person, I could just tell him the truth. But to leave a message like that on a machine? I guess I was afraid he wouldn't call me back.

You could have driven a truck through my silence, and just as I was about to speak, the machine beeped and the line went dead. *Damn.*

I redialed. This time, I was expecting the message: "You've reached Devlin Brady. Please leave a message." I did as asked and said, "Um, hi. Agent Brady? My name is Jennifer Crane. You, um, might remember me because we met once about a year ago. Actually, you confiscated my laptop, remember? I was Melanie Prescott's roommate? Anyway, I really need to talk to you. Can you call me back right away? It's urgent. Thanks." I left my home and cell numbers, then called his cell phone and the number listed as his direct dial at the FBI. I got dumped into voice mail in both cases. I hate that.

I left my messages, then hung up, feeling (rightly) like I hadn't accomplished a thing. More, I wasn't sure what to do next. Should I hang out and wait? Should I go to his apartment? For that matter, was it safe for me to leave my apartment?

I paced from kitchen sink to bathroom, running these questions over in my head. In response to pretty much all those queries, I decided I should give him an hour to call me back. My reasoning was that for all I knew, he already knew about the game, knew who I was, and was on his way to my place. That's what FBI agents did, right? Rode to the rescue of damsels in distress?

The other reason was that I wasn't really a damsel in distress (though I had to keep reminding myself of that). Sure, I was in deep doo-doo, and there was a definite possibility that I wouldn't get out of this situation alive (with that thought, I had to remind myself to breathe), but I wasn't the target. This may seem like a technical distinction given the overall fucked-up-edness of the situation, but I was clinging to whatever good news I could find.

Once I hooked up with Agent Brady, not only would I not be the focus of the assassin's bullet (or whatever), I'd also have the added protection of a Fibbie at my side. I can't say that I thought this rendered the situation ideal or anything, but having someone else shoulder the burden was a definite step in the right direction.

While I waited, I tried Mel again. Still no answer, which made me concerned about the state of national security. If an NSA employee isn't answering her cell phone, that seemed to me to be very bad indeed.

About five minutes into the "wait an hour for Agent Brady" plan, I began to have second thoughts. I wasn't good at waiting around. I wanted to be out doing. Possibly even running. Mexico sounded appealing, I could use a tan and a fruity alcoholic beverage, and that was an option I very specifically intended to discuss with the elusive Agent Brady. At the moment, getting the hell out of Dodge sounded like a mighty fine idea.

Since I still had fifty-one minutes to go, I busied myself by zipping my laptop in its Neoprene sleeve and shoving it down into my tote. Then I rummaged in my closet until I found my favorite light jacket, along with the pair of Nike Airs I'd bought during my brief fascination with jogging in Central Park. My enthusiasm had waned after, oh, about seven minutes, and I'd shoved my running shoes into the closet, vowing to devote myself to Pilates at a women-only center.

Now, I'd get my money's worth out of the shoes. Running, I figured, was very likely in my future.

Other than that, I didn't know what to take with me. My lovely Marc Jacobs tote was plenty big enough to double as an overnight bag, but I wasn't heading out on a typical overnighter. I mean, I had a complete list of what to take on a first date—everything from makeup to emergency tampons to emergency condoms—but what to take on a deadly scavenger hunt through the city? That was a new one on me. I pondered for a while, then decided on a toothbrush, deodorant, a clean shirt, and fresh underwear. Then I checked the batteries on my iPod and tossed that in as well. I might be on the run, but I didn't intend to be without my show tunes.

All of that took about fifteen minutes, and I was just about to say fuck it and head out the door forty-five minutes early, when the phone rang. I bolted across the room and snatched it up, my heart pounding so hard in my chest I thought it would explode. I'm good at shoving emotions down inside me, but poke even the tiniest crack in my armor, and it all explodes out of me in one big, gooey mess.

"Agent Brady!" I cried. "Thank you so much for calling me back. I've been—"

A long, sustained beeping noise interrupted me, and I realized that I wasn't talking with Agent Brady at all. I didn't have a clue who was on the other end of the line, in fact, but I did have a very bad feeling. Paranoia? Maybe. But it turned out I was right. Like the saying goes: it's not paranoia if they really are out to get you.

The beeping stopped and suddenly I was being serenaded. The music from *The Rocky Horror Picture Show*'s "Eddie" trickled across the phone line, and even though the situation was a bit odd, I couldn't help but hum along. I'd seen the movie at midnight screenings an embarrassing number of times, and I'd played Janet in two productions and Magenta in another. The music was practically branded on my brain. And this particular song—about poor Eddie who didn't love his teddy bear—was one of my favorites.

So there I was, filling in the words to the go with the tune, when all of a sudden, the lyrics kicked in, and there was Eddie telling me to "hurry or *you* may be dead."

What the fuck?

The voice had specifically said "you," which undoubtedly referred to me, because that wasn't in the song. Even more, that voice—the one who'd piped in for just that one word—wasn't on the original recording.

I realized I was staring terrified at the phone. Then a voice came on, the sound far away since the handset was no longer pressed to my ear. With trepidation, I pulled it close and listened. One of those computerized voices. The kind that says "please press or say 'one' now." Only this time she said: "Tick, tick, tick. The countdown has begun. Ten tomorrow morning, and your time is up."

The line went dead, and my stomach clenched. Forget what I'd thought about being a tiny bit safe. I needed to hurry or, in the immortal words of Meatloaf, I might be dead.

My stomach wrenched and I clapped my hand over my mouth as I raced for my bathroom. The porcelain of the toilet felt cool against my arms as I literally hugged the toilet, empty-ing my stomach of the coffee I'd had for lunch.

Weakly, I stood, then walked on shaky legs to the sink. I turned on the faucet, bent over, and sucked down two handfuls of water. Then I splashed water on my face and held myself up-right as I inspected my reflection in the mirror.

The girl who looked back at me appeared calmer than I felt. And why not? That girl now had a plan.

Back in the living room, I rummaged on the coffee table until I found the card Mel had given me. I'd had no luck with either Agent Brady or Mel.

Now I was pinning my hopes on Andrew Garrison.

I dialed carefully, then held my breath as the phone rang twice, then three times.

On the third ring, I heard someone pick up, followed by an impatient "Hello?"

I almost fainted with relief. "Mr. Garrison? Andy? My name is Jennifer Crane. I'm a friend of Melanie Prescott. And—oh, God—I really need your help."

Chapter

12

BIRDIE

>>http://www.playsurvivewin.com<<

PLAY.SURVIVE.WIN

>>>WELCOME TO REPORTING CENTER<<<

PLAYER REPORT:

REPORT NO. A-0002

Filed By: Birdie

Subject: Status update.

Report:

- Secondary subject located and encounter successfully orchestrated.
- Time-release toxin delivered.
- Initial message to primary subject in transit.

- Warning and incentive message to secondary subject in transit.
- Game currently proceeding on schedule.

>>>End Report<<

Send Report to Opponent? >>**Yes**<< >>No<<

Block Sender Identity? >>**Yes**<< >>No<<

I shut my newly-acquired laptop, then get up from the Chippendale writing desk. Almost distractedly, I pace naked in my hotel suite at the Waldorf-Astoria, my head filled with so many thoughts that I can hardly sort through the noise.

I let my fingers trail over the fine silk upholstery of the love seat, then linger on the lilies and roses that are the centerpiece of the ornate flower arrangement that sits atop the coffee table. The suite is stunning, resplendent in genuine antiques and fine textiles, and I take it all in, enjoying these amenities as if I were a starved person.

And I have been starved. But I have the game to thank for letting me recover my soul in a bit of luxury. My reward will be even more satisfying when I complete the game, terminating the target and claiming my victory. But the initial payment is sufficient. Certainly enough to allow me to acquire supplies and enjoy a few of the finer things.

Almost without thinking, I pluck a rose from the arrangement, holding it delicately between two of my fingers. Then I slide the stem down, allowing the hook of the thorn to draw a thin line of blood up from my palm.

Once the soft petals rest inside my hand, I make a fist, thinking about my ultimate victory in this game as I claim this small bit of beauty as my own.

Silly, I know, but I shiver, experiencing a delight so physically intense that it is almost sexual in nature.

Then again, perhaps that isn't silly. After all, what is sex but the coupling of two individuals designed to create a rush of hormones and stimulate a physical response of ecstasy? That I can create my own ecstasy is both amazing and thrilling, and only underscores my own superiority over those that I hunt.

And it is through the hunt that I will experience the most exquisite ecstasy. Physical, mental, spiritual.

And, most important, I can exact my revenge.

That pleasure, however, must wait. The game has certain rules. Having set the clock in motion by poisoning the girl, now all I can do is stand back and wait, hoping that the lovely Jenn and the industrious Agent Brady solve the qualifying clue in time. Until they do, they are not my prey.

Of course, I'm tempted to strike early. In fact, it took all my willpower to not strike when I was in the man's bed.

But I won't break the rules. That's *my* rule: never break the rules.

But that doesn't mean I won't find satisfaction.

I run my finger lightly over the top of my computer, remembering the message that came only minutes before, just as I'd been filing my report. Instructions, along with an address and a photograph.

I dress carefully, then check my makeup. I dab on an extra touch of lip gloss, then brush some blush on my cheeks. Prison has made my skin so sallow.

Finished, I do a pirouette in front of the mirror.

I tuck my weapon into my purse, then head out the door.

Time to go to work.

ndrew opened the door before I even knocked. "Jennifer?"
I nodded, and he pulled me inside. The place was sti-
fling hot and I felt myself start to sweat.

He was tall and rumpled, but cute in a geeky sort of way.
Behind his thick glasses, narrowed eyes peered at me. His hair
spiked up in a thousand directions, probably from hours spent
running his fingers through it.

"You weren't followed?" he asked brusquely.

"I was careful," I said. "Just like you said."

"Good." He turned and moved toward a seating area on the
far side of the room where, I saw, a window stood open.

"Damn heater's on the fritz. The place is an oven. Not so
bad over there, though."

I followed him through the room to the other side. And
that's really all it was. Just one big room with metal beams pro-

truding in various places, apparently to hold up the ceiling. Chain link fencing ran down the center of the room, and cables and wires twined through it, originating from dozens of computers scattered across battered tabletops. The place had absolutely no artwork except for a dozen or so posters of Devi Taylor, the movie star, plastered around. Also one of those cardboard standup things from her last movie. Weird.

I must have stared, because he just shrugged. "I'm a fan. And it's not like I'm trying for *Better Homes & Gardens.*"

"Right," I said, a little embarrassed. "Thanks for letting me come over. I couldn't get in touch with Brady or Mel, and I didn't know what else to do."

"She's in Geneva."

"Excuse me?"

"NSA sent her on some spur-of-the-moment training thing in Geneva. They're incommunicado for I don't know. Three, four days maybe."

"And Matthew?"

"Beats me. He's Homeland Security now. For all I know they sent him over there, too."

"Oh." I stood there, not sure if I was relieved or disappointed. Disappointed Mel wasn't going to be any help to me. Relieved she was safe.

I decided that relief won out. After all, I had Andrew here to help me. "Like I said, thanks for helping me. You *can* help me, right?"

"I'll try," he said, snagging the chair closest to the window. "Tell me about the call."

I sat on the little sofa across from him. Cooler, but still too warm for my taste. I resisted the urge to fan myself as I started to tell my story. I'd hit the high points on the phone, but I'd been a tad on the hysterical side. Calmer now, I told the story straight through.

I squirmed a bit when I got to the part about the Eddie and his teddy song, but I made my way through it. "It just doesn't make any sense," I said in conclusion. "If the song had said to hurry or *Agent Brady* might be dead, that fits. But why me? Isn't the protector supposed to be safe? I mean, more or less?"

"That's the way the game works, yeah."

"Well, then what's happening? What's going on at ten to-morrow? Why am *I* the one getting a threat?"

"Dunno," he said. "But we'll try to figure it out." He squinted at me. "You're sure you didn't give the cops your name or address, right? When you called 911?"

I stopped, looked at him sideways. "No. I swear. I already told you."

He nodded. "Good. But I gotta say, I still wonder . . ." He trailed off, then waved a hand, dismissing his thought.

"What?" I demanded, alarmed.

"Nothing. Nothing."

"Andrew . . ."

He exhaled. "Look, I'm glad you came to me. I really am. I can help you. And by coming to me, you're probably helping others, too."

"But . . . ?" I prompted.

"But nothing. It's fine. I was just wondering—what with Mel working at the NSA and me working with Mel—I was just wondering if maybe I'm . . . well, if maybe I'm considered an authority, too."

"Oh, shit," I said. "I didn't think. I didn't know." I stood up, mortified and ready to go—where I didn't know. He made push-ing motions with his hands, gesturing me to sit back down.

"No, no. It's okay."

"Is it? What happens if I call in the cops, anyway?"

"The rules change," he said. "Call in the cops, and suddenly the protector is fair game, just like the target."

"Oh." Considering I was the protector in this particular game, I didn't much like that scenario. "Well, then."

And right then, someone pounded hard at the front door. I screamed.

"It's okay, it's okay," Andrew said, hopping to his feet. "It's just my dinner."

My hand was over my mouth, and I nodded. I was wiped. Ripped apart from the inside. And even though Andrew had said it was okay—that he wanted to help me—I still felt com-pletely alone.

Andrew came back with a plastic bag and a Styrofoam cup. He sat them on the table, then started pulling out containers of Chinese food. "Want some?"

I shook my head.

"Up to you." He sat back in the chair and took a long drag of the soda through the straw.

"So what do we do now?" I asked. "Find Agent Brady, right? And then what?"

"Then, I think the best thing would be to—*shit!*"

The soda tumbled to the ground, and his free hand went up to slap at his neck.

"Oh, shit. Oh, God. Get it out. Jesus, Jenn! Get it the fuck out of me!"

I jumped to my feet, but I didn't know what he was talking

about. Then he shifted, the hand moved, and I saw it. A dart, the metal end stuck deep in his neck, and blood trailing from the wound.

I was beside him in seconds, but his eyes were already rolling back in his head.

"Tired," he whispered, as I yanked the thing out. "The window. God, the open window."

I should have been worried that there was a dart out there with my name on it, but all I could think about was making sure Andy was okay. I raced across the room to the kitchen area, hoping I'd see a phone. I did, then called 911. I stayed on long enough to make sure the dispatcher understood that someone had been shot and to confirm the address. Then I hung up and went back to Andy.

This time, I was more cautious, staying below the windowsill until I reached him. Then I grabbed him by the shoulders and pulled him out of range.

He moaned, and I said a silent prayer.

"Tranq," he whispered. "Get out. Before they get here. Find Brady. No more cops. Dart probably meant . . . for you . . ."

He was struggling for words now, and I had to lean close just to hear him. "No choice, Jenn . . . Play . . . the game . . ."

And then he was gone.

I heard a whimper and realized it was coming from me. I leaned over, listening to his chest, relieved to hear the slow but steady pulse of his heart.

And then, in the distance, I heard something else.

Sirens.

I stood up, my legs shaky as I glanced back at Andy. I hesitated only a second before grabbing my tote.

Then I ran.

Chapter

14

JENNIFER

Agent Brady lived on the Upper East Side on 77th near John Jay Park, and that meant a thirty-minute taxi ride from Andy's place. I spent the first ten minutes calming myself down, then the next ten trying to think. As much as I didn't want it to be true, I knew that I was on the run now. And that meant I needed cash. The truth may not have sunk in before, but after watching Andy get shot, it totally had. This game was for real. And I needed all the resources I could get.

I leaned forward, told the driver to take a detour, then sat back until we reached my bank. During the short ride, I pulled out my cell phone to call the hospital, then realized I didn't know which one Andy was at.

But surely he was okay. I'd got the dart out, and his heart was beating—and strongly—when I left. He had to be fine. He had to be, because I wasn't willing to believe anything else.

The cab pulled up in front of the bank, and I paid, then got out, telling the driver to wait. Then I went in and flashed my ID at the nearest teller. And that, despite everything, was actually kind of fun. A girl only has so many times in her life when she can withdraw twenty grand in cash.

Blood money, maybe, but that didn't change the fact that I totally intended to spend it. I watch television. I know not to use my credit cards. The bad guys can always find you if you use a credit card. You use cash if you want to disappear. And that's exactly what I wanted to do at the moment.

As soon as the girl returned with my money, I headed to the ladies' room. I stuffed two grand into my wallet, another three into my laptop case, then put the rest of it into my jeans' pocket, my bra, and my tennis shoes. The cash (especially the shoe cash) would end up rumpled and stinky, but that wasn't something I intended to worry about.

And then, once I was loaded down with cash in much the same way a scarecrow is stuffed with straw, I hurried back out to my cab. While the driver whisked me through the streets of Manhattan, all the while mumbling into the hands-free set on his cell phone, I tried to locate Andy again, finally succeeding on the third try. Since I knew that hospitals hardly gave any information out these days, I pretended to be his sister. "I know you're not allowed to release information," I said. "But it'll take me a few hours to get there. Can you just tell me if he's going to be okay?"

I heard the hesitation, and when the nurse spoke, her words were soft, like someone who knows they're breaking a rule. "The prognosis is quite good. He's in observation, and they anticipate he'll be discharged in the morning."

I sagged back against the seat, a little giddy with relief. A ridiculous emotion, I suppose, since I was exactly where I was before. Andrew might be fine (thank goodness) but I was still alone. And ten tomorrow was coming as fast as ever.

A few minutes later, the cab pulled up in front of Agent Brady's place, a completely refurbished and totally stunning pre-war building, complete with art deco masonry and the original mullioned windows. I stared at it and decided that FBI agents made a better living than struggling divas marking time working as singing waitresses. Which, again, probably comes as no great surprise, but I like to tally these things up. So far, I've got to say that in the relative NYC hierarchy, I'm pretty low on the pole. The notable exceptions being homeless people and busboys. (That's not *entirely* true. On any given night I earn pretty good tips. Sometimes, though, you just have to bitch about the status quo.)

An elegant porte cochere fronted the building, under which stood a white-gloved doorman. Inside, undoubtedly, I'd find a concierge. And unless I was seriously mistaken, there were elevators in that building. I felt a little tinge of jealousy. *My* flat was a sixth-floor walk up, and I considered myself lucky to find a building I could afford that had the basic necessities like, oh, walls. I figured a bathroom was a plus. Doormen and concierge service were out of the question.

I paid the driver, then got out. I took a quick look around, scoping out the neighborhood for bad guys lurking in the bushes. I didn't see any lurkers, so I headed into the building, nodding politely as the doorman, bedecked in a dark green suit with military-style piping, opened the door for me. I marched across the gleaming marble floor to the concierge desk, where a dark-haired man (this one in a blue blazer) held up a finger, signaling for me to wait while he finished a phone conversation.

So I waited. I shifted my weight from foot to foot, drummed my finger on the desk, and did everything short of writing "S.O.S." in lipstick on my forehead to try and get him to hurry up. No luck.

When he finally did hang up the phone, though, he was all smiles and attention. "May I help you?"

"Yes, thank you. I'm here to see Devlin Brady."

He asked my name, I gave it, and then he picked up a nearby phone and dialed three digits. I expected him to say something into the phone, but he didn't. Instead, he just hung it up and looked at me. "Is Agent Brady expecting you?"

Okay, that wasn't in the script I had running through my head. "I called and told him I was on my way over." True. But what I didn't mention was that Agent Brady may not have gotten the message.

"I'm sorry, but there's no answer now."

"Oh." I'd known that was a possibility—I mean, the man hadn't answered his phone—but the scenario I'd concocted had him coming home. Or screening calls. Or something. "So, do you know where he is?" Maybe I'd get lucky.

"No, ma'am."

"Oh." I thought for a while. "Maybe he's in the gym? You guys have a health center, right? Could you check?" He just stared at me, so I added, "It's really important that I talk to him."

Another long stare, probably as he tried to decide if I was a jilted lover, come to seek revenge.

"Really," I insisted. "It's about one of his cases. Tell him it's about PSW." I had no idea if that would move Agent Brady to action or not. But it was the best shot I had. Not that it made any difference if we couldn't actually get the guy on the phone.

"About what?"

"PSW," I repeated. "You know. The computer game?"

He raised an eyebrow.

"Just *tell* him," I begged.

The concierge eyed me up and down with a frown (I tried not to take it personally). Then he apparently came to a decision. Unfortunately, I wasn't informed of what that decision was, so when he picked up the phone again, I didn't know if he was once again trying to call Agent Brady, or if he was calling security to have me booted out.

It turned out he was calling Marissa (whoever she was). "Is Agent Brady up there?" He listened to the response, then looked at me, shaking his head slightly. "I'm sorry, miss, he's not in the gym."

I exhaled, torn between frustration and fear. What if he was in there rotting? I had to at least know. If Agent Brady was gone—or dead—then my last ally was gone. And since alone wasn't an option I wanted to contemplate, I leaned up against the concierge desk, doing my best to look desperate. Which, under the circumstances, wasn't too hard.

"Could I just head up?" I asked, aiming my best ingénue smile at him. "It's really important that I see him, and he's probably just asleep. I'll pound on the door, and he'll let me in and everything will be just fine. Please?"

"Lady, I'm sorry."

So much for the ingénue role. "His regular phone, then. Have you called his regular phone?"

He nailed me with a squinty-eyed stare. "Have *you*?"

"As a matter of fact, I have. No answer. But that was at least a half hour ago. Can you try again?"

Surprisingly, he didn't argue, just dialed the number, then left a curt, "Please call the front desk" message. After he hung up, I stared at the phone for a full minute. Surely Devlin would call.

He didn't.

I cursed, then considered sneaking upstairs. I had Devlin's profile, so I knew he lived in 12A. And there had to be a back door to this place. Some sort of service entrance. Probably even a service elevator. So all I had to do was get past the doorman and the concierge . . . and the locked doors and the security cameras.

Okay, so maybe that wasn't the best plan, but I was getting desperate enough to try anything.

I was just about to tell the concierge that I was heading to the corner to get a Diet Coke (a total fabrication since what I really wanted to do was scope out the rear-entrance potential), when a messenger trotted in, his bike helmet still on his head and his pouch slung crossways over his chest.

"Hey," he said to the concierge, not even noticing me. I decided this was as good a time as any to make my escape. If I hurried, maybe the concierge would be so involved with the messenger that he wouldn't check the monitors that were undoubtedly broadcasting everything going on near the back doors. I'd moved two feet away from the doorman when I heard the messenger say "Brady, 12A. I'm supposed to wait until he signs for it."

I stopped. More specifically, I froze. And it doesn't take a genius to know what I was thinking: This skinny cycler with helmet hair was holding the message that would shove Devlin Brady full force into the game.

I sidled back until I was leaning against the concierge desk. While I did, my good friend the concierge dialed the house phone again. Once again, there was no answer. The messenger and the concierge looked at each other. Then the concierge held out his hand. "I can sign for it."

Helmet Head made a face. "Sorry, man. I'm supposed to make sure it's delivered. Urgent document or something. Customer even paid extra. I'll get ripped a new one if I don't get a confirmation."

"Maybe we could all go up," I suggested. "Knock on the door."

"Who are you?"

"Miss . . ." The concierge sniffed. Apparently my good friend the concierge was getting a little pissy.

"Look," I said, trying to appear reasonable and rational. "I'm pretty sure that message is related to my business with Agent Brady. So let's all go up and knock on the door. What can that hurt?"

"I gotta get the man the message," Helmet Head said. "If I go back without trying everything, my boss is gonna—"

"Rip you a new one," I finished. "Yeah. We know." I turned to the concierge. "Please?"

He scowled, then picked up the phone, this time dialing enough numbers that I knew he wasn't buzzing Devlin on the house phone. But I didn't know who he was calling. A psychiatric ward, maybe?

While he concentrated on the phone, I focused on the messenger. "So, um, who's the message from?"

"Beats me."

"Does it say on the envelope?"

"Lady, you want to give it a rest?"

"I'm just curious. And what's the big deal, anyway? You can't even look?"

He did look. But he didn't say a word to me.

"Well?"

"Is your name on this envelope?" He didn't wait for me to answer. "Then I guess it ain't any of your business, is it?"

"Since you won't let me see the envelope, how do I know if my name's on there or not?"

"What is your problem?"

"There are too many to list. But it's important. *Really.* Now who sent the package?"

He sighed. "There's nothing on the envelope, okay?"

I nodded. "Thanks."

He gave me a curt nod back.

"So who brought it to your office?"

Every bone in his body seemed to go slack, and he let out the loudest sigh I've ever heard. I swear, I've never seen such a stunning example of exasperation. Truly. The guy should be an actor.

Behind us, the concierge started speaking, telling Agent Brady in very polite tones that he would be escorting a delivery man to the door, that it was a priority package, and that he hoped Agent Brady would answer when he and the messenger came calling.

"What about me?" I asked.

The concierge ignored me. Instead, he signaled to the doorman, asked him to watch the desk for a moment, then headed toward the elevator bank.

I tagged along.

The doors slid open and they stepped on. Once again, I followed, only to find myself foiled by a firm hand held out by an equally firm arm. If I took one more step, the concierge would be copping a feel, and that really wasn't something I was in the mood for.

"Dammit! I told you, it's urgent. I need to see Agent Brady."

"And I told you no. Not unless Agent Brady wants to see you."

I shifted my weight from one foot to the other, wondering what I should do now. I've gotten used to being rejected at auditions, but except for that, I tend to get my own way. And I can't say I was too keen on not getting it right now.

Unfortunately, I didn't see a way around it.

"Fine," I said, mustering as much pride as I could. I turned to Helmet Head. "Will you at least answer my question?" I was standing in the doorway, and the elevator door was doing that number where it's trying to close but can't. Any second now, the thing was going to start squawking.

"What question?"

"Who gave you the package?"

"My boss."

It was my turn to be exasperated. "Who gave it to him?"

"Her," he said. "My boss is a woman."

The concierge took a step forward. "Miss, if you don't step back now, I'm going to call the authorities."

That did it. Frustrated and defeated, I stepped back. But as the doors slid closed, I did manage to catch a glimpse of Helmet Head's satchel: Speedy Delivery.

Well, I thought. That was something.

Chapter

15

DEVLIN

Devlin stared at his answering machine, the red flashes almost blinding in the dim light of the apartment. He almost erased the messages, but then he squared his shoulders and pushed PLAY instead. A whir, a beep, and then, "Yo, Devlin. It's Mark. Agent Bullard if you want to get official about it, and since I hear you're sitting on your ass, I guess we'll make this an official request. I outrank you, after all." A pause, then, "I'm worried about you, buddy. I know you're not dirty, man. And a lot of the other guys are rallying for you, too. So just give me a call, okay?"

The message clicked off and Devlin drew in a breath. He'd known Bullard for going on three years now, and the guy was a decent enough agent. But he'd never been investigated by OPR. Never shot his partner. As far as Devlin knew, Bullard hadn't ever even fired his weapon outside of training.

Still . . . he picked up the phone. Almost called back. Then he slammed down the receiver and, for good measure, he hit the ERASE button, effectively deleting the rest of the messages from the machine. Why not? He'd already interacted with the human race today. As far as Devlin was concerned, his quota for the week was filled.

He stood there and counted to ten, trying to calm down. When that didn't much work, he headed to the kitchen for a beer. Or bourbon. That's when he heard the knock.

For a second, he considered ignoring it, but he dismissed the idea. Most likely Annabel again, and he figured he could put up with her for at least a few more minutes.

But when he pulled open the door, it wasn't the elderly lady he saw. It was Evan, the concierge, standing beside a skinny guy in cycling gear who immediately shoved an envelope into Devlin's face. A standard brown clasp envelope adorned with a crisp white label. Devlin noted his name, and also noted that there was no return address. He didn't take the envelope.

"You're Agent Devlin Brady?" the messenger asked.

"Who wants to know?"

"Agent Brady," Evan inserted, in the smooth tone of a man used to working out problems, "this gentleman insists that this delivery is of the utmost importance and that he was strictly instructed to deliver it only to you."

"Tell him to get the hell out of my way, or my fist will deliver something meant only for him."

"Come on, man," the messenger said. "I'm going to get so fucking fired if you don't sign for this thing."

Devlin looked at Evan. "You fell for this shit?"

"I'm sorry, Agent Brady. You've received so many official papers these last few weeks that I thought this might be urgent or expected. But now that I see it's not, I'll escort the gentleman back downstairs, and apologize for the inconvenience."

"No way, man. Just take the thing, would you? I'm going to get so busted."

Devlin was just about to say that wasn't really his problem when he heard the locks click on Annabel's door. Then it opened and the woman's head poked out, her eyes wide behind her glasses.

"I was wondering what all the fuss in the hall was about. Is there a problem?"

She looked at Devlin while she spoke, her voice and expression just a tad too innocent. He sighed and held his hand out for the envelope.

"Thanks, man. Sign here." The messenger shoved a clipboard at him, and Devlin dutifully signed. He tucked the envelope under his arm and dug in his pocket for his key as Evan and the messenger headed back toward the elevator bank.

"By the way," Evan said as Devlin pushed his door open. "There's a young lady in the lobby who wants to see you. I called to announce her, but you didn't answer."

"I'm not interested in seeing anyone," Devlin said.

"She said it was about a game."

Devlin paused, for a moment wondering if it was the woman from the bar, come to play find the panties. "Tell her it's a bad day. She can try back later."

"Certainly, sir."

Devlin didn't think any more of the woman. Instead, he shut the apartment door and flipped the dead bolt. He tossed the envelope onto the foyer table, and was just about to leave it sitting there when one small oddity caught his eye. A water-mark, barely visible, on the pure white label. He hesitated, wanting to simply leave it be. But Devlin had learned a long time ago to trust his instincts, and the fact that he'd been living in a cave for the last few weeks hadn't changed that.

He took the envelope, then angled it slightly, so that he could just make out the mark: PSW.

Devlin reached for the gun he wasn't wearing as his mind raced to Melanie Prescott, his first thought that she was in danger. He hadn't been on the case in over six months, his reassignment inevitable once the case had gone cold. Was this a break? Or was it something else entirely?

The thoughts ripped through his head almost as quickly as he ripped the seal on the envelope. Then he reached in, carefully extracting the single piece of paper with the very tips of his fingers. He laid it on the table, then felt his stomach tighten as he saw what was written in bold at the top of the page: PLAY OR DIE.

He drew in a breath, steeled himself. This was something else entirely, all right.

And this something was a hell of a lot worse.

"No way," I said. "I'm staying. Consider this a hunger strike." I'd been pacing the lobby, but once Mr. Concierge returned and told me that Agent Brady refused to see me and that I'd have to leave, I'd plunked myself down on the fancy brocade sofa. Now I kicked my feet up onto the polished wood coffee table, crossed my arms over my chest, and dug in for the long haul. Agent Brady had to come out sometime. And until then, I was staying put.

I wasn't entirely sure what I was going to do about food or bathroom breaks, but I was kind of hoping we wouldn't get that far. Of course, the second the thought entered my head, I realized I desperately needed to pee. So much for mind over matter.

"Let me be a bit more specific," my concierge friend said as he loomed over me. "If you don't vacate the premises by the time I count to five, I will call the police. One . . . two . . ."

Okay, obviously he'd figured out my weak spot. So I got up—slowly—and headed toward the revolving door. Mr. Concierge Asshole Dude continued counting, which really pissed me off. I was going, wasn't I?

"Three . . . four . . ."

I was just about to step into the revolving door when I heard the phone ring. Since he stopped his counting, I stopped walking. Call it a matter of principle.

I couldn't hear what he had to say, but I did see the way he looked at me. Annoyed and maybe even more than that. Maybe downright pissed off. Then he nodded, hung up the phone, and walked toward me. I held up my hands in defense. "I'm going, already. Just get off my case."

"Agent Brady will see you now."

I balked, but I recovered quickly. I lifted my chin high as I moved away from the door. Then I walked with a grace and dignity I didn't feel toward the elevator bank. I stepped into a waiting car, pushed the button for twelve, then turned to aim my very best stage smile at the concierge. The kind that the guy on the last row of the balcony can see. "Thanks *so* much. You've been such a big help."

And then—with timing that couldn't be more perfect—the elevator doors slid closed, effectively erasing his prissy, sour face.

A minor victory, maybe, but at the moment, I was taking whatever I could get.

Chapter

17

JENNIFER

Only a few moments had passed from the time I stepped into the elevator all agog with victory to the time I emerged on the twelfth floor, completely and totally terrified once again. Under the circumstances, a victory was like a drug. During the moment, all was perfect. But once the drug wore off, reality slapped back, and even harder than ever.

I'd barely knocked when Agent Brady yanked the door open. He stared at me, not the pillar of strength I'd expected at all. Instead, he looked lost, his pale eyes cloudy with distrust. For an instant, recognition flickered in his eyes, and he stood back from the door, a silent invitation if not exactly a welcome.

I almost ran the other direction, I swear to God I did, but right now, this was the only person I knew who could help me. And I desperately needed help. So I stepped inside. The thud of the door closing seemed to echo in my head as Devlin stared me down. I just stood there in the dimly lit foyer, my hands at my sides.

"You," he finally said. "I know you."

I nodded. "Jennifer Crane. I was Melanie Prescott's room-mate last year."

"What do you know about the game?"

I took a step backwards and casually rested my hand on the doorknob. After what happened with Andy, my faith in the safety of my surroundings had diminished to zero. Agent Brady might be the target, but I was still going to be careful.

Brady didn't move a muscle. He just stared right at me, his face etched in stone, his eyes penetrating. The man scared me and, unreasonably, that made me feel better. This was a hard man. And a man like this could keep me safe.

"Talk to me, Crane. I need to know what you're doing here."

There was no denying the sharp edge of anger in his voice, and I cringed. "I got a message," I said. "About PSW. I'm . . . I guess I'm playing the game now." I licked my lips. "And I guess you are, too."

His face never softened, but I saw a flicker of something cross his eyes. Then he shoved his hands into his pockets as he moved out of the foyer. Not knowing what else to do, I followed, silently congratulating myself on only looking back toward the door once. There was no place to run, after all. Ever since I'd left Andy, I'd been telling myself that this apartment was safety. Now that I was here, I was clinging to that, and nothing was going to make me change my mind.

Not even Devlin Brady.

DEVLIN

"You're here about PSW," Devlin said. He examined her face as she nodded, her lips pressed together as if she wasn't going to say another word until she was sure he was on her side. Smart woman. "It's okay," he said. "I don't bite. Just tell me."

She hesitated, then drew a breath and spoke. "You're the target. And . . . and I'm the protector."

He looked her up and down. A mane of coal black hair framing a thin, worried face. A delicate body, but with a solid layer of muscle. He thought back, trying to remember her file, and he seemed to recall the theater. A dancer, maybe, in which case she might have a hell of a kick.

A kick wasn't going to do a lot of good against an assassin's bullet. Finally, he just laughed. A weak, tired, time-to-quit-all-the-bullshit kind of laugh.

She took a step back, her green eyes wide, her expression terrified.

"Forget it," he said.

"Forget it? Forget what?"

"The whole goddamn thing," he said. "I don't need a protector. I'm not playing the game."

"What do you mean?"

"What does it sound like?"

"So you're just going to sit here? A target, literally, for some freak? You're going to end up dead!"

"Maybe," he said. Then he turned and headed down his small hallway to the living room. She followed. "Would you like coffee?" he asked, the sarcasm coming naturally. "Soda, water? Anything I can do to make you feel more comfortable?"

"You wanna make me more comfortable? Quit acting like an asshole."

It was a gutsy response, and accurate. And he liked the girl all the more for it. "Sorry. Asshole is my natural state of being."

"Work to overcome your limitations," she said.

"Feel better?"

Her brow furrowed. "What?"

"Do you feel better?" He spoke slowly, the way his mother had always talked to the hired help who didn't speak English, as if a slower speed would somehow make the unfamiliar words comprehensible.

She shook her head slowly, clearly *not* comprehending.

"Anger," he said. "Sometimes it takes the edge off of fear."

"I . . . Oh." She squinted at him, probably trying to decide if he was okay, or even more of a jerk than she'd originally believed.

While she pondered that mystery, he moved into the kitchen

and came back with a Diet Coke. He hadn't asked what she wanted, but in Devlin's experience, most women wanted Diet Coke.

She popped the top without even looking at the can, took a long sip, and then grinned. "You're right," she said. "Getting pissed off at you totally made me feel better."

"Happy to oblige."

She glanced around his apartment, her nose wrinkling in disgust as she did so. He stifled a shrug. *Women.* The place wasn't that bad yet. Nothing was breeding in the mess on the floor, and to the best of his knowledge, he hadn't yet discovered penicillin in its natural form.

He waved at the couch. "Sit if you want. We should probably talk."

"Well, duh!" She turned and glanced at the couch, then moved to his desk and pulled out the hard wooden chair and sat there.

He shrugged and moved to the sofa, shoved aside the takeout containers, beer bottles, and crumpled bags of chips, then sat in the space he'd offered her. Then he stared at her.

She managed to keep still for a good sixty seconds. Then she got up, went to the curtains, and pulled them open. Since it was late afternoon, the light was dim, but it was still more than his apartment had seen in weeks. His pupils shrank to the size of pinpricks, and he flinched, squinting even as he glared at her. "Come on, lady! You want to ask next time!"

"It's like a tomb in here."

"Maybe I like it that way."

Her brow furrowed. "I remember you," she said. "What happened to you?"

"Shit happened," he said. A pretty accurate assessment of the situation, he thought. Pithy. To the point. And a lot more direct that blathering on about a drug deal gone bad. About discovering that his partner had thrown in with the assholes they'd been tracking. About the FBI thinking maybe he'd gone dirty, too. About shooting his partner, so his buddy wouldn't shoot him first. Except maybe Randall wouldn't have shot him at all. He didn't know, not anymore. Not for certain. Especially not after he'd seen Randall's daughter, three years old and dressed in black, coming up to him after the funeral and hugging him. Loving him still, even though Devlin had killed her daddy.

What was left of his heart had just about ripped in two.

"Shit happens all the time," he said.

She stared at him, then slowly shook her head. "Nice philosophy."

"I can't claim that it's original." He watched her, then tried to pull something resembling social skills up from the depths of his gut. "Look, just go."

"I can't do that," she said. "I don't have anyone else to help me. And something's going to happen to me. Tomorrow. The voice said I had until ten tomorrow."

Hysteria had crept into her voice. The last thing Devlin wanted to deal with was a hysterical female. He had to give this one credit, though. She'd been thrust into an untenable position. Worse, she'd ended up stuck with him. Right now, that was a fate he wouldn't wish on anybody.

So maybe he could understand her mood.

His mood wasn't particularly chivalrous, but that didn't mean he had to be an ass. Especially since there was apparently more to the whole story than she'd told him so far.

And before Devlin even realized what he was doing, he was standing in front of her, his hand on her shoulder. He led her to the couch, then sat her in the clean spot. He sat himself on the coffee table in front of her, first using his arm to wipe all the detritus to the floor. "Tell me," he demanded.

"I got a message," she said.

"That much I gathered. So what was it? Transferred money and my profile?"

"No. I mean, yes. I got all that. Then later, when I was trying to figure out what I should do, I got another message. It . . . it was *Rocky Horror*."

"Excuse me?"

"A phone call. It was a line from Eddie's song in *Rocky Horror*. The voice on the phone was singing Eddie's line about hurrying, or he might be dead. Only the line was different. It was a warning to me. Hurry, or *you* might be dead. Talking about me. Talking *to* me. And then after that, there was this freaky ticking noise and a computerized voice told me I had until ten tomorrow."

"Shit."

That actually earned him a grin. "That was pretty much my reaction. And the thing is . . ." She trailed off with a shake of her head. "Never mind."

"You figured that even if you weren't cut out to be my protector, at the very least I could help you."

"It seemed reasonable. But then I couldn't get ahold of you. So I called Andy."

He felt an absurd pang of guilt for erasing the messages, then quashed it and focused on what she was saying now. "Who did you call?"

"Andrew Garrison. He works with Mel on all the PSW research she does on the side. You know about that?"

He nodded, and she continued, telling him about how she contacted Andrew, then went to his apartment. When she got to the part where Andrew got shot, he winced.

"I called the hospital," she said, summing up, "and he's doing okay. But I still needed help."

"And I was all that was left."

"Pretty much. So I came here." She looked around his apartment. "But I didn't know."

"Know what?"

"That shit happened." She stood up, then hauled her huge tote bag over her shoulder. "I'll be fine. I'll get ahold of Mel. I'll figure this out. And right now, I'll just leave you alone. So sorry to have bothered you, Agent Brady."

She started to take a step, but he caught her arm. She looked up at him, a question in her eyes.

"Call me Devlin," he said.

"Fine. Good-bye, Devlin."

"And stay."

"Why?" she asked.

Redemption, he almost said. But he didn't. "I'll help you," he said. "And then we'll see where we are."

Chapter

19

JENNIFER

"**A**nd that's all the phone call said?" Devlin asked.

I nodded. I was pacing his apartment again, a trash bag instead of a Diet Coke in my hand as I used the tip of my forefinger and thumb to pick up all the crap and toss it in a bag. Honestly, the man should arrest himself. The apartment was stunning—all gleaming wood, expensive furniture, and fabulous artwork —and he'd totally trashed the place.

I didn't know what had happened to this man, but I did know that he'd come over to my side. Or maybe his cop instincts had just gotten the better of him. I didn't know the reason, and I didn't care. All that mattered was that he was going to help me.

He passed by me, taking the trash bag from my hand. I was about to argue—I *really* didn't intend to hang around in that mess—but then he started picking up the trash himself. Good.

I didn't come here to be his maid, and I settled myself back in front of his window, looking out onto the terrace that overlooked the East River.

"A few lines from *Rocky Horror*, a warning that you might be dead if you don't hurry, and then a voice telling you the clock is ticking and that your drop-dead deadline is ten tomorrow."

"Except for the fact that I'm not crazy about the term 'drop-dead,' yeah. That about sums it up."

"It's the *Rocky Horror* thing that I think is really interesting."

"Well, gee, me too. Who doesn't love a great transvestite musical?" I was dripping sarcasm now. I think he could tell.

"*My* clue," he said, "is overflowing with Broadway musical references."

Okay. He was right. I was interested. "Let me see."

He disappeared back into the hallway and returned with a manila envelope I'd seen before. He handed it to me, and I pulled out the single sheet that was inside. When I saw it, I gasped:

PLAY OR DIE

Annie

Brigadoon

Cabaret

Damn Yankees

Evita

Falsettos

Gigi

Hair

I'd Rather Be Right

Jesus Christ Superstar

Kiss Me, Kate

Lady, Be Good
Mary Poppins
Nine
Oklahoma!
Pippin
Quilt
Rent
Show Boat
Titanic
Urinetown
Vanities
Wonderful Town
You're a Good Man, Charlie Brown
Ziegfeld Follies

If the understudy becomes the lead, then: ANA RNERNEN
AKKI NAIVA IEKAVHHDKINAAO & HVNEAAVA AKE AVE
OADIV IIDIAI KI IAV EDAVE, HAV OKRAA ANAV AKRIA AVE
NIHOVE ADAAVI DI N ANAV ODIA AKREIARA VOVH

"We've definitely got a Broadway theme going here," he said.

"No kidding. But why?" I asked.

"What do you mean?"

"The whole point of PSW is that the clues are based on the *target*'s profile. Right?"

"Right."

"But my *Rocky Horror* message and your Play or Die message all have Broadway musical references."

"So?"

"So the clues are supposed to be related to *you*. But Broadway's my thing. That's why I'm in New York. I don't intend to be a waitress forever. One of these days I'm going to win a Tony award."

"Good luck," he said, and I didn't think he was being facetious. "But that's not a mystery." He turned his head toward the massive mahogany entertainment center. And right there, above the television on the center shelf, stood the familiar statuette. I think I started to whimper.

"You have a Tony award?"

"Got it when I was thirteen," he said. "That was my seventh production, I think. Second nomination."

I swear I had to manually shove my jaw back into place. "You were on Broadway when you were a kid? Holy shit." I was gaping at him, but that was just too damn bad. "Wait. Wait a second. Devlin Brady. Of course! I just never made the connection. Oh my God! Oh. My. God."

He just stood there staring at me. I had a feeling he'd been subjected to the gushing fan thing a few times before. I wasn't a gushing fan so much as an envious wannabe. But I could still see why Devlin wanted to keep his distance.

I cleared my throat and tried to calm down. "So why do you work for the FBI?" I couldn't imagine quitting Broadway. Not in a million years. And especially not if I'd won a freaking Tony award.

What kind of planet was this guy from?

"I wanted a low-stress career," he said.

"Ha ha. Seriously, why—"

But he cut me off with a wave of his hand. "We can discuss the pressures and foibles of a career in theater after we keep you

alive. Right now, all you need to know is that Broadway musicals fit my profile, too. Except, of course, I never submitted a
profile."

I blinked. "You must have."

"Nope. I'm not into computer games. And after I landed the
case, I wasn't inclined to jump on the PSW bandwagon, you
know?"

"But I saw it!"

"Fake. I entered one in the course of the investigation in
order to access the game, but no legitimate information was
used. Second of all, even if I had submitted a profile, I would
never have included my address and phone number. I may be
fucked up, but I'm not stupid."

He had a point, actually. I know I hadn't put that kind of information on my PSW profile. For that matter, I wasn't even
sure the profile form had asked for those kind of details. Except
it must have because that's how I got Devlin's address and
phone number.

I lifted a finger. "Just hang on a second." My tote bag was at
my feet, and now I rummaged inside and pulled out my laptop.
I started it up, cursing it softly to try to make it boot up faster.
Since that wasn't happening, I shifted gears, moving on to other
things while the computer warmed up. "And here's something
else that's off. Don't you think it's a little freaky that I'm involved in this game? You, too."

"I'll bite," he said. "Why?"

"Because we know the score. We know that Mel and
Matthew actually won. Plus, we know about that lawyer you
guys suspected for a while." By "you guys" I meant the FBI.
Since Devlin was nodding, I figured he knew that.

"Thomas Reardon," he said.

"That's the one. I can't believe you didn't arrest him."

"No proof," Devlin said.

I snorted. From what Mel had told me, Archibald Grimaldi's attorney had been at the very end of the game she'd played. And somehow—I'm not quite sure how—he'd been the catalyst for both Mel winning her prize money and for calling off the assassin. That seemed to me to be proof enough.

I guess my disbelief showed on my face, because Devlin kind of half-smiled. "We had no proof that the attorney was doing anything except holding materials for Grimaldi. Since Grimaldi is dead, if he's behind all of this, then obviously someone else was helping him. It might be Reardon, it might be someone else. We just don't know. And we can't arrest without sufficient evidence."

"Fine," I said. I wasn't a lawyer; how was I supposed to argue with that? "But it still seems weird to me that you and I are sucked into this. We know stuff. And if we were chosen randomly, then it's *really* weird."

"Especially since I've never played the game."

"Exactly," I said. "Except according to that, you have." I pointed to the laptop, which had finally finished doing its thing. I hunched over and pulled up the document, DB_Profile.doc. I turned the machine and pointed. "Take a look."

He did. "You're right," he said. "This is fucked."

"You really didn't do it?"

"I really didn't. And look at this." He tapped the screen and I leaned over to see the photo embedded in the document. "That's a candid shot." He met my eyes. "Someone's been scoping me out. And someone knows me well enough to put together a profile."

"Someone wanted you to be the target," I said. "Wanted you enough to make sure you had a profile in the system."

"Looks that way."

"Have I mentioned I really don't like this?"

He smiled, but didn't answer. Instead, he just said, "What else?"

"What else is weird? Other than the whole situation? Well, the insinuation that I'm going to be dead before lunch tomorrow is a little off-putting."

"I can see that it would be."

"It doesn't make any sense."

"Considering the whole game is about killing people off, I think it makes a lot of sense."

"Thanks," I said. "Your support is overwhelming."

He just smirked. I tell you, I was starting to like the guy.

"Look," I said. "Killing *the target* off is what the whole game is about. But I'm not the target. That's you," I said, poking him in the chest to make my point. "So why am I the one with the ticking clock?"

"I don't think I've got a free pass here. For one thing, we don't have any idea what that message says. I can't even pronounce it, much less interpret it."

"Devlin! That's not the point. I'm supposed to be the protector. I may be entirely lacking in qualifications—sorry 'bout that—but that's still my role. And the protector isn't supposed to be the target. That's the whole point of having those nice descriptive names."

"Kill switch," he said.

Since that seemed like a total non sequitur, I stared at him. "Kill who?" I finally asked.

"The twenty-four-hour kill switch," he said, this time speaking slowly, like I had a learning disability or something.

That ticked me off. "Okay, Agent Brady, let's get something straight, okay? I don't play this game. And I didn't spend months investigating some psycho who shoved the game into the real world. So don't treat me like an idiot just because I don't know what the hell you're talking about. Okay?"

He held up his hands in a gesture of surrender. "In the online version of the game, if you don't start playing in twenty-four-hours, the target is terminated and the players can all move on to another game. The point is incentive. So that the protector and the assassin aren't waiting around waiting to play a game with some target who's dragging his ass."

"Nice," I said.

"Not so nice in the real world," Devlin said. "What kind of incentive is there to play, after all?"

I cocked my head, remembering. "Kill the target," I said, remembering what Mel had told me. She'd been poisoned. And she had twenty-four hours to interpret the clues that led her to the antidote. And let me tell you, according to Mel, that was some slam-bang incentive to getting her ass in gear.

I frowned, then, because the pieces still didn't fit. "But that's just what I've been saying. Mel was the target. I'm not. So why am I being threatened?"

"Because it wouldn't do any good to threaten me."

He spoke nonchalantly, his voice level. I didn't have to ask what he meant.

"So whoever's pulling our chains knows us both really well. Knows enough to fill out a profile for you. And knows enough to know that threatening to kill you right off the bat isn't going to get you up and moving any faster." I kept my voice as flat as his, but I have to admit my heart was breaking. Something had happened to Agent Brady. The one time I'd met him before, he'd seemed vibrant. Now, he just seemed broken. I wanted to ask, but I didn't want to offend. I needed him to keep me alive. But he didn't need me at all.

"Threatening you, though . . ." He trailed off with a shake of his head. "Well, welcome to my weakness."

"Serve and protect," I said, dully.

"That's the police. But yeah, the sentiment's the same." He stood up then, and moved to the window. He stared out over the city, his hands shoved deep into the pocket of his jeans. "So what's going to happen to you tomorrow at ten, Jennifer Crane?" he asked.

I didn't know. And so help me, I didn't really want to find out.

Chapter

20

BIRDIE

I arrive at the white stone skyscraper after most of the staff has cleared out. The quarry I'm currently tracking will still be there, though. Of that, I'm sure. That's the lovely thing about lawyers; they don't keep bankers' hours.

I sign in—with a false name, of course—then walk the short distance to the elevator banks. The inside of the car is mirrored, and during the express ride, I take the opportunity to check my wig and freshen my makeup. This isn't a job where I expect to call upon my feminine wiles, but one can never be too careful.

A receptionist still mans the desk, probably counting the minutes until she can leave or counting the dollars in overtime she is earning. I identify myself, then sit down and start to riffle through a copy of *The New Yorker* while she announces me.

I'm chuckling over one of the cartoons when my quarry steps through the glass doors, his hand held out and a smile on his face. "Miss Paroti," he says. "A pleasure to meet you. I'm Thomas Reardon."

I rise and take his hand, my smile full of charm. I know that I'm attractive, all the more so when I smile. High cheekbones, arched eyebrows, a wide mouth. All features that light up when I'm happy. According to my mother, I was never happy enough. My response? With a mother like her, why would I be?

His grip is firm, but cold. And as I study his face, I decide that I don't like him. There's weakness in his eyes. A sense of self-loathing.

I never find my job distasteful; far from it. But in this case, I find my mission to be even more palatable than usual. I will be doing the world a favor.

I continue to smile as he leads me to his office, my expression fading only a bit when Thomas steps toward his desk without shutting his office door. I clear my throat, and he stops in his tracks.

"I don't mean to silly," I say, "but I was hoping we could keep this just between us. At least until I sign a retainer. I'm so very particular about my privacy."

"Of course." He moves back to shut the door, and when he does, I pull the gun from my purse. It's well hidden in the folds of my skirt by the time he turns back and then gestures to one of the guest chairs.

I sit, then adjust my skirt to cover the gun and show off my legs. He sits as well, behind the desk, and his gaze drops to my knee. Oh, yes. This one will be so, so easy.

"You mentioned you had some business concerning a friend," he says, referring to some handwritten notes on a yellow legal pad in front of him.

I nod, and try to look sad as I make a mental note to take that pad with me when I leave. "Yes. More of an acquaintance, really. But I respect the man and I'm trying to tie up some loose ends for him. At his request, you know."

"You were rather vague on the phone. Why don't you give me the full story now."

"I'd be happy to," I say. I lean back in my seat, my hand still hidden in the folds of my skirt. "I think you know my acquaintance, actually. The one who needs my help."

"Do I?" He looks appropriately interested. "Who is it?"

"Archibald Grimaldi."

That gets him moving. He sits up straight, his eyes flashing with alarm. "Archie's dead. He's been dead for well over a year now."

I nod. "I know. Such a pity. A brilliant man, cut down in the prime of his life. A brilliant man who left so many loose ends hanging."

"What loose ends? " he says, and as he speaks, his hands creep toward the edge of the desk.

"I wouldn't do that if I were you," I say, and as I speak, I stand. The gun in my hand is aimed right for his heart, and the expression of stunned disbelief on his face is priceless. *That*, my friend, is what makes my job so rewarding.

He holds his hands high in the air, well away from the panic button that is surely under his desk.

"Roll backwards," I instruct, because once I was burned by a clever executive who tripped the signal with his knee. That wasn't the incident that landed me in prison, but the experience had been too close for comfort.

He complies—who wouldn't with a gun aimed at his heart?

"Who the hell are you?" he asks.

"I told you. I'm doing a favor for an acquaintance." I don't know much about what is going on, just the limited information that has been transmitted to me in the form of this additional assignment. But I do know that Thomas Reardon wasn't the only one helping to keep the game alive. Beyond that, I have nothing but supposition. And what I suppose is that Reardon knew too much. That others had played the game before me (lucky bastards) and that the authorities were closing in.

"If someone put you up to this . . ."

"Someone did," I assure him. "Did you think you were the only one helping Archie out with his game?"

"Archie is *dead*."

"So," I say, "are you."

Chapter 21

JENNIFER

"Maybe it's a hoax," I said, not really believing it. Someone was serious enough to shoot Andy. I was sure they were serious about getting me, too. "I mean, how? How can they say ten tomorrow with such certainty?"

"Sniper? Poison?"

I frowned, feeling lost and sulky. Not that he'd said anything I hadn't already thought myself. I just can't say that I was too keen on thinking it.

He sat down beside me. The beard stubble made him look sexy and dangerous, and I was desperately glad that he was there. For better or for worse, I knew that Devlin Brady really would protect me. He might not protect himself, but for me, he was willing to go the distance.

Except for my parents, was there anyone else in the whole world who'd do that for me? Was there anyone I'd do it for? I'd been "assigned" to protect Devlin. If it came down to it, could I? Would I? Even more, would he let me?

I squeezed my eyes shut. I didn't want to think about bloody conflicts or being a protector or even my parents. Especially not my parents. Because if I thought about them, I'd want to call them. And if I called them, they'd worry. Worse, they'd call the cops.

All these thoughts were raging through my head when Devlin took my hands in his. He squeezed, and I looked up at him, trying for a stalwart smile, but managing only a grimace.

"We don't have enough information to know what's going to happen tomorrow. All we can do is follow the clues. It's a kill switch. An incentive."

"To make us play the game," I said, the prize pupil.

He touched the tip of my nose, a ridiculous, silly gesture that had me wanting to cry. "Exactly. So we play. We solve my clue. We follow where it leads. And along the way, we'll figure out how to stop whatever it is that's going to happen to you."

"Oh hurry," I sang, "or I may be dead."

"Exactly," he said, then passed me the message. "Be brilliant."

"Speedy Delivery," I said.

"Excuse me?"

"That's who delivered it. He wouldn't tell me who dropped it off, but he did tell me that his boss gave it to him. Maybe we could call. Talk to his boss. Figure out who's behind all of this, and then we can—"

"Wait."

He spoke with such firmness that my mouth closed automatically. And believe me, that's not something that happens often.

"Maybe," he said. "But not yet. First we figure out the clue. First, we make sure you're safe."

Since I was behind that plan one thousand percent, I didn't argue. I didn't argue, but—"I don't know what to do with this," I said, tapping the message. "Do you know what to do with this?"

" 'Play or Die' is pretty clear," Devlin said. "But I don't have a clue what this gibberish means." At this, he pointed to the weird combination of letters like "ANA" and "AKKI."

"Or this," I said, also pointing. "What does 'If the understudy becomes the lead' mean? Other than my life's dream, that is."

He looked at me with interest. "You've been an understudy?"

I scowled. "You really need to learn not to take me so literally. *If* I ever get a job, and *if* I'm ever assigned as the understudy, *then* it'll be my life's dream."

"Maybe you'll nail the lead right off the bat," he said.

I was liking him more and more. And I was just about to say so when he held up a finger. "Actually, you may be on to something."

"I may?" That was news to me. "What?"

"If the lead in a show is the first, then the understudy is the second. Right?"

"Okay." I said the word slowly, wishing I knew what he was talking about.

"This list of shows is in alphabetical order," he said, his finger once again tapping on the paper.

"Right. Broadway musicals in alphabetical order."

"And these nonsense words have to be in code."

"I certainly hope so," I agreed.

"And I think we have the key to the code right here. Understudy, lead. Second, first."

I made a whooshing gesture over my head. "Not following."

To Devlin's credit, he didn't roll his eyes, look away, or do anything else to suggest that he thought I was an idiot, and he feared for his mortal safety with me cast in the role of protector. Then again, considering his doom and gloom persona when we first met, maybe he didn't give a shit about whether I could protect him or not. But since that wasn't our current problem, I wasn't going to worry about it. Instead, I just scooted closer, focused on the paper, and said, "Show me."

"Take this one," he said, pointing to the first weird word in the sequence: ANA. "The understudy becomes the lead, or the second becomes the first. So we look down the list of musicals— the *alphabetical*—list, and find titles with the second letter of A."

He did that, his finger stopping at *Cabaret.*

"So since the second becomes the first, then the letter we're looking for to undo the code is the first. So the letter is C." I said all that, and when Devlin nodded, I sat up straight, just as proud as if I'd recited all fifty states from memory (which is not, for the record, something I've ever managed except before my tenth grade social studies midterm).

"And N is the second letter of *Annie,*" he said. "So the second letter of our interpretation is A for Annie."

"Right. And we've already translated the A in our code and we know it's C. So that means the word is CAC."

Our eyes met and the apartment fell completely silent. Not even the creak of the walls or the thud of feet in the apartment above. And then the silence was broken. I broke it, actually. I said, "Well, shit. We're screwed."

And you know what? He *laughed.* He actually laughed at me.

"What," I demanded, "is so funny?"

"You," he said. "Stick with theater. I'm thinking you don't have the patience for investigative work."

I made a face. "In case it escaped your attention, I never claimed to be interested in the detective arts."

"If you're going to survive through tomorrow, I suggest you develop an interest really fast."

That sobered me up. "Right." I frowned at the message. "So what are we doing wrong?"

"Maybe it's—"

"Wait!" I had it. I was right. I *knew* I was right. "There are a whole bunch of options. We have to set them all out and then choose."

"Show me."

He grabbed a felt tip pen off the table and handed it to me. Then he shoved a copy of *Men's Health* in my direction and tapped the cover. "Scratch paper."

I was tempted to suggest that he actually read the issue, but this really wasn't the time for levity or advice regarding healthy living. Instead, I ran my finger down the list of Broadway titles and wrote the following:

A	N	A
C	A	C
D		D
F		F
H		H
L		L
M		M
V		V

Then I started working across to see what words I could come up with. I ended up with these: CAL, DAD, DAM, FAD, HAD, HAL, HAM, LAD, MAD

"Go with 'had,'" Devlin said.

"Why not 'mad'?"

"Looks like a sentence," he said. "That's the most likely word to start a sentence with."

I could think of a lot of sentences that started with Dad or Ham, but I wasn't inclined to argue. And I had a gut feeling he was right, anyway. I wrote HAD in big letters across the top of the magazine.

"This isn't going to work," Devlin said.

"Are you kidding? It *has* to work. It's the only clue we have!"

"Not that," he said. "The magazine. Hang on." And then he got up, disappeared into the back room, and came back with a yellow legal pad.

Okay. Much better.

I moved on to the next word:

R	N	E	R	N	E	N
B	A	J	B	A	J	A
		R			R	

"Barbara," Devlin said, before I'd even written the final A in my chart. "This one's easy. You can practically see the word."

It took me a second longer, but he was right. The word had to be BARBARA. I wrote that on the legal pad, just after HAD.

Had Barbara . . . what?

We kept going. I thought the next word would be pretty easy since the only translation for the KK in AKKI was OO.

Unfortunately, A and I both had a lot of options. The word list we came up with was COOK, COON, COOP, COOT, FOOT, HOOK, HOOP, HOOT, LOOK, LOON, LOOP, LOOT, MOON, and MOOT.

All well and good, but none of those words really seemed to fit. Had Barbara cook*ed* might make sense. Or look*ed*. But to just sit there? I had to wonder if our tormentor cared about verb tenses. More important, had we screwed up on the HAD BAR-BARA part of the equation?

I was just about to suggest to Devlin that we move on to the next word—figuring maybe that would give us a clue to this one—when he tapped the paper. I looked down, saw that he was tapping COOK, and then looked back up at him.

"That's it," he said.

"You're sure."

"Positive."

I wasn't and so, being both reasonable and nosy, I asked.

"Barbara Cook," he said. "Broadway musical star. Starred in—"

"*Any Wednesday, Carousel, Candide, The Music Man,*" I fin-ished. Then I leaned over, took both his cheeks in my hands, and kissed him. He looked surprised, but not annoyed. Score one for my team. "You're brilliant," I said.

"Duly noted." He nodded at our notes. "But we still have a long way to go."

"At least we know the theme. And we know we're doing this right. We've got a list of Broadway musicals, and now the name of a star. That can't be a coincidence. We must be on the right track."

My enthusiasm was like a living thing, pushing me along as

I moved on to the next word and the next and the next. Unfortunately, living things die, and this was seriously hard. We were still making progress, but it was slow going. More to the point, the message we were revealing wasn't striking lightning in either of us. After working our tails off for two solid hours, all we had was HAD BARBARA COOK ACTED PROFESSIONALLY & SEARCHED FOR HER WHITE KNIGHT ON THE RIVER.

I was starving and discouraged and, frankly, I was a little pissed off. "I thought the first clue was supposed to be *easy*. Get the game rolling, and all that."

"*Relatively* easy," he said. "Maybe this is a breeze compared to what's coming next."

"Oh, thank you. Thanks so much for helping me feel better."

He grinned, and then we split up the words and went to work. Another hour later, we'd solved the entire puzzle—for all the good it did us.

HAD BARBARA COOK ACTED
PROFESSIONALLY & SEARCHED FOR HER
WHITE KNIGHT ON THE RIVER, SHE WOULD
HAVE FOUND HER ANSWER HIDDEN IN A FACE WITH
MOURNFUL EYES.

I read it out loud, then looked up at Devlin. "I'm so screwed," I said. And, damn the man, he didn't disagree.

Chapter

22

JENNIFER

"Well?" I said.

"We're not beaten yet. We just need to break it down. Figure it out one piece at a time."

Which, I figured, was a nice, polite way of saying that I was dead meat.

"We also need to eat," he said. "We've been at this for hours. It's no wonder we can't think. What do you want?"

"I don't know. Pizza," I said. "Pepperoni. Mushroom. Extra cheese. And sausage on half, too."

"I thought you didn't know?"

"I figured it out," I said. It's a bad habit, I know. I say I'm undecided, when I really know exactly what I want. It drives boyfriends nuts. I think it's a girl thing.

Devlin didn't look annoyed. But he did point to the decoded message. "You're on a roll. Figure that out."

And then he took the phone and disappeared toward the front of the apartment. If his place is like mine, I figured that was where he kept the delivery menus.

I, meanwhile, grabbed my bag and went the opposite direction to the bathroom. I'd washed my hands and was searching for my makeup kit when my cell phone rang.

I snatched it up, hoping for Mel but getting Brian.

"I thought we were going to have drinks tonight! Where are you, and why have you left me alone with Fifi?"

"You're going to kill me."

"If that means you're leaving me with him for the evening, I have to agree. The little queen is driving me nuts. I swear I don't know how people survive with roommates. Much less with spouses."

"I'm sorry. I really am." He didn't know how sorry I was.

"I can't possibly forgive you. Unless it involves sex. If you're getting laid, I can find it in my heart. So long as he's cute and I can live vicariously through you later."

"I'm not getting laid," I said, though I wouldn't mind.

"Then you're screwed," he said.

"You don't know the half of it," I muttered. Then I added, "But I am with a guy."

"So there's still hope," Brian said.

"Yes," I agreed. "There's hope." I thought about the bizarre clue. A tiny, dismal ray of hope, but hope nonetheless.

"Then I forgive you for standing me up."

I almost grinned at that. Even in the crappiest of circumstances, Brian always made me feel better. "I promise you a rain check," I said. And since I had every intention of surviving, that was one promise I absolutely intended to keep.

"I'll let you get back to almost getting laid," he said. And he was just about to hang up when I had a brilliant idea.

"Brian!"

"Jenn?"

"Hang on a sec. I need a favor."

"No way. That's way too kinky for me."

"I happen to know that *nothing* is too kinky for you."

"True," he said. "Shoot."

"The guy I'm with, he's into puzzles and stuff. And we're doing one, and I'd like to impress him, you know? But I'm clueless." I wasn't entirely sure Brian would buy that, but I wasn't about to tell him the truth. I know Brian, and Brian would call the cops, no matter how much I begged him not to.

"Puzzles," he said. I could hear the curiosity in his voice. "What kind of puzzles?"

"Like crosswords and stuff. The kind of crap you get off on." I was whispering now, just in case Devlin had moved back from the kitchen and was hanging around outside the bathroom. "I don't want him to know I'm asking you. So can you hurry?"

"Not if you don't tell me the puzzle."

"Right." I felt a quick twinge as my mind went blank. I should have brought my notes back to the bathroom with me. But then I took a deep breath and forced myself to calm down. I'd been looking at the damn thing now for hours. I'd memorized entire songs in less time than that. The words were there in my memory. I just had to pull them out.

A sharp knock at the door made me jump. "Jenn? You okay in there?"

"Yeah. Yeah, I'm fine. Just freshening up, and then a friend called. We were supposed to get together tonight."

"Oh." A pause, then in a lower voice: "You're not telling him about—about all of this, are you?"

"Hello? No! Duh! Of course not."

In my ear, Brian was humming the theme from *Jeopardy!* On the other side of the door, dead silence. Then, "Right. Okay. Well, the pizza should be here in about forty minutes."

"Great. Terrific. Be right there."

"I'm not hearing a lot of passion from you," Brian said.

"First date."

"And you're hoping that solving a puzzle makes him hot?"

"Just shut up and help me." Since he stayed quiet, I assumed that meant he was okay with the shutting-up plan. "Okay, here's the puzzle." I closed my eyes and tried to picture the legal pad. "Had Barbara Cook acted professionally and searched for her white knight on the river, she—"

"Come on," Brian said, cutting me off. "Tell me the truth. This is really something kinky."

"Just *help* me."

"Okay, okay." I heard the eraser end of a pencil tapping against his teeth, a terrible habit I wish he'd break. Then I heard a beep.

"Your phone?"

"Hang on." A pause. "I don't recognize the number. God, I was hoping it was Larry. I could handle Fifi if I didn't have to do it alone."

"Brian . . ."

"Sorry. The puzzle. Right. Well, the first part is easy."

"I'm listening."

"Barbara Cook, right. She's an actress, so there's your 'acted' reference. And the professional bit is a hint that we're talking about one of her roles. One of her most famous ones, actually."

"How do you know?" I asked.

"Because of the next part. The search for the white knight. That's what she—"

"Did in *The Music Man!*" I finished. "The white knight song! You're a genius." I paused—a moment of silence as we both paid tribute to his brilliance. "Except. . . ."

"Right. The rest of it. What did you say? Looked for her white knight on the river?"

"Yup. Mean anything to you?" I knew it didn't mean anything to me.

"No, but—"

"Something's familiar," I said, once again butting in on his thoughts.

"You, too?"

"Yeah. I can't get my head around it, but something."

"Okay, let's think about what we know. She's a librarian. She's looking for a knight on a river. What knight? For that matter, what river? The East River? The Hudson? The—"

"Wait!" I almost dropped the phone I was so excited. "She's a librarian, and the Library Bar's at The *Hudson* Hotel! That's got to be it! It's so obvious!" Convoluted and weird, but obvious. Especially when you know that the game is basically one big scavenger hunt across the city.

"So how do we know if we got it right?" Brian asked.

"I'm sure," I said. "It has to be right."

"And that's it?"

"Hell, no," I said.

"Good. Because this is way more interesting than watching reruns of *Trading Spaces* with Fifi."

Actually, I'd happily settle into a boring night of television. But I didn't bother telling Brian that. Instead, I just moved on to the second part of the clue. "So the next bit is 'she would have found her—' "

Beep. Again with the phone.

"Hang on." And then he was gone. Two seconds later, he was back. "Larry," he said. "Thank God. He's going to save me. I swear, I'm going to owe the boy kinky sexual favors, but I don't mind because he's saving me from home decorating hell."

"Bri—"

"Love you, babe. Have a fabulous date. I hope it gets steamier than solving puzzles."

"Brian! Wait!"

But he'd already made *kiss kiss* noises, and was gone.

Damn!

I dialed him back, but I just got his voice mail. I left a message to call me back, but I didn't think he would. With a choice between a date or solving puzzles, I'd have chosen the date, too.

I felt a little snarly that he'd abandoned me, but I couldn't hold onto the emotion. For one, he thought I was just playing first date games. For another, he did help me with the first half of the clue. That was good, right?

Devlin looked up as I came back into the living room. "I tried to track down the source for the message from Speedy Delivery. No luck. The guy's boss wasn't there. I left a message asking her to call me, but they said I probably wouldn't hear back until tomorrow."

"Well, I managed to make a much bigger splash than you," I said. "I figured out the first half of the clue."

"No shit?" He looked at me with respect in his eyes, and I felt like preening. "Spit it out."

More than happy to oblige, I told him.

"Brilliant," he said, and I preened some more. "But what about the rest of the riddle?"

Leave it to a Fibbie to rain on my parade. "Still working on that," I said. "Any ideas?"

"It says she'd find her answer," he pointed out. "I think that may be a reference to us."

"If we go to the Library Bar, we can find our answer in . . . something," I said, just to make sure I was clear on the point.

"Exactly."

"Any idea what the something is?"

"Not a clue. You?"

I shook my head, desperately trying to force myself to think. More than anything before in my life, I knew that this Mattered. You know. With a capital M.

This was real, and this was bad, and I needed to figure this out—and fast—or I could end up dead. Just like poor Eddie who didn't love his teddy.

The thing is, I was having a hard time making this all *feel* real. I don't know about you, but I haven't been tossed into that many life and death situations. If someone were standing there pointing a gun to my head, well, I think I'd have no problems feeling the pressure. This, though . . .

Somehow, I'd ended up in the wrong role. You know: Tonight, the part of the Female in Peril will be played by Jennifer Crane. And I didn't even get a kick-ass solo. Except I didn't want to play the female in peril. I wanted to be the kick-ass heroine. The Lara Croft of musical theater. Appropriate, I thought, since she was a video game heroine, and this whole thing started with a computer game.

The thing is, Lara wouldn't run. She'd walk straight into danger. And she'd win. After she'd kicked a little butt, that is.

Time to do some butt-kicking of my own. "Maybe we should go there. The Library Bar, I mean. We can try to figure it out on the way." I glanced at his cable box to read the time. Not quite ten. The bar would be open for hours yet.

"Works for me. Let's go."

I looked him up and down. I still didn't know what had happened to this man, but I could tell that he'd been pretty much locked in a hole for days. But here he was, stepping out into the world for me.

I gotta say, that made me feel pretty damn good. And so I hooked my arm through his and off we went to see the Wonderful Wizard of Oz. Or Marian the Librarian. Or something like that.

I am by far the luckiest girl on the planet. I know this, because why else would Providence be smiling on me with teeth so bright they're blinding? The game, the encounter with Reardon.

It's just all so perfect. How, I wonder, can it get any better?

That's a question I ponder as I sit in my room at the Waldorf, painting my toenails with the polish I picked up at Sephora. I've already re-done my makeup. Twice, actually, and I've decided to go with peach tones for both my face and my nails. I considered red, but ruled it out. Not only is red really not in my palette, but it also tends to stand out.

As the base coat on my fingers dries, I focus on my toes, particularly my little toe. It's tricky, and I'm concentrating intently when my computer beeps, signaling an incoming email.

Now, for most girls that may not be a big thing. But I've been in prison for five years and don't have that many correspondents. At the moment, in fact, I'm receiving emails from only two sources: PSW and a young man I'm cyberfucking. At least I think my online lover is young and male; considering the propensity of the Internet for hiding reality, I really can't be certain. Not that I care. I'm having a blast no matter who he is.

The little *ping* excites me, and I finish my toe quickly, then head across the room to the machine. If it's my lover, I'm more than up for a romp. But I'm hoping it's from PSW. The success of my earlier assignment has made me giddy, and I want a repeat performance.

Of course, I know that the odds are against me. After all, the rules of the game are clear, and I'm not to make a move on my target until after he solves the qualifying clue. Since he's only been in possession of the message for a few hours, I know just how unlikely it is that my part in the game has commenced.

Still, I know Devlin Brady. And I know that he's smart. He was the force of nature behind the team that landed me in prison, after all. And any man who can do that must have brains and balls.

So maybe a man like that really has aced the first portion of the game.

All those thoughts zip through my head as I heel-walk to the computer. And then, when I look at the screen and see that the message really *is* from PSW, well, I have to admit I fall a little bit in love with Mr. Devlin Brady. A man who can work his way through this game so quickly is one hell of a worthy opponent.

My lust fades, though, the second I click over to the message. Brady hasn't made progress. Not yet. But someone new has been added to the mix.

And, frankly, that is even sweeter.

So sweet, in fact, that as I stand here, waiting for my toes to dry, I have to read it once again:

>>http://www.playsurvivewin.com<<

PLAY.SURVIVE.WIN

>>>WELCOME TO REPORTING CENTER<<<

You have one new message.

New Message:

To: Birdie

From: Identity Blocked

Subject: Additional Player

Protector has obtained assistance from outside source. Source identified as Brian Reid, address included in profile.

Fate of Additional Player: Discretionary to Assassin

>>>*Audio File Included: Telephone.wav*<<<

>>>*Additional Profile: BR_Profile.doc*<<<

I hug myself, loving those three little words: Discretionary to Assassin. Why do I love them? Because they mean I can do whatever I want to do. Jennifer Crane dragged someone else to the party, and now that someone else is fair game. And the most lovely thing about it? It's a totally guilt-free kill for me (well, frankly, they're *all* guilt-free). Because I didn't bring the boy in. Jennifer did. His death is on her head. I might be the one who pulls the trigger, but she's the one who made the next move mine.

Chapter

24

DEVLIN

During the drive to the Hudson Hotel, Jennifer curled up in the far corner of the taxi, possibly just thinking, but more likely scared. Terrified, really.

Devlin knew he should reach out to her, tell her it was going to be okay. But that wasn't a connection he wanted to make. He was willing to *make* it okay. To make sure she was safe and secure and getting on with her life.

But to discuss it? To get all warm and fuzzy about it and hold her in his arms and let her cry on his shoulder?

No.

He couldn't go there.

Instead, he could only go as far as the hotel.

She fidgeted a bit, then dug in her purse and pulled out her cell phone. As Devlin listened, she made a call, then asked for status on Andrew Garrison. After a pause, she frowned, then hung up the phone and looked at him.

Instantly, he was on alert. "Trouble?"

"I don't know. They said he'd been discharged. I thought he was supposed to stay overnight."

"They can't hold him if he wants to leave," Devlin said. "And under the circumstances, he probably wanted to get out of there. I bet he's on the way to Washington. You said he works out of Mel's house sometimes, right?"

She nodded, her thumb stroking the phone. "I want to call him, you know? Call and make sure he's okay. And say I'm sorry. But . . ."

She trailed off, and he nodded in understanding. "But you can't risk contacting him again. I know." He put a hand on her leg and met her eyes. "I'm sure he understands, too."

"Thank you," she said.

"For what?"

A tiny smile flashed, then was gone. "For being home. For letting me in."

"No problem," he said, only slightly surprised to realize he meant it.

They rode in silence for about a block, then he said, "We should—"

"I know. The clue. Let's see if we can't figure it out."

They batted a few ideas around, but nothing much stuck. Then Jenn looked up at him again, her eyes sparkling. "The clue's about Broadway musicals, right? And we've both performed in musicals. And the clues are supposed to be kind of personal. Geared toward the target and all."

"Right . . ."

"Well, since this first clue is supposed to be a little bit easier than the ones that come later, maybe we should be thinking about shows that you've actually been in. You'd know those the best, wouldn't you? So that would make the clues the easiest."

He nodded. "Not bad," he said. "Okay, let me think." He started to list all the productions he'd been in, counting them out on his fingers as she stared at him, obviously in awe. So in awe, in fact, that he had to work to hide his grin. ". . . *West Side Story, Falsettos, Into the Woods, Man of La Mancha, Cabaret*—"

"Hang on," she said. *"Man of La Mancha?"*

"Summer stock," he explained.

"There's a song, remember? 'Knight of the Woeful Countenance.' "

"Right," he said. "And *Man of La Mancha* is based—"

"On *Don Quixote*," she said, triumphantly. "Which is a really old book. And doesn't the Library Bar have a bunch of old books?"

"They probably prefer to think of them as rare books. Old just sounds like something in your grandmother's closet."

"Your grandmother, maybe," she said. "My grandma keeps her closet filled with boxes of Estée Lauder. A lifetime of free gifts with purchase."

"At any rate, that's got to be it." He gave her a huge grin. "We're good."

"Good? Screw that. We're awesome."

They reveled in the high of being awesome for about three more minutes, and then the cab dropped them off in front of the nondescript entrance. Basically a door-sized hole cut into a white wall. Even more nondescript because of the scaffolding—

the stuff seemed ever-present in New York—set up to allow workers access to the upper floors of the building.

They paused in front of the entrance for a second, and Devlin got a good look at the fear in Jennifer's eyes. And the determination.

This whole situation was completely fucked up, but she was hanging in there. He had to hand it to her. His life had been screwed up even before today, and he'd barely been hanging on by his fingernails.

They rounded a tight corner then got on a claustrophobic escalator. Devlin hadn't been to the hotel before, though he'd been on several dates that had *almost* ended up at the Library Bar or the Hudson Bar. The job had interfered though, his pager going off at an inopportune time and hauling him away. When Uncle Sam signed your paycheck, you learned to deal with interrupted dates and a fucked-up schedule. His dates, unfortunately, never learned the lesson as well. They always got pissed off when he had to cut the evening short.

For just a second, his mind drifted back to the woman from the pub. Maybe that was the best way to connect with a woman. In a bar. Juiced up. With no names, no strings, and no memory.

"Devlin?"

He looked up, surprised, and realized that he'd been rubbing the aching spot at the back of his neck.

"You okay?"

"Yeah. Yeah, sure." He stood up straight and tried to shake it off. "Just a memory."

"Bad?"

"No. Yes." He closed his eyes and took a breath. "Just something I'm not very proud of."

She answered with a curious look, but he was spared a response because the escalator had reached the top, and they emerged in the center of a lobby that—even in his current jaded mind-set—he had to admit was impressive. A reception counter spread out in front of them, and the facing wall was glass, but mostly covered with climbing vines of ivy that seemed to engulf the entire room. A déjà vu moment from his first trip to the tropical rainforest room at the zoo. Except the rainforest wasn't so loud. Here, the din from a nearby bar filled the room as much as the ivy did. The plant, Devlin assumed, was a necessary acoustical accoutrement. Without it, the bass thrum from distant speakers would be almost nuclear.

Beside him, Jenn was clearly in awe. "Isn't it great?" she said, practically shouting. "I absolutely love this place."

"It's impressive," Devlin said. But he was thinking: *chick pick*. Give him a sports bar any day.

A boy in black with a Euro accent greeted them and offered assistance, but Jenn was already leading the way. Just a quick shift to the left, then a right turn and down a short hallway.

They moved that way, passing the Hudson Bar, which was apparently the source of the music. Filled to the brim with beautiful people, the bar seemed to vibrate with energy. Glass tables sat on a glass floor where colors flashed then faded.

Devlin took a quick look as they passed, grateful they weren't going in there, then exhaled in relief when they rounded the corner and he realized he could hear again. "Hello," he whispered.

Jenn stopped and looked at him. "See someone you know?"

"Just testing. I really can hear myself think now. Nice."

She rolled her eyes and continued on, past the table and

chairs set up against a windowed wall overlooking a stone patio. Devlin shrugged and followed, wondering when he'd gotten old. He still wasn't forty, though. So maybe it was a curable antiquity.

Unlike the too-loud-to-think music coming from the Hudson Bar, the Library Bar was quiet. Old-world elegance coupled with a hint of whimsy. Specifically, overstuffed leather chairs, lots of woodwork, and some paintings of cows. Devlin got a particular kick out of the cows.

A freestanding bar filled one corner, a tall woman with curly black hair manning the thing. A few men leaned on the bar rail, apparently fascinated with the way she mixed a martini.

They squeezed in and waited to catch her attention.

Jenn had her head tilted back as she turned slightly, taking in the entire top section of the room. Although it was called the Library Bar, the place was different from any library Devlin had ever seen. The ceiling was high, with a catwalk about ten feet up. The upper portion of the walls was made up of built-in bookshelves, and they seemed to hold a wide variety of old books. Dusty books, actually. And Devlin supposed that made sense. The point, after all, was that they were old. And rare.

As the bartender turned to them, Devlin leaned in closer. "Have you got *Don Quixote?*"

She cocked her head. "That's with pineapple juice and tequila, right?"

"It's a book," he said, and she looked so blank he almost laughed. He waved his hand, encompassing the room. "You know . . . books."

"Oh. Right." Her forehead creased. "I don't know what we've got."

He exchanged a quick glance with Jenn, who shrugged. Then he turned back to the bartender. "Well, what if I want to read a book?"

The girl stared back at him, her eyes narrow behind her fashionable fuchsia frames. "Read?"

"Yeah. You know. Read. I think it's the traditionally accepted thing to do in a library."

"This isn't a library," she said, her mouth quirked all funny. Like maybe he was the dangerous sort and she had to keep her distance. Well, maybe he was and maybe she did.

"It's called the Library Bar."

She rattled a martini shaker. "I think the emphasis is on the *bar*."

"Devlin . . ." Jenn had eased in, and now had her hand on his shoulder. He wasn't even tempted to move away. In fact, he kind of liked it—the feel of her hand and the whole good-cop bad-cop groove they could get going if they tried. He thought of the woman from the pub—the woman whose panties had found their way to his couch. For about thirty-seven seconds, she'd made him feel alive. Maybe with Jennifer Crane the moment would last a full minute.

And maybe this wasn't the time to be thinking about it.

"So the books are only for show?" he asked.

The bartender nodded.

"Is there a staircase up to that catwalk or anything?"

"No," the girl said, a little sulkily, Devlin thought. "And I think the point was atmosphere. It's not like a sports bar has to have a baseball team hitting foul balls in the back corner."

"Can't hurt," he said, earning him a scowl from both Jenn and the bar girl. A doubleheader.

"And as a matter of fact, we *do* have an exhibit."

"You do?" Jenn managed to ask the question before Devlin could get his mouth around the words.

The girl pointed somewhere toward the center of the room. "All those big cushy leather chairs? You gotta have someplace to set your drinks, don't you?"

"You set them on rare books?"

That earned him another scathing look.

"Display tables. They're glass. I guess the powers that be started thinking like you, so they've pulled some of the coolest old books and they've put them on display."

"The powers that be are very astute," Devlin said.

"Want me to run a tab?" she said, in a not-so-subtle attempt to end the conversation and send him and Jenn on their merry way.

"We're not drinking." He stepped away, ignoring the bartender's irritated snort, and considered the room. Jenn had already moved across the room, and was peering into a waist-high display table that was set up against the back wall. She turned to him and shook her head. So much for easy.

If anyone else cared that there was no "library" in the Library Bar, they didn't care enough to stay away. The place was packed. Every overstuffed leather chair filled, every brocade couch stuffed full of people. Even those standing were packed in so close that the traditional American rules of personal space seemed no more to apply.

Since Devlin didn't give a flying fuck about personal space, he barged into the nearest group with a brusque "excuse me," then peered down at the table centered between the couch and two armchairs.

"Do you mind?" That from a woman in fabulous silk suit, with legs of equal quality.

"Not very well," he admitted. As the bartender had promised, books were on display in the case. *David Copperfield,* some C. S. Forester, even a first edition of *Alice in Wonderland.*

No *Don Quixote.*

He backed out from the crowd—smiling at the woman with a curt "I'll call you"—then moved behind the group to get a look at a side table nestled between two nearby armchairs.

Again, nothing.

He was just about to move on to the next display case when Jenn slid up beside him, taking his elbow and tugging.

"I found it!" she whispered. "It's right over there." She pointed to the far corner of the bar, where two wingback chairs sat, a drunken couple holding hands over an ornate display table. "That's it," Jenn repeated, her face practically glowing. "That's *Don Quixote.* Now all we have to do is get it."

We'd found the book, which was good.

The book was behind glass. That was bad.

The glass was part of a table nestled between a particularly amorous couple. I edged closer, craning my neck to see. "Can I get a quick peek?" I asked.

The man, who reeked of alcohol, shrugged. He also eyed me in a way that should have really pissed off his date. Me, I just ignored it and pressed forward. And there it was, just inches away. A leather-bound volume, underneath which had been placed a typed index card that set out all the particulars of the book, and also announced that it had been donated by Paul S. Winslow.

I reached over to flip the latch on the case, not terribly surprised when I found it locked. Not surprised, but still annoyed. I looked back at Devlin, but he was already heading to the bartender. I hurried after him.

"Any chance of getting inside that display case?" he asked the girl. "We need to take a look at that book."

"Um, no. I mean come on, dude. What's your problem?"

"How about the manager? Maybe we could speak to him?"

"No manager on duty tonight. What you see is what you get." And then she flashed a winning—if not entirely sincere—smile.

"Hotel manager?"

Her shoulders slumped as she exhaled. "Hold on." She finished making a drink for someone, then told another customer that she'd be right with him. She rolled her eyes as she said it, and the customer smirked, clearly bonding with the girl in sympathy about the crazy people she had to deal with.

She reached below the bar and pulled out a cordless phone. She dialed, waited, and then she was talking with Harry, presumably the night manager. She explained—without any of the required urgency, I thought—that some patrons wanted to see one of the rare books. She listened, nodding, then said, "Okay, thanks." And hung up the phone.

"Well?" I demanded.

"He said sure. Just come back in the morning when Mr. Banister is here. He'll take care of you."

"But we—"

"Okay," Devlin said. "Sure. Thanks."

He pulled me away, his firm grip annoying me almost as much as his words. "What are you doing?" I asked. "We can't wait until morning. My deadline's ten! Can't you just shoot the lock off? Or better yet, just shoot that bartender."

"That's one idea," Devlin said. "Another would be to go find Harry and convince him to let us have a peek. Maybe tell him it's a scavenger hunt and we just need to see the book."

"Can't you flash your FBI badge?"

His face hardened, and he shook his head. "If I had it, I'd flash it. But no. Right now, that's not a possibility."

"Oh." I figured I'd discovered Devlin Brady's sore spot. But now wasn't the time to poke at it.

His mouth quirked. "Or maybe you should just hit a high C. Break the glass. Then we run like hell."

I crossed my arms and stared him down. "That's a myth, you know. Even if I could hit the note, the glass wouldn't shatter."

"Actually, I was kidding."

"But it could work," I said. "An obnoxious woman singing at the top of her lungs is sure to draw the manager. And fast." Plus, the plan was dramatic. I, of course, am all about drama.

"I'm not so sure—"

But I was already shoving my tote bag into Devlin's arms. "Be ready," I said.

"Jenn, you're not—"

But I didn't have time to answer. I was already into my role, shifting from kick-ass Lara to vixen Lola. And as the guy sitting by the book gaped, I settled myself on his lap and started with the sultry tones of "Whatever Lola Wants," one of my absolute favorite songs from *Damn Yankees.*

"Excuse me!" The girl part of the couple didn't seem too happy with my plan. But since that was part of my plan, I was A-okay with her irritation.

The guy, I noticed, wasn't complaining at all. Too shocked. And that, also, was just fine by me. I pulled my legs up and pressed against his chest so that I was snuggled close as I sang about how he was a fool and I was irresistible. "*Give in,*" I sang. Then I poked him in the chest. "Give. In."

By this time, people were staring. Also what I'd wanted. Except that in my fantasies about singing solo numbers, I'd always been on a stage. Not in a bar.

"Enough, already!" the bartender called. "I swear, if you don't shut down the disturbance, I'm calling security."

Devlin frowned, and I knew what he was thinking—security was no help to us.

I reached the end of the song, and was trying to decide if I should stop or keep going when I caught Devlin's eye. *More,* he mouthed. So I kept going. I wasn't sure what he had planned, but I trusted him. I was also happy he'd gotten into the spirit of the plan.

I segued neatly into "Who's Got the Pain," still in my Lola character, and on the word "Mambo," I grabbed date guy's hand and tugged him out of the chair.

The song's bouncy and fast and, hey, it's about the mambo. So that's what we did. Or, rather, that's what I did. And since I had his hands tight in my own, he reluctantly joined me. We weren't going to win any awards, but the exhibition did have the desired effect. Namely, the girl jumped out of her chair—absolutely furious—and tried to cut in. I wasn't having any of that, and danced him across the room to another little cluster of chairs. Not that there was anyone sitting there. By that time, they were all gathered around us. Me and date guy, and the girl trying to horn in on our good time.

I heard the bartender howl from across the room. "I'm calling right now! I mean it!" And then I saw her yank up the phone. I tried not to worry about that because I now had more important things to worry about. Like the fact that I'd glanced toward the *Don Quixote* table and found Devlin through a break in the crowd, busily shoving the blade of his pocket knife under the top of the table.

Oh, shit.

Since I didn't want anyone else looking where I'd been looking, I turned back to my captive, stepping lively and moving his arm up and down in an exaggerated motion as I sang at the top of my lungs that immortal question of *"who needs a pill when they do the mambo?"* Then I flipped my leg up in a flirty little kick just as the song hits an *UGH!*

Honestly, this isn't the easiest song to sing without accompaniment, and I think I was doing a kick-butt job. Considering how everyone was staring and laughing, I figured I wasn't being too conceited. If those guys from the *Carousel* audition could see me now . . .

I glanced back toward the table where Devlin had been, and saw that he wasn't there now, and figured it was time to wrap this up. I yanked us to a stop, pulled the guy close, and planted a big kiss on him. (On his cheek. After all, I didn't want to mess things up for his girl.) Then I pushed him away and turned to the girl. "Great dancer," I said. "He's a keeper."

And then, with the hum of the crowd buzzing behind me and the bartender calling out, "Hey, *hey!*" I hauled ass out of there.

Devlin (thank God) was waiting for me at the end of the hall, and he took my hand and we raced across the lobby, the ceiling of ivy looming above us and the music from the bar pounding all around us. We skidded across the floor, then raced down the escalator until we emerged onto the sidewalk.

My heart was pounding in my chest, and I leaned back under the scaffolding, breathing hard. In front of me, Devlin was leaning over, his palms pressed against his knees, and his eyes on me.

"Tell me you have the book," I said between gasps.

"I've got it," he said. "Keep moving." And he took off at a clip toward Seventh Avenue, me keeping pace behind him.

I glanced back before we turned and didn't see armed security guards barreling down on us. That was a good thing.

Finally, we quit running, but still walked quickly, and Devlin took my hand. "You've got one hell of a voice on you, that's for damn sure. But have you ever heard of subtlety?"

"It worked, didn't it? And I didn't see you coming up with any other brilliant ideas."

"No," he said. "You didn't. You did good in there. Not subtle. But it worked."

"Oh." I stopped on the street. "So you weren't being critical?"

"Just stating facts. Don't stand there. We need to keep moving."

Right he was. I kicked back into step beside him. "Where are we going?"

"Someplace we can sit down and look at the book."

"Right." It suddenly occurred to me that we'd just committed theft. Not something I would have *ever* considered doing before. Now, though, I didn't even feel a twinge of guilt. We needed the book to keep me alive. We got the book. That deserved a pat on the back, not handcuffs and a mug shot. For that matter, it deserved a standing ovation.

He rounded a corner, then ducked into a bar. The place was elbow-to-elbow with people, but Devlin miraculously snagged us a table, conveniently tucked away under a bronze crawfish rotating on a pedestal. I kid you not.

We collapsed into the chairs, and Devlin shoved the previous occupants' dirty glasses aside. Then he pulled the book out from under his jacket and plunked it on the table.

I have to admit that I did feel a tiny bit of guilt at this point. Not for stealing the thing—we'd give it back when we were done with it—but for taking it out of its sealed and locked little homestead. I don't know much about books and preservation and all that kind of stuff, but I couldn't help but wonder if we'd just consigned this poor book to mold and worms and other versions of bookish hell.

The cover was red leather, with a stylized drawing of a knight all in black on the cover. Gold gilt bordered the cover and also decorated the spine. All in all, it was a pretty book. And solid. And probably incredibly expensive.

Devlin had just opened the cover when a waiter appeared. "What can I get for you?"

"Nothing!"

Devlin looked at me sharply. "Scotch. On the rocks. Single malt."

"Nothing for me," I said. "But could you take those away?" I nodded toward the dirty glasses. They still had some liquid inside them. "What if he spills your drink when he brings it? What if *you* spill it?"

"I won't." He was slowly flipping the pages.

"How can you be so sure? That book has to be, what, four hundred years old?"

He stopped his inspection of the pages and looked up at me, curiosity in his eyes. "You know Cervantes?"

"When you were on stage, did it bother you when people thought you were dumb? Does it bother you now if they think you're just some FBI flunkie with no brain, a black suit, and the party line?"

"Point taken." He tapped the book. "But this isn't a first edition. It's in English."

My cheeks warmed a little at that. I mean, I know Cervantes wrote *Don Quixote* back in the 1600s. During the years of torture that my father called a liberal arts education and that I called twelve years of hellish private schools complete with uniforms, I'd studied Cervantes on more than one occasion, though I can't admit to retaining all that much of it. I'm very proud of my straight-C average. But I'm not going to be discussing the impact of fifteenth-century literature at cocktail parties anytime soon.

"So, what does that mean? It's not really rare? Does that matter? We got it from the Library Bar. There's no way we got that clue wrong. It was too freaky and obscure. And the book was there. We have to have gotten it right."

"We got it right. And if it makes you feel any better, I still won't spill anything. The book may not be four hundred years old, but it's still old and spectacular." He closed the book and inspected it. "I don't know how much this baby is worth, but considering its condition, I'm thinking a lot."

"A lot? How much a lot?"

"Enough that you and I just committed a felony."

"Oh. Great."

"Don't worry."

"I'm not. Unless we find the clue, I'm going to be dead before they arrest us, anyway." I blinked, and sat back in my seat, the reality of the situation blindsiding me. I'd stowed it away, pretended I was playing a part, but this was real. Real and deadly, and I was scared.

"Jenn? Are you okay?"

I looked at him, my eyes unnaturally wide as I tried to keep myself from crying.

"It just hit me. Something bad is going to happen to me. In just a few hours. It's not a drama. It's not the theater. And nothing's going to swoop down in the third act to save me."

"I will," he said, with such conviction that I actually managed a smile. He pressed his hand over mine. "I like happy endings, Jenn. And I promise you that you'll get one, too."

I swear I almost melted on the spot. But I gave myself a little shake and tried to come to my senses.

"Right. You're right." Brooding wasn't going to get us anywhere. And I didn't have time for self-indulgent depression or momentary lapses into lust.

"Right," I said again. "I'm fine." He didn't look convinced, but I pointed to the book. "Do you see anything in there?"

He paused, but then shook his head. "Not yet," he said, still flipping pages.

"Do you think maybe it's some combination of words? Something from the first message? Do we have to use that code key to unscramble something else?"

"If that's the case, we really are screwed." His eyes met mine. "Are you up to translating all of these words using that code?"

I shook my head.

"Me neither. But I don't think it matters. The code we had before turned nonsense into legitimate words. I can't fathom how it would work backwards. And even if there's a word or two in here that would become something else if we applied the code, how are we supposed to know which word to use?" He shook his head. "No, I think the key has to be somewhere in this book."

"Or in another one," I said. "Oh, shit, Devlin. What if the bar had more than one copy of *Don Quixote*?"

"No panicking," he said. "And no making up worst case scenarios. The clue's here," he said.

"How do you know?"

"Because it says so."

I gaped at him. "It *says* so? What are you talking about?"

"Didn't you read the card?"

"The notecard? Yeah. Sure." I frowned, trying to remember it. "It was just a card."

"Not exactly," he said, and then he smiled, reaching into the back of the book to pull out a card and pass it to me. "Lucky I snagged it, too."

" 'Privately Printed for the Members of the English Biblio-philist Society and Printed by Morrison & Gibbs Limited, Ed-inburgh,' " I read. "No date, but it says that it was probably published between 1892 and 1894. It's part of a limited edition of one hundred copies, and this one was donated by Paul S. Winslow." I looked up at him, definitely missing the big picture. "So?"

"Paul. S. Winslow," he said, slowly. "PSW."

"Oh my gosh!" I said. "That can't be a coincidence."

"That's what I'm thinking." He tapped the book. "Let's see if we can't prove it," he said, and then we started going through the book, page by meticulous page.

Flip. Nothing.

Flip. Nothing.

And then—

"Shit! Devlin! Look!"

Right there, tipped in between the pages about two-thirds of the way through the volume, was an almost transparent sheet of onion-skin paper.

"I can barely read this," I said, leaning closer and trying to make out the words.

Devlin leaned close, too, but admitted he couldn't do a much better job. The clue had been typed on what must have been an antique manual typewriter with the original ribbon. Coupled with the dim lighting, it was almost impossible to see.

He held it up, and we both squinted at it, finally making out the text:

VISIT THE HOME OF THE CREATOR OF *FUNNY BOY, THIS TOO SHALL PASS, THE KIDNEY STONE,* AND *100 DOLLAR LEGS*

"*The Producers,*" I said. I love that show, and I recognized the list of titles right away. "Those are all shows that Max Bialystock produced," I added, naming the musical's lead, a shyster Broadway producer involved in an elaborate scheme to produce a flop.

"Yeah," Devlin agreed. "But what does it mean by 'the home of the creator'?"

"I'm not sure," I admitted. "Maybe we're supposed to go to the St. James Theater? That's where *The Producers* is running, right?"

"It's worth a shot," he said. "I sure as hell don't have a better idea."

I didn't waste time pointing out that it was well after midnight now. In my experience, everyone clears out of the theaters pretty fast. I was afraid we were going to find the place dark, but that didn't mean I wasn't willing to try. Maybe we'd get lucky. Or maybe there'd be a message for us graffitied on the side of the building. I don't usually hope for vandalism, but in this case, I'd make an exception.

Since we couldn't find an empty taxi, we ended up walking the few blocks back to the theater district, and then over to the St. James on 44th Street. Like I'd expected, the theater was deserted, and even though we pounded on the stage door, no one came to answer. Not even a security guard.

"Closed up until morning," Devlin said.

I didn't say anything. I was too busy telling myself that it didn't matter, because the clue was somewhere else. But where?

"Mel Brooks' house?" I suggested.

"How would we know where that is?" He looked back at the theater. "And I still think it's Bialystock. Otherwise, why not say the creator *of* Bialystock."

He had a point, and I certainly didn't have any ammunition for arguing. So while Devlin dialed the number for the theater, hoping to find some night manager to come let us in, I tried to think about all the various possibilities where the clue could be hidden. If this was a musical, and I was the female lead, I'd probably have a big solo right now, bemoaning the fact that we were stuck. I figured this would come somewhere around the end of the first act, and I'd bust a gut belting out how frightened I was and how I couldn't find the clue. And then I'd throw myself up against the wall—which I did right then, just to get in the spirit of the thing—and then, when I looked down, I'd see the clue etched into the glass covering the theater posters.

I stopped, considering that, and checked the glass. No etchings.

So much for my playwriting skills.

Or maybe the heroine drops her purse, and something rolls out, then down into a grating, and *that's* where she finds the clue.

I half-considered dropping my tote just to test that theory, but I wasn't inclined to torture my Marc Jacobs bag that way. Plus, my laptop was still in the bag, and if I dropped it, I'd surely smash it, and then where would we be? From what I could tell, even stuck in the real world, most of this game played out on the computer, and—

That was it!

"Devlin!"

He rushed to my side, his face painted in concern. "What? Are you okay? What happened?"

I didn't even bother to reassure him. "A web page," I said, tugging at his arm. "Come on. We don't need to be here. We just need to get onto the Internet."

Fortunately, that was easily arranged. Since my parents— bless them—express their love through expensive technological gifts, I'm the happy recipient of an air card. Which basically means I don't need anything but my computer in order to snag an Internet connection. No phone lines, Internet cafes, or T-Mobile hot spots for me. (And if I sound like a commercial, it's because I love my computer. More, I love my mom and dad.)

I dragged him around the corner to the Howard Johnson's, and as I booted up my laptop, I explained what I was thinking. "It says the home of the creator, right? Well, that's Max Bialystock. So I bet we're supposed to go to the Max Bialystock home page!"

The waitress was looking at us funny, but Devlin ordered two coffees and a plate of french fries, and she vanished up the aisle. He came around from his side of the booth to sit next to me.

"What do you think?" I asked, since he'd been quiet, and I was starting to descend into insecurity.

"I think you're brilliant," he said.

"Yeah?" My descent changed directions, and I was almost grinning as I pulled up the browser and typed in the web address, http://www.maxbialystock.com. I pressed ENTER. "Here goes nothing," I said.

And, in fact, I was right. Not a damn thing happened. Nothing except a DNS error, anyway.

"Try it with an underscore," Devlin said, leaning over me to type it himself: http://www.max_bialystock.com.

Again, nada.

"Well, damn," I said. "I was so certain. Maybe melbrooks.com?"

"Try Bialystock.com first."

I did and seconds later, we knew that we'd hit it right. "Shit," I said, looking at the words on the screen. "What do we do now?"

If Memory serves, the answer is Practical-ly on the knight's production.

And will be found by following One Thing After Another

to the gathering place
of the patroness of Candide, as she dances among the Italian
canals, and of those who dine on the meal named by Morgan and
Catiline when they sat on The Love Set and When [they were] In
Rome.

Chapter

26

BIRDIE

I don't wait well. I find boredom tiresome. Lines and queues only irritate me, and so I often find myself not attending any function that requires me to wait.

In that particular aspect, I found prison especially unappealing.

Now, I have my freedom, but I am still waiting. And even though I have had some lovely diversions, those tasks are now complete, and I'm left waiting for the main event to begin.

My computer is open, the browser pointed to a GPS map with no indications of activity showing on it. I glare at it, then pick up my PDA. It shows the same map and, also, the same lack of activity. I sigh. How much longer will it take for them to figure out the qualifying clue? Am I dealing with idiots here?

I hope not. And once the game begins, I want them to be

clever. I want to win, of course, but not too easily. There's no fun in a slaughter. The fun is in the chase. In the game.

I return to the bed and open the bottle of nail polish. I've decided to go ahead and splurge on Devilish Red this time, and I think that's appropriate. I prop my feet up and go to work on my toes. Just something to keep my mind occupied while I wait.

After all, the tracking software was truly a gift. I think about the message I received along with the email that included the software: **Your vision will be clearer as you track them through the town, but keep in mind, my pretty, inconsistencies will abound.**

I don't know exactly what that means, but from the software alone, I'd been able to tell that I was installing a tracking system. Considering the microchip I'd placed earlier, that made perfect sense. The reference to inconsistencies will, I assume, become clear over time. My guess is that the software is designed to work only intermittently, with random periods of blackouts where I won't be able to track my quarry's location.

If I were running the game, that's what I'd do. True, it makes it harder for the assassin, but it also increases the fun. Adds to the thrill of the chase, the beauty of the hunt.

At the moment, though, I don't give a fuck whether it's continuous or intermittent. I just want the chip to turn on. I just want the location to register on the screen. I just want to start the game. I only have ten toes, after all, and I can change the color of my polish only so many times.

I finish my toes and I'm moving on to pissed off. Don't they know I want to get started? Don't they know that time is of the essence? There's a toxin in the girl's blood, after all. Why the hell aren't they moving faster?

I'm working myself up into a full-blown snit—staying on the bed, of course, so I don't smear my polish—when a wondrous thing happens. My computer and my PDA both chime. A high-pitched tone that brings me such joy that I leap off the bed. Screw my toes, this is what I've been waiting for.

I race to the far side of the room, but pause just in front of the desk, my eyes cast down at the floor. What if I was wrong? What if the noise meant something else? An email, perhaps, or simply another message from PSW.

I almost don't want to look, because I need this so much.

But I have to know and so, slowly, I lift my head. And there, flashing on the screen, is the most beautiful thing I've ever seen: a single red dot, marking with an accuracy within fifty yards the location of Agent Devlin Brady within the island of Manhattan.

I smile. I twirl. I let myself dance giddily around the room.

And then I take the PDA and my gun and slide them into my brand-new Fendi bag. Without worrying about my toes, I slip on socks and a pink pair of sneakers. Comfortable, fashionable, and practical.

Then I slide my purse over my shoulder and head out of the hotel. Time to go meet an old friend.

Devlin stared at the words, wishing the meaning would leap from the screen. But instead, all he was seeing was nonsense.

If Memory serves, the answer is Practical-ly on the knight's production.
And will be found by following One Thing After Another
to the gathering place
of the patroness of Candide, as she dances among the Italian canals, and of those who dine on the meal named by Morgan and Catiline when they sat on The Love Set and When [they were] In Rome.

"What on earth does that mean?" Jenn's eyes were wide and concerned, and he made an effort to seem reassuring.

"We'll figure it out," he said. And then, just for extra measure, he reached over and gave her hand a quick squeeze. "Don't worry."

"Easy for you to say. Your neck isn't on the block. Yet." Her brow furrowed as she spoke. "Or is it?"

"What do you mean?"

"Qualifying clue."

He knew where she was going with that. In PSW, the target had a free pass until he (or she) solved the qualifying clue. Once that happened, a signal was sent to the assassin, who was then allowed to begin the hunt.

On the computer, it was all done electronically and signals were sent instantaneously. In real life, it was a bit dicier. In Mel's case, they'd realized that an electronic signal had been triggered when she'd handled one of the clues. But he had no way to know for certain if that's the way the signal was always transmitted. For all he knew, they had a tail; someone who was reporting back their every movement to the psychopath who was running this show.

He glanced around the restaurant, memorizing the faces of everyone looking his way. And, more important, of everyone who'd turned away the second he'd met their eyes.

"Devlin?" She closed her fingers around his wrist. "You okay?"

"Fine." He drew in a breath, made a decision. "Ever take a class in self-defense?"

"Sure. Nothing major. Just a Learning Annex thing."

"One of the things they should have taught you is to always be aware of your surroundings."

She looked around, perhaps not as subtly as he'd done, but he wouldn't fault her for that.

"Take note of who's around you. Try to remember things. And if you see a familiar face somewhere else, don't shake it off as coincidence."

She nodded, her face deadly serious. He felt a twinge of guilt for scaring her, then immediately quashed it. She needed to be scared if she wanted to stay alive. She also needed to be smart. And they needed to get off the stick and interpret a seemingly uninterpretable clue.

"This," he said, tapping the paper. "We need to focus."

"Answer my question first," she said. "Have we solved the qualifying clue? Is the assassin after you? Could he be one of the folks in the diner? Or do you think one of them is hanging out, waiting to take a sniper's shot at me?"

"I don't know who's in here with us," he admitted. "But yeah. The first clue gets the game going. And the second clue is the qualifying clue. Solve that, and the target emerges from the woodwork, ready to take a shot at you. And I'm pretty sure we just solved the thing."

She looked around, clearly alarmed. "Then we need to get out of here. The killer might be out there. Watching us."

"Could be," he said. "But if so, he's after my neck. You're safe until ten tomorrow, remember?"

"Today," she said, then pointed to her wristwatch. "It's already tomorrow. Besides, I'm fair game now, too, remember? I contacted the authorities. And Andy took a dart probably meant for me."

"You're right." He shifted in the booth, felt the familiar comfort of his spare piece in his ankle holster, then stood. "Let's go."

She finished packing her things, then moved quickly in front of him. He pressed a light hand to her back as she headed for the front door. "Back," he said, steering her toward the kitchen.

"What?"

"We're going out the back way."

She nodded, and her sudden acquiescence warmed him. His life might be a total mess, but at least he could still earn the trust of a beautiful damsel in distress.

They wended their way through the kitchen, picking over the rubber mat flooring and easing around waiters with trays of food and busboys with tubs of dirty dishes. A few people shot them curious glances, but no one seemed interested enough to stop them. More important, no one was following.

The back door opened onto an alley filled with the stench of rotten food and urine. They moved carefully toward the street, emerging from the dank wasteland of the alley to the vibrancy that was Times Square. They cut back over to Broadway and Devlin paused, considering their options. He didn't like being tugged along on a string, impotent and at the mercy of some asshole who wanted to play a deadly game of cat and mouse. Over the last few weeks, he'd gotten used to the sensation of spinning out of control, of having no purchase on his life. Gotten used to it, but that didn't mean he had to like it.

And this . . . well, this was different. This was fucked.

And while part of him wanted to stand on the sidewalk, and yell for the s.o.b. to just take him out right then and there, the bigger part of him knew that he couldn't do that. He had Jenn to consider. And if that meant that he was coming back to life—slowly defrosting—well, then that was something he'd have to deal with, too.

He glanced over at Jenn, who was watching him curiously. "Well?" she said. "Where to?"

"Here, I think. We'll stay in Times Square for now."

"Why?"

"Lots of people, and lots of hotels with decent evening security. Not great," he added. "But decent." He looked around, located the Marriott right across the street, and headed that direction. "Come on."

" '*If Memory serves,*' " she said as they rode up the elevator to the lobby level. "What do we think that means?"

"We're talking about Broadway, so maybe an old show?"

"Could be," she said. "But what show? I'm not that familiar with the really old ones, not if they're obscure. And are we talking only musicals? Or plays, too?"

"I was only in musicals," he said. "Got an offer for a play once, but turned it down. Musical theater was always my thing."

"Are you gay?"

The question didn't take him by surprise. That was just the nature of the business. "I'll be happy to prove to you I'm not."

"Oh." She completely avoided his eyes as her cheeks flushed even more.

Devlin didn't even bother to hide his grin. "I'm a rare breed. A heterosexual male who sings and dances on the Great White Way."

"Had to go and strap on a gun to prove your manhood, huh?"

"Something like that," he said, just to keep up the banter. In truth, it was nothing like that at all.

"Maybe the reference to a knight has to do with Don Quixote?"

"That would make sense," he agreed.

"Another song from *Man of La Mancha*? A lyric from 'Knight of the Woeful Countenance?' "

He started running the lyrics through his head. "Well, the Innkeeper sings the song. So maybe we're looking for a hotel?"

Jenn lifted her chin, hope in her eyes. "That's good. That's very smart!"

He accepted the praise, but didn't point out that he had no idea *which* hotel. "It also talks about the knight's glorious deeds, and how he battles the villains."

"We're battling villains, all right. But I don't see how that helps us know where to look for the next clue."

"Me neither," he admitted, as they stepped off the elevator and started toward the front desk.

"And what about this *memory serves* crap?" Jenn asked. "Does that make any sense at all to you?"

"Not really."

"Shit," she said, and his heart broke just a little.

He wasn't exactly batting a thousand here, and he paused in the lobby, took her hand in his, and squeezed. "It's going to be okay."

"Promise?"

"Yeah," he said, "I promise." The force of his words surprised even him. Because as he spoke, he realized that he meant it. He'd started on this path to help her out. Because that was the right thing to do. Because it was what he'd been trained to do. But quirky Jennifer Crane had gotten under his skin. He cared. And he kind of liked the way that felt.

It wasn't obligation anymore. It was personal.

And God help any son-of-a-bitch who took a shot at the girl.

Chapter

28

JENNIFER

I had to admit he had the right idea about the hotel. I would have dragged us to some fleabag motel, something deep in Harlem, maybe. The kind of place that rented rooms by the hour, and where you didn't sleep on the mattress because you didn't want to bother the bedbugs.

Instead, we ended up in the lap of luxury, complete with a linebacker-looking guy blocking the elevator bank and holding back any and all traffic that couldn't produce a room key.

I flashed ours, then pranced to the elevator button, enjoying the momentary high that came from building security. My mood was surprisingly light, a combination of being in a clean hotel with the illusion of safety, and Devlin's promise that we'd get through this. He'd been lying, of course. But it had made me feel a lot better.

It had also made me confident.

We *could* through this. And, somehow, we would.

"Crap security," Devlin said as we waited for the elevator. "But better than nothing."

I deflated immediately. "Thanks. Thanks a lot."

"Sorry. But there are about a dozen easy ways our assassin could penetrate that security."

"And you now feel it necessary to recite each and every one to me?"

"No. I was just thinking about them. Occupational hazard. We're safe. I promise." The elevator arrived, and we stepped on, Devlin moving immediately to push the button for the 43rd floor.

Occupational hazard. I considered that. I spent my days humming show tunes. Mundane, maybe. But pleasant overall. What must it be like to look at murder and mayhem and drugs and criminals every day? Exhausting, I figured. And satisfying? I guess it must be. I mean, I knew *my* career was satisfying. My real career. The one I hadn't officially started yet, but would soon.

But Devlin had held that career in his hand. Hell, he had a freaking Tony award on his bookshelf. And if the buzz that came from working—*starring*—in musical theater could be matched by joining up with the FBI, well, then maybe I ought to turn in an application to my local field office.

Or not.

I frowned at my reflection in the mirror-lined elevator. There was only one job I wanted, and I was unreasonably pissed off that someone was stepping in and risking my dream. I could hardly open in the next Sondheim if I was dead.

For that matter, I could hardly deliver a cheeseburger and

fries if I was dead. And that happy thought made me remember my job. Which, as it turns out, was only a few blocks down the street.

Proximity is a great purveyor of guilt, and all of a sudden, I felt a wallop. (The guilt was stupid, I know, but sometimes emotion is unreasonable.) I needed to call in for tomorrow because there was no way I was picking up my shift. And now with Brian cut loose from the wonderful world of food service there wasn't anyone I could call to cover my hours. (I was not bitter, I was not bitter . . .)

My boss was just going to have to improvise. Lord knows, I was getting the hang of it.

With no effort at all, I pushed the problem aside. In the grand scheme of things, the current state of my employment was way low on the totem pole. At this moment in my life, frankly, nuclear holocaust, sexually transmitted diseases, and a takeover of high fashion by Sears were all low on my list of concerns.

The only things flashing neon in my brain, in fact, were knights, *Candide*, Rome, and the rest of that goddamn ridiculous clue.

The elevator door opened, and Devlin and I stepped out, got our bearings, and headed left toward the room. He slid the plastic key in and the door opened on the first try. I was impressed—those doors never work for me—and we stepped inside a clean room that looked like every other hotel room on the planet.

It had one bed, a king-size, but at the moment, I wasn't particularly concerned with the sleeping arrangements. (Which, frankly, goes to show you how much this whole experience was messing with my head. Under normal circumstances, sleeping arrangements are tops of my list when I hook up with a cute guy.) Instead of sleeping, I planned on working, and so I dragged the floor lamp closer to the bed and turned the light on so that the bed was illuminated.

"You really think we're safe here?" I asked. "Mel told me that Lynx had some sort of tracking device. Maybe our assassin has one, too."

"I thought of that," Devlin said. "But I stand by my decision. We can't stay on the move and work out these clues. We need a base. And a large hotel works perfectly. Those devices don't have pinpoint accuracy. There are at least a thousand rooms in here. He won't find us."

"I think that makes me feel better," I said, trying to block the image of an assassin wandering the halls in search of us.

"And what would the device be in, anyway?" he asked. But he answered his own question. We both did, turning in unison to look at the bed, where he'd left the book laying on the spread.

"Right," he said. "I want to check the rest of the book for clues, anyway. I'll look it over for electronic devices, too."

"Cool." I sat on the edge of the bed and took off my shoes, then pulled the wad of cash out of the bottom of each. Devlin watched, his brows raised, as I tossed the bills onto the middle of the bed. "If that amuses you," I said, "you're going to love this." And then I reached into my bra and pulled another wad out of each cup.

Devlin's mouth twitched. "I'm sure there's an appropriate smart-ass remark to make at this point, but I'm not entirely sure what it is."

"That's okay," I said. "I won't hold it against you." I pointed to the cash. "Take some. We should both have a supply of cash and it's your blood money anyway."

He nodded. "If it's all the same to you, I'll take the bills that were in your bra, not your shoes." He leered a little, but he almost laughed at the same time, and that sort of destroyed the effect. "Want to see where *I'm* going to hide the money?"

"I don't want to hear about your kinky fantasies," I said primly. I pointed to the book. "Now get to work."

"Yes ma'am," he said, with just a hint of a chuckle.

I shook my head in mock exasperation, then moved to sit at the desk as Devlin settled in to scour the book. I pulled my iPod out of my tote first, and set it to play the soundtrack to *Into the Woods.* It's Sondheim, which means the lyrics are fast and fun and smart. Normally Sondheim draws my attention so much I can't focus on anything else, but I know that show really well, and it made good background noise. Fast enough to keep me moving, familiar enough to keep me concentrating on the clue.

As the Narrator started to set the story up, I opened the drawer, took out some hotel stationery, and broke the clue down into sections. By the time Cinderella was singing at the grave, I wasn't even hearing the music anymore. Instead, I was annotating my notes. Here's what I ended up with:

If memory serves—Memory? The song?
the answer is Practical-ly —"Practical"? A musical? A play?
capital letter important? Hyphen important?
on the knight's production —man of la mancha (?)

And will be found by following—a note to us??

One Thing After Another—a title?? play? musical? Check web

to the gathering place—??

of the patroness of Candide—Candide = musical. But who's the patroness?

as she dances among the Italian canals—Venice?

And of those who dine on the meal—????

named by Morgan and Catiline—characters? Actors? Writers? (the "named" reference???)

when they sat on The Love Set—another show? Check that

and When [~~they were~~] In Rome.—right? Doesn't [ ] mean to cut??

I sat there, tapping my pen against the paper in time with "I Know Things Now," going over my notes. Okay, if it is "Memory," then what did that mean? I had no idea.

Then again, maybe I did. Because "Memory" is the famous song from *Cats*. And *Cats* is based on T. S. Eliot's collection of poetry called *Old Possum's Book of Practical Cats*. Which could be where the Practical-ly came from.

Not bad deducing, if I do say so myself, and I was feeling pretty smug. Except, of course for the fact that I had no idea what any of that had to do with *Man of La Mancha*. Or what any of the last part of the clue meant.

Frustrated, I switched off my iPod, then twisted around in my chair to watch Devlin, who was meticulously flipping pages, then examining each one for markings, tipped in notes, or messages scrawled in blood. "How's it going?" I asked.

"Slow," he said, looking up. "You?"

"Not bad," I said. "But not there yet. Can you think of any connection between *Cats* and *Man of La Mancha*?"

"The theater?" he said. "I don't know where *La Mancha* was staged, but that's my best guess."

"Works for me," I said, then pulled out my laptop once again. As soon as it booted up, I went to the Internet Broadway Database at www.ibdb.com. Not as well known as the movie database, but way more useful to a theater buff like me. There, I checked the theaters where *Cats* and *La Mancha* played. "No luck there," I said. "Different theaters."

Since I was online, though, I checked *One Thing After Another, The Love Set,* and *When in Rome.* All plays. Old ones—from the twenties and thirties—which explained why I'd never heard of them before. Now that I'd become acquainted with them, though, I still didn't know what to do with the information.

I sighed. "I hate this. I can't get a fucking clue."

Devlin came over behind me and put his hands on my shoulders, then looked down at the paper I'd been scratching my notes on. "Actually, you've got the fucking clue. You just can't find the fucking answer."

I couldn't help it. I'd been so certain he was going to offer me platitudes that when he didn't—when he laid that smart-ass remark on me—I burst out laughing.

"How about you?" I finally asked. "Did you check the spine? Any clues? Any electronic chips?"

He picked up the book and showed me the slot between the leather binding and the bound pages. "Nothing there."

"You're positive?"

He didn't even answer me that time, and I took that for a yes.

"So, is this what it's like? Working for the FBI, I mean."

"Can't say I've investigated that many rare books," he said. "And I've never once obtained evidence by resorting to sexy musical numbers."

"Yeah, I can see how that probably doesn't come up too often." I frowned and shook my head in mock despair. "Sounds like a pretty boring job, then."

"Terribly," he said. "Tedious and dull."

"Really?"

He shrugged. "A lot of the time, yeah. But the point is for the tedium to pay off."

"I can't imagine trading the theater for tedium," I said. Then I immediately backpedaled. "I mean, theater can be tedious, sure. Lighting checks and technical rehearsals and all that b.s., but the payoff . . . standing on that stage, drawing energy from the crowd. Don't you miss that? How did you walk away from that?"

"I didn't," he said.

"You . . . what?"

He laughed, low and soft. "What I mean, is I may have left theater, but I still have that rush. When the evidence pulls together, when you finally get to the heart of the case—well, that's a rush more powerful than any I felt on stage."

"Really?"

"I know it sounds hokey, but I like helping people. Flashing a badge and packing a gun's not too bad either." A shadow crossed his face, and I realized we'd taken this conversation a little too far.

"So," I said, trying to cover. "You really think the book's okay?"

A pause, but then he nodded slowly. "I'll rip it apart page by page if you really want me to, but this book is intact. If there's something hidden inside, then someone would have had to rip it apart to put it there."

He had a point. "Okay. You're right. We have the clue. Now we just have to find the answer."

He took my hand and squeezed. I held on, wishing I didn't ever have to let go. "We'll find it," he said, and I have to admit, I liked his positive thinking.

"Right," I said. "I know. I just wish I knew what was supposed to happen today."

"Doesn't matter," he said, and I felt my eyebrows rise up behind my bangs. He grinned. "I mean it doesn't matter because we're going to stop it with plenty of time to spare. Okay?"

I nodded. "Okay." I stood up, then started to pack up my laptop. "We should get out of here."

"You know where we need to go?"

I shook my head. I didn't have any idea where the clue led, but I did know that I was supposed to be the protector. That was a part I was playing by ear, but I had a feeling my instincts were dead-on. No pun intended. "All I know is that we need to move." I pointed to the bed, and the book that was still on it. "But the book stays here."

We'd paid for the room with cash—not a common thing these days, but since I'd foisted so much cash on the clerk, they really couldn't argue.

It was enough money, in fact, that I knew we were covered for a few days. So while Devlin looked at me like I was a nutcase, I wrapped the book in one of the hotel-provided laundry bags, dropped down to my belly, and crawled under the bed to inspect the setup. After a few seconds of that, I crawled back out, turned on my side, and peered up at him. "Got any string? Rubber bands? A belt you're not using?"

He stared at me, head cocked, a completely perplexed expression on a face that I was becoming quite fond of.

"Never mind," I said. "The laundry bag has a drawstring." I took my bundle, unwrapped it, tugged the cotton drawstring out, then wrapped the book tight again in the bag. And then, with Devlin staring at me like I was a loon, I inched back under the bed. This time, I made a little sling, using the drawstring hooked around one of the metal slats that held the boxspring in place. I tied the book into the sling, tightened it up so that it would stay nice and firm, then shimmied back out.

This time, Devlin had a grin on his face. "Clever. If there's some sort of tracking gizmo in that book, the assassin's going to come here. And we'll be long gone."

"Exactly. And if it turns out we need the book, we can come back and get it," I said. "An old trick from church camp. Well, not the tracking device part. But we hid our romance novels and chocolate under our bunks that way."

I stood up and brushed the dust off my clothes—no worries that the maids would find the bundle under there. "Now we go to another hotel. And when this mess is over, we can send it back to the Library Bar." I frowned, then. "Do you think if we just leave a Do Not Disturb sign on the door that they really won't disturb us?"

"I think so," he said. "At least for a couple of days." I must not have looked convinced, because he continued. "I could call down and tell the front desk to not bother us because we're having hot sweaty sex in here."

"Don't even tease about something like that unless you plan to follow through."

"Not right now," he said, his voice like honey. "You look to be in a hurry. And I like to take my time."

"Oh." I grabbed up my tote bag, my face flaming. I couldn't believe I'd laid such a come-on line at his feet. More, that he'd taken it. It was tempting. Too tempting, when you consider that Devlin Brady was hotter than sin. Especially now that he'd stopped being surly.

But he was right. Now just wasn't the time.

Chapter

29

BIRDIE

The Marriott Marquis looms over Times Square, a huge hotel complete with a Broadway theater included within. I pace the perimeter, trying to decide the best option. They've chosen an excellent place to hole up my quarry, and I'm both frustrated and pleased.

After all, I wouldn't want the game to be too simple.

Still, I anticipate that the tracking device will go black soon, and right now, it's of little use to me, the red dot utterly still on the GPS grid. I stand there on the corner, my back to Times Square, the late night revelers surging around me. I'm oblivious to everything but the hunt, my concentration split between the hotel and my PDA.

Move, I think. Damn it, get going.

And then, miraculously, the blip shudders.

They're on the move. And like a spider in a web, I'm right here waiting for them.

Chapter

30

JENNIFER

We hung the Do Not Disturb sign on the door, headed down the elevator to the first floor, then stepped out onto the bright lights of Broadway. (It might have been past two in the morning, but the lights were still bright.)

"Faces," Devlin said as we walked.

I nodded, and scoped out the features of everyone who passed us on the street. And there were a lot of them. Mostly college-aged and mostly drunk. That was okay. The crowd made me feel safer.

A throng had gathered on one corner to listen to the street-band sound of some guy making music from ordinary kitchen items. It was loud, it was funky, and it was also oddly compelling. Not enough to stop walking for, though. Once we stopped, we were a stationary target; I much preferred being a moving one. And so we pushed through the crowd, shoving and bumping our way through the people just like everyone else who was more interested in moving from point A to point B than they were in hearing the music man.

I heard a couple of curses come from behind us, and Devlin and I both turned. The crowd had tightened up, and a few people were having trouble getting through. I could make out the top of a woman's head and a blur of baseball cap on the man beside her. They looked pretty stuck, and I was glad we'd made it through when we did. Crowds can be brutal.

The cross-street light was green, and we paused at the corner long enough for traffic to clear away.

"So tell me," Devlin said, pointing to the theater marquees that seemed to surround us, "why isn't your name on one of those?"

"Oh, God, Devlin. Don't tease me."

"I'm not teasing," he said, sounding truly serious. "You have a strong voice. You're smart. You're resourceful. And you seem to want it. So why don't you have it?"

"I guess I just haven't gotten that break yet," I said. I tried to keep it light, but honestly, I wasn't too keen on having this conversation.

The last taxi zipped by, and Devlin stepped out into the street. "What does your agent say?"

"I, um, haven't found an agent yet."

He looked at me sideways. "Really." He made it a statement, not a question, and all of a sudden, I felt this overwhelming urge to smack him. To tell him that I hadn't gotten a break as a cute kid, and that Broadway was a really hard place, and that he had no business judging me.

The thing was, though, I don't think he was judging me. I

think *I* was judging me. Because every time Brian or my parents or my sister or anyone tried to ask me these questions, my immediate reaction was to go hide in a corner. Which was stupid, because I always told them the truth: I was working my ass off.

But if that was the truth, then why did I always end those conversations feeling like a big, fat liar?

Honestly, though, that was a level of self-analysis that I was so not going to jump to. Especially since I wasn't going to have a self to analyze if we didn't get a handle on these clues.

I was spared telling him to drop it by the scream that ripped through the sky, followed by a word that turned my blood to ice. "Gun! Oh, shit, a gun!"

"Go!" Devlin yelled, and he practically pushed me out into the street. We raced across Broadway, dodging cars until we were over the median and standing in the middle of Seventh. Behind us, I could still hear the people clamoring. I didn't know if the gun had been for us, but I was guessing it had. And I kept expecting a bullet to whiz past my ear and lay Devlin out flat.

A taxi slammed to a stop, and Devlin wrenched the door open, ushering me in next to a terrified couple.

"Sorry!" I said. "Sorry!"

Devlin got in after me, ignoring the rattle of curses from the driver. "We'll pay their fare," he said. "Where are they going?"

"Waldorf," the driver said.

"Fine. Great. Go."

And we went, with Devlin giving the tourists a novel-length apology, only to realize they only spoke German. At least they'd go home with a Those Crazy Americans story.

As soon as the Germans were safe at the Waldorf, Devlin

told the driver to head back to Times Square, this time the Crowne Plaza on 49th.

"We're going back?" I said. "I thought we'd head downtown. Or Brooklyn. Queens has hotels, too."

He just shook his head. "Times Square. If that was the assassin—and I think we can assume it was, although how we got so lucky, I don't know—but if it was the assassin, he's going to expect us to do exactly what you suggested."

"So we're pulling a fast one? How? He must really have a tracking device. I mean, how else could he have found us?"

"I don't think it works consistently. When I interviewed Mel and Matthew, that was one of the things their statements seemed to suggest. And when we located and analyzed the chip, even though it was damaged, the lab confirmed that it appeared to be designed to send a signal only intermittently, on a randomly generated schedule."

"Which means it might be black now."

"Right. And even if it's not, he found us in front of the Marriott Marquis. So if the tracking device was in the book, that's where he's going to continue to look."

"Okay," I said, not so much because I agreed, but because I was processing information. "Okay, so basically, you think we'll be safe at the Crowne Plaza either because the tracker has gone black or because the little blip will show us at the Marriott?"

"Right."

"I can live with that," I said. And I hoped to hell I could.

Like so many Manhattan hotels, the street level lobby of the Crowne Plaza was basically empty, and we had to go up to check in. Unfortunately, we were stymied in that effort by a man behind a podium who was letting only those with keys enter. Great for security, bad for us.

Devlin explained that we didn't yet have a room, but we would like one, and after a short interval, we were escorted up to the registration desk. I paid with the blood money, and five minutes later we were ensconced in a room. A minor victory— very minor—since my problem wasn't living quarters. It was *living*.

We needed to figure out where to go next. And soon.

Frustrated, I scribbled a second copy of the clue onto Crowne Plaza stationery and handed it to Devlin. "Be brilliant," I said.

He took it, then headed for the bathroom as I settled back with my notes, this time focusing on the second chunk of the clue. I was just about to Google "Morgan" and "Catiline" when my cell phone rang. The shrill sound echoed through the silence of the room, making me jump.

My fingers closed around the phone, and I yanked it up without checking the caller ID. "I'm here! Hello! Who is it?"

Even as I said the words, dread washed over me. I'd assumed the caller was Brian or my parents or any one of a number of people who calls just to chat any number of times each day. But as I answered, I realized the caller could be the assassin. And with that single thought, my mouth went dry and my body stiffened. I fought the urge to hang up, but I managed to wait it out.

Then I heard the familiar "Jenn?"

I just about sagged in relief.

Mel continued, speaking so fast I almost couldn't understand her. "Oh, God, Jenn! I'm so sorry. I'm in Geneva, and we're on a communications blackout. They gave us an hour to check messages and return calls and so I did and WHAT THE HELL IS GOING ON?"

I opened my mouth, but nothing came out. My throat was too dry. I swallowed, then tried again, realizing as I did that I'd moved to the side of the bed and practically collapsed there. "Mel! Thank God! I didn't want to leave the details in a message. I was afraid—I'm not sure what I was afraid of. That you'd freak out, maybe."

"Dammit, Jenn, I'm freaking out now! You mentioned PSW! You sounded hysterical! I swear if you don't tell me exactly what's going on right now I'm going to reach right through this phone and strangle you!"

"A message," I squeaked. I cleared my throat, and managed to sound more normal (albeit terrified). "I got a message, Mel. I'm playing the fucking game."

"What?"

"PSW," I said. I started to mention Andy, but I didn't want to her to worry her any more than necessary. Especially since she was stuck in Switzerland, totally incommunicado.

"No." The word came out with such conviction that I could practically see her shaking her head. "No. That's not possible."

"Believe me, it's not only possible, it's true."

"I'll make some excuse. I'll get out of the training. Special dispensation or something and I'll be there as soon as I can. Where are you?"

"Right now, we're at the—*hey!*" I fell backwards onto the bed as Devlin yanked the phone out of my hands. My heart pounded in my chest and I glared at him and scrambled to my knees as I reached for the phone. He moved deftly out of the way, then pressed his palm against my chest and shoved me back on the bed when I managed to scramble close again.

"Jenn? *Jenn?*" Mel's voice filtered from the phone. "*What happened? Are you all right? Jenn!*"

"She's fine," Devlin said into the phone. I could hear her voice, but I couldn't make out her words. "Mel, it's Devlin," he said. "Devlin Brady. I'm with her. She's fine. For now. Don't come up here. Don't call back. You don't need to get drawn back into this shit, and I don't want to put you at risk." Another pause, and then, "Yeah, well, I'm already at risk. I'm the target."

He opened his mouth, apparently wanting to say more, but I could hear the hum of Mel's voice cutting him off. Finally, he just jumped into the fray. "Mel! Mel! Calm down, okay. She'll be fine. We'll be fine. . . . I know you don't, but I do. And Jenn does, too." He scowled at the phone. "I'm hanging up now." And then, without giving her a chance to say anything more, he did just that.

I stared at him, completely flabbergasted. "What the—"

He shoved the phone into my hand. "You can't pull her into this."

I lost it. "Why not? Damn it, Devlin, why the fuck not?" I shook my head, not comprehending. "She's brilliant at this kind of thing. She could totally help us. I need—"

He pulled me roughly into his arms, effectively shutting me up. I pressed my face against his chest, and his arms tightened around me. My body fired in response. Dear Lord, one minute, I was riding a wave of terror, and the next I was surfing on lust. Red hot and desperate.

I'm not so stupid to believe it was real. I'm not. But the *sensation*. The *need*. That was real. And so was the fire building between us. I wanted to dive right in and burn myself in that fire. Flame purifies, right? And that's what I wanted. A few minutes of absolute, blissful purity.

I pulled back just enough so I could tilt my head up. And in a bold move that really isn't my style, my lips found his and—oh, yes!—he responded wholeheartedly. His mouth opened, and his hand moved from my back to my ass. He pressed me tight against him, tight enough that I could tell this wasn't an act—the man was definitely turned on.

I wove my fingers through his hair, clinging to him, wanting to just lose myself in him. God, I wanted to forget everything and just feel. Feel his hands on me, his cock in me. Anything and everything. Mostly, though, I wanted to feel safe.

He shifted, and somehow my back ended up against the wall. My fingers fumbled at his belt, and all I could think of was the *yes, please, now* chorus that was singing in my head.

His hands closed on mine. "Wait."

"What?" I pulled away. "Why?"

His face, so full of lust only moments before, now seemed lost and a little sad. Immediately, I felt like an idiot. I shouldn't have come on to him. I shouldn't have kissed him. I shouldn't have—

"I want to," he said, and I closed my eyes in relief. "So help me, I want you so much right now I think it might just kill me."

"Then why not?"

"Because the timing stinks. You're scared. You don't know what to do next. You don't want to think about what's going to happen if we don't solve this damn clue. And so you're trying to forget all of that, even if just for a few minutes."

"No, I—" But I closed my mouth. It was true. Everything

he said was true. I was desperately—*desperately*—attracted to this man. But right then—right at that particular moment—I think any man would do.

I turned away, suddenly unable to meet his eyes, and my arms crossed automatically over my chest.

He stroked my cheek. "It's okay. It's okay to be scared. To want to feel that rush so you know you're alive, and somehow manage to forget the fear at the same time. But it's hollow." He sighed, moved a step away. "Trust me. I know what I'm talking about. And I don't want hollow with you, Jenn."

Something in his voice reached out to me, and I turned, looking up at him curiously. The corner of his mouth lifted. Barely a smile, but enough that I was willing to count it. "What are you saying?"

"I'm saying I want you. But not now. Not in a rush. Later, when we have the time to do it right. And when it's about us, and not about a killer."

I didn't know what to say, so I nodded. I probably ought to have been mortified, but I wasn't. Instead, all that danced through my head was the realization that he really did want me. And not as a quick fuck. In a day full of horrors, I chalked that up as a minor miracle.

I wandered away, a bit aimlessly, as I wasn't sure what to do now. I'd lost my balance, and I didn't know how to find it again. We needed to worry about the clues, but I didn't know how. I was lost, and right then, all my focus was on this man.

"What happened to you?" I asked, when I couldn't stand it any longer.

"We don't have time for this," he said, his face closing up on me.

"We do," I insisted. "Don't you know? If you just take your mind off a problem, the solution always comes. My subconscious is doing its thing. So's yours. So while our brains are working their tails off, tell me. I want to know, Devlin. What happened. A man like you, alone, in that dark apartment. It's like you were in prison or something. Only you'd stuck yourself there."

"I guess I had," he said. He looked up, his eyes hitting me with fierce intensity. "I killed my partner."

I let out a little gasp, but he went on.

"I lost my badge, my gun. I guess you could say I was having the pity party to end all pity parties."

I swear, my heart was breaking. "But where are your family? Your friends?"

Considering the question was perfectly serious, I was surprised when he laughed.

"What?" I demanded.

"You," he said.

"Excuse me?"

He just chuckled. "Anyone else would have zeroed in on the fact that I offed my partner. Not you. You're wondering where my support network is." He stroked me cheek. "You've got a special way of looking at things, Jenn."

I lifted my chin, a little flattered, a little embarrassed. "You didn't kill him on purpose."

"Why do you say that?"

"I know you."

He shook his head. "No, you don't."

"Not completely, but enough. And I'm right, aren't I? You didn't kill him on purpose."

THE Manolo MATRIX

"I shot him on purpose," Devlin said, his expression tight. "But you're right. I wasn't trying to kill him. I was trying to save my ass."

I hesitated, then sat beside him and took his hand. "Do you want to talk about it?"

"No. Suffice it to say I learned that he'd gone dirty. And he knew that I knew. And he was setting me up."

"So the shooting was self-defense."

"Damn straight."

"Then why did they take away your badge? Is that like standard operating procedure?"

His face tightened. "No, not at all."

"Well?"

"Jenn . . ."

"I want to know, Devlin."

He ran a hand through his hair. "Randall was trying to blackmail me into not turning him in. So he did a few things that made it look like I'd thrown in with him."

"And even after you shot him, they still thought you were bad?"

"Essentially. I've spent my whole adult life with the FBI and have a service record as clean as a whistle, but still they pulled my badge and sicced OPR on me."

"Opie what?"

"O. P. R.," he repeated, rubbing the back of his neck. I almost offered to give him a neck massage, but my hold on my libido was still too tenuous. "Office of Professional Responsibility. Like Internal Affairs for cops."

"Oh. I'm sorry."

"Yeah. So am I."

"What about your job?"

"Suspended pending investigation."

"But you'll be cleared? I mean your partner really was dirty, so it'll all be okay in the end."

" 'Okay,' " he repeated, as if he were exploring the sound of the word. "I'm being investigated for the very thing I deplore and have spent over a decade fighting against. My former partner's dead—by my gun—and his little girl doesn't have a father. So I'm not really sure that it's ever going to be okay."

"*His* choices," I said. "Not yours. And you'll get your job back."

"I'm not so sure I want it anymore."

"You could always go back to the theater," I said, trying to lighten the mood.

"No thanks. Although it would certainly thrill my mother. She's always said my biggest mistake was leaving the theater. She'd consider my current situation God's way of balancing the scales."

"She doesn't know?"

He rubbed the back of his neck. "We don't exactly have a warm, fuzzy relationship."

"Oh." Okay, so we weren't dealing with my overly involved, overly boisterous family. "Haven't you got anyone to dump on about all this? I mean, if it were me, I'd be on the phone to my mom or my sister or Mel in a heartbeat. Surely you've got someone. Father? Siblings? Friends?"

"Dead, none, quiet."

"Quiet?"

"After a while on the job, you realize that all your friends are agents, too. And when something like this happens, the bulk of them scatter."

"Then maybe they aren't really your friends."

"Maybe not."

"You picked a hard life," I said, once again wondering why. I couldn't get that Tony award out of my head.

"So did you. Theater's brutal."

"So far, I haven't had the pleasure of suffering for my art." I met his eyes. "I promise, I'll drop it if you don't want to talk about it. But I'm really curious. Why the change? You were on the stage. You won awards. That's just so, so *incredible*."

"It is," he agreed. "And I loved it in a way. But it wasn't in my blood. My mother's blood, yeah. But not mine."

"Stage mother."

"To the nth degree. Don't get me wrong, I did enjoy the work. Stayed in it even after I'd fired my mom. But once I hit college, I knew it wasn't the life I wanted. My mom considered it a slap in the face. It would have been bad enough if I'd just given up theater. I had to pursue my dad's career."

"He died in the line of duty?"

"Cancer," Devlin said. "But their marriage was over even before I was born. There was so much bad blood between them it was like a thick red curtain. It—" He cut himself off with a shake of his head. "You know what, it doesn't matter. I am who I am today, and I don't regret any of it. I worked my ass off in the theater, but I wanted something more. Being an actor is amazing, but I wanted . . . I don't know. I wanted to be out there fighting the fight, not just playing a part. My mother always said I had an overdeveloped sense of justice, but I think hers was just on the puny side. But maybe she was right. Maybe that's what the pull was. Some corny need to get out there and save the world."

"Serve and protect," I said. "Sure worked in my favor."

At that, he actually smiled a little. "All I know is that it hurt like hell when the whole goddamn agency turned on me. All those years, all that work, and then it's just fuck you, your hearing's in a month. Fucking bastards."

"You'll be reinstated, right?"

He rubbed the back of his neck, his expression tense. "Will I? If I fight and pull together the evidence to prove Randall set me up, yeah. I could probably get back in."

"If?"

"Awful lot of goddamn hoops."

"Jesus, Devlin. You just told me how much you love the job. More than Broadway, which I find so hard to believe. And all this stuff you're talking about is just bullshit. It's not the job. It's bureaucracy. Like getting a bad review or having to go to cattle calls. That's the sucky part. But it's not the job. And if the job's really in your blood, you need to fight for it."

Even as I spoke, I had to wonder if I'd been following my own advice. I frowned. This was about Devlin. "I'm right," I said to him. "I know I am."

"Maybe." He drew in a breath. "But I still have to deal with killing Randall."

"You need time," I said. "But I'm sorry your friends haven't been there."

"Just as well. I haven't exactly been in the mood to talk about this." He met my eyes, his hard at first, and then softening. "I can't believe I'm talking about it now. I'd say it's the situation, but I think it's you."

My face burned and I focused on the carpet. "Yeah, well, I'm glad you can talk to me, but I still feel bad for you. I mean your friends—"

"I'm a reminder of what can happen."

"Maybe. But that's not an excuse. Friends should be there for you. That's the whole point of having them. And good friends want to be there no matter what."

He didn't answer, but I saw him look toward the cell phone he'd dropped to the bed.

"Mel can help," I said. "More, she wants to help."

"All right," he said slowly. "Call her."

I felt ten pounds lighter, as if he'd just wrenched an anvil off my heart. I pretty much leaped toward the phone.

"But just remember that you're pulling her into the game and putting you both at risk. She survived once. If she doesn't survive this time, who's going to have to carry that guilt? It's a heavy burden. Believe me. I know."

My finger was over the TALK button, but I stopped, the anvil dropping back down on my chest. My finger trembled; I really wanted to push that button. But Devlin's words . . .

"Explain," I said.

He reached out and plucked the phone out of my hand. "Two things. Call in the authorities and the protector can get picked off, remember?"

"Yeah, but I already did that, remember? Pulling in Andy was a huge mistake. But it means that the assassin's already after me. I've got a big, fat bull's-eye painted on my back, and getting Mel's help won't make it any worse now."

"All right," he said. "But what if she's not an authority?"

"Andy said she was."

"She's not a cop," Devlin countered.

"She works for the NSA. That sounds pretty authoritarian to me."

"She's only an analyst," he pointed out. "And if she's *not* an authority, and she steps in to help us . . ."

He trailed off, but from the tone of his voice, I could tell he expected me to pick up the thread. Unfortunately, I wasn't sure of the pattern he was weaving.

"Outside help," he said. "The rules."

"What are you talking about?" I asked, dread icing my blood.

He looked at me sideways, his expression curious. "A player can pull in help," he said. "That's allowed by the rules. But once they do, the help is tagged, too."

"Tagged?"

"They're fair game," he said. "I thought you knew that."

"No, I . . ." My mind churned, processing the information. "Then that dart might really have been meant for Andy," I said slowly. "Not for me at all." And then the worst hit me. I clapped my hand to my mouth, fighting back a wave of bile. "Brian," I whispered. "Oh, dear God. Brian."

"Please be okay, please be okay, please be okay." I just kept repeating that over and over during the entire taxi drive to Brian's house. It was just after three in the morning, and the streets were clear, so the cab driver was moving fast. Not fast enough to suit me, though. Especially since Brian wasn't answering his cell phone.

I wanted to lose myself in a role—the ingénue who believes her friend is dead, only to discover he's alive—but I couldn't do it. The reality was too close, and as much as I wanted my fantasies to help me cope, I couldn't do it.

All I could think about was Brian.

"He has to be okay," I babbled. "Because how could they know? So what if I asked him to help solve a clue? I was in your bathroom for Christ's sake. No one could know. They couldn't."

But as soon as we turned the corner into Brian's Chelsea neighborhood, I knew that I was wrong. Everything shifted, the world seeming to change into black and white, and I heard myself whimper. Devlin's arm went around me, and I leaned in close, turning my face away from the spectacle we were approaching: flashing lights, crime scene tape, and dozens of gawkers.

"I killed him," I whispered. "He's dead because he helped me."

"It's not your fault," Devlin said. But I knew it was. And I think Devlin knew it, too.

He pulled away from me, then turned me so that I was facing him. He pressed his hands against my cheeks. "Jenn. It's not your fault."

He spoke firmly, his eyes never leaving mine, and I so desperately wanted to believe him. I couldn't, though. I'd opened my big mouth and Brian had died.

"Come on." Devlin took my hand and tugged me out of the taxi. He leaned back in to pay the driver, who was mumbling something under his breath and looking a little too excited to suit my taste. I wanted to lash out, to shout at him, to tell him that someone was dead in there. But I didn't. I just kept quiet and let Devlin lead me away.

"Maybe he's not dead," I said. "Maybe it was just an attempt. Or maybe it's something else entirely. One of his neighbors dealing drugs. Someone falling off a balcony."

"Maybe," Devlin said, but I could tell he didn't believe that. I didn't believe it myself.

He held tight to my hand as we walked the short distance to the crime scene tape. Even though it was silly, I craned my neck and tried to see—as if I could somehow channel an image of the inside of Brian's flat. Of course, I saw nothing. Nothing to make me feel better, anyway. I did see an ambulance, pulled up close to the door. And I watch enough television to know that an ambulance just sitting there is a bad thing. Moving ambulances mean that someone is alive. They might be in trouble, but they're alive.

When you're dead, there's no need for the ambulance to move very fast.

I heard a whimper and realized it came from me. Devlin must have heard it, too, because he squeezed my hand. I squeezed back, grateful for the support. Then Devlin raised a hand and signaled for one of the uniformed officers. She came over, her face tight, as if she was expecting trouble from some neighborhood asshole.

"What happened?" Devlin asked.

"Sir, are you a resident of the building?"

"No, I'm—"

"Then I'm going to have to ask that you stand back and let us —"

"I'm FBI."

Her eyes widened, and I decided that she was actually quite pretty despite the too-severe haircut and the complete lack of makeup. "Got identification?"

"Not on me." He nodded at me. "I was delivering my girlfriend to her friend's place. He lives here. She's concerned."

I could see the tension play out across her face. Should she believe he was on the job? Did it really matter?

After a moment, her face cleared. She turned to me. "Who's your friend?"

"Brian Reid," I said. "Apartment 7G."

"We've been trying to reach him," the officer said. "Have you been in touch? Does he have a cell phone?"

"I . . . *what?*" I heard the words, but my brain didn't quite process the information. I blinked. And I must have looked particularly befuddled, because a whole array of expressions flashed over the officer's face. Confusion, irritation, surprise. And then, finally, mortification.

She reached over the tape and put her hand on my shoulder. "Your friend's not in there, honey. It's his apartment, but a neighbor confirmed that Mr. Reid isn't the victim."

Relief ripped through me with such fury I felt my knees go weak.

"Who is?" Devlin asked.

But I knew. Dammit all, Brian might be safe, but I still had blood on my hands. And even before the officer told Devlin the answer, I could hear her voice echoing in my head: Felix Donnelly. Aka Cousin Fifi.

Devlin held up a hand, signaling the officer to wait. She could have told him to go fuck himself, but she didn't. Instead, she was looking at Jenn with the same compassion he was feeling.

"Honey, are you okay?" she asked.

Jenn nodded. "Yeah. I'm . . . yeah." She looked up at Devlin. "I'm going to go sit down a sec, okay?"

He pointed to the curb. "Right there," he said. "Don't go where I can't see you."

"Don't worry."

If the officer thought their exchange was odd, she didn't say anything. But when he turned his attention back to her, she launched in with, "Are you really a Fed?"

"I really am," he said. He didn't bother to announce that he was a Fed without a badge or a gun. Well, except for the clutch piece he'd tucked into his ankle holster before they'd headed for the Hudson. He nodded toward the building. "What can you tell me about what happened in there?"

"You a friend of the vic?"

"Never met the guy."

She considered that, then nodded. And then she turned slightly, giving Jenn her back. It was a considerate move, ensuring that Jenn didn't overhear the gory details, and Devlin realized with a start how grateful he was. Anyone who went out of their way to protect Jenn was okay in his book.

"A clean slice across the throat. Someone got close. And they had a steady hand."

"Shit."

"Lot of folks looking for your girl's friend."

"A lot of folks, and one killer," Devlin said.

She nodded. "Yeah, I heard the detectives talking. They're working that angle, too. The vic is an out-of-towner. They're thinking the perp got the wrong guy."

"Fuck."

"You said it." She turned away to chastise a drunk who was leaning too heavily on the crime scene tape, then returned her attention to Devlin. "Get the cell number from your girl," she said. "And leave me your names and numbers."

"No problem," he said. He gave her his boss's name instead of his own, then gave her the name of the first girl he ever kissed. For phone numbers, he gave her the numbers for the Thai place down the street from him, as well as his neighborhood pizza place. Why not? She was surely going to be hungry when this was all over. He got Brian's number from Jenn and gave that to her as well, though he did transpose two numbers. They'd track down the number soon enough, but maybe this would slow them down. In the meantime, he wanted to track down Brian himself. He needed to tell the guy to be careful. Cooperate with the cops, but watch his back. Better, get the hell out of town and stay there. At least until he or Jenn called and told him it was safe to return.

Good advice, and he hoped Brian would take it. Even more, he wished that *Jenn* could take it. She couldn't, though. Because hell had already started to descend on her.

And until they put the brakes on that, nothing else mattered.

>>http://www.playsurvivewin.com<<

PLAY.SURVIVE.WIN

>>>WELCOME TO REPORTING CENTER<<<

PLAYER REPORT:
REPORT NO. A-0003
Filed By: Birdie
Subject: Status update
Report:
I failed.

I still cannot quite believe the magnitude of such failure, and I have only myself to blame.

I was so anxious, so *eager*, that I didn't take into account the effect of the crowd around me. I took my weapon out too early, hid it under my jacket, expecting that it would remain concealed, and I would have the warm security of its weight in my hand.

I hadn't anticipated the crowds—bumping and banging and stumbling, drunk on youth and alcohol.

And the one bitch who shoved me. Who pushed my jacket aside.

Who saw the gun. Then screamed.

I tell myself the failure stemmed from a lack of practice—five long years during which my skills atrophied. But in my heart, I know the fault is entirely my own. I was careless. I was sloppy. And in the end, I was discovered before I could get a shot off.

A failure, yes. But also a lesson.

And so now I'll wait, patiently biding my time until the tracker blips again. And this time, when I go after my quarry, I will not fail.

>>>End Report<<
Send Report to Opponent? >>Yes<< >>**No**<<

"It was him, wasn't it? The assassin did this?" I was still sitting on the curb, numb, ignoring the hand that Devlin had offered to help me up.

He stood there for a moment, then he bent down to sit beside me. He didn't answer, but that was answer enough.

We both were quiet for a while. I don't know about Devlin, but I was fighting a whole whirlwind of emotions. Euphoria that Brian wasn't dead. Anger and desolation that Fifi was. And guilt. Lots and lots of guilt.

Most of all, though, I was scared. There was a man in there—dead—by the hand of the same person who had me on a hook. Who had a gun aimed at Devlin's heart.

And who was still looking for Brian. Or, maybe, had already found him.

No. I couldn't—*wouldn't*—believe that. Brian was safe. And

since I was the one who got him in to this, I was the one who was going to get him out.

I started rummaging in my tote bag, found my cell, and began to dial. Once again, Devlin ripped it out of my hands.

I glared at him. "You're starting to make a habit of that."

"We need to get another phone."

"Excuse me?"

"Think, Jennifer."

Okay, now that just pissed me off. But I thought, and it only took me about two seconds to understand what he meant. "Oh."

"*Oh* is right," he said. "If the assassin came after Brian, it's because somehow he found out about your phone call. Found out that Brian helped you with the clue."

"And how could he have done that unless he's intercepting my cell calls," I added, a statement, not a question.

"Exactly."

"There could be a bug in your apartment," I suggested.

"Possibly," he said, easily. "But since we don't know for sure, we should probably avoid using your cell. Or mine, for that matter. If you call Brian, the assassin's going to hear. And if he doesn't already know Brian's still alive, he will then."

He was right, of course, but I didn't want to waste any time. "We need a phone." I pointed randomly into the crowd that was starting to dissipate now that they knew there wasn't going to be a raucous arrest or a violent shoot-out. "Ask someone for a phone."

"And drag someone else into this mess? No way. We find a pay phone."

He had a point, but I didn't know where a pay phone was.

For that matter, for all the times I'd come to Brian's place, at the moment, I couldn't even remember where the closest deli was. I stood up, turning in a circle as I scoped out the neighborhood. "Dammit, this is New York. Why is everything closed?"

"This is a pretty residential street," Devlin said. "Come on. There's got to be a twenty-four-hour diner nearby."

"Yes!" Thank God the mush I call my brain was starting to gel again. "Yes, there's a little coffee shop around the corner. I'm almost positive it's an all-nighter."

"Let's go."

The place really was just around the corner, and we were settled in a booth in no time. I pulled my notes about the clue out of my tote and slapped them on the table in front of him. "I never got the chance to tell you what I figured out," I said, then ran him through my thinking about "Memory" and *Cats* and the fact that *One Thing After Another, The Love Set,* and *When in Rome* were all old shows. "And *Candide* is a musical, of course," I added. "But I haven't put it all together yet."

I hauled out my laptop again and pushed it to his side of the booth. "Maybe you'll have better luck."

While he got the computer going, I rummaged for some change, then headed off to warn Brian. In a perfect world, he'd answer his phone, I'd tell him calmly and firmly to go take a Club Med vacation, he'd do it (and screw the Broadway debut), and I'd return to the table to find that Devlin had solved the clue.

Needless to say, I was not living in a perfect world. I couldn't get through to Brian, and Devlin's frustrated expression when I returned suggested that he'd made no progress whatsoever.

"Nothing?" I asked, just in case he was, you know, teasing

me. Maybe he'd figured the whole thing out, located the assassin, and took him out of action.

He looked up, but didn't say anything. Didn't have to.

"Well, hell," I said as I slid into the booth.

"How about you? Any luck?"

"No, goddamn it. I left him a message. Told him not to come home, to lay low, and that I'd call him back soon." I ran my fingers through my hair, then twisted it into a knot that I held in place with the pencil sitting across Devlin's notes. "We have to get another cell phone. One of those pay-as-you-go things."

"Stores aren't open yet," Devlin said. He leaned across the booth and plucked the pencil from my hair, then tapped the paper with it. "This is our priority right now."

He had that right.

The truth was, I didn't even know if Brian was still alive. But if he was—and I hoped to hell he was—the only way he'd stay safe was if we played this game to the end.

A waiter swung by and delivered two sodas and a basket of fries, food I assumed that Devlin had ordered while I'd been on the phone.

I grabbed a fry and munched on it, my thoughts in a scramble. "Memory" leads to *Cats* leads to . . . *Man of La Mancha*? That just didn't make sense.

I tapped my pencil against the table top, looking at the clue again. "The knight's production," it said. Okay, sure. But what does that mean? Did Don Quixote put on plays? He did in the story, but—

That's it!

"It's not *Man of La Mancha*," I said, practically yelping.

"It's Andrew Lloyd Webber. *He's* the knight who put on *Cats*."

His grin shot straight down to my toes. "Awesome," he said. "That's got to be it."

I sat back and took a long sip of my soda, feeling almost smug. We'd worked our way through the first part, and now we were on something of a roll. The rest, I thought, would be easy.

Famous last words.

Five minutes later we'd gotten nowhere.

"We have to approach this methodically," I said. "Step by step."

"Agreed."

"Right." I sat up and straightened my shoulders. "So this part here talks about how the answer is on the knight's production. So it's on *Cats*. Backstage, maybe? Or something during the show?"

"I doubt it's backstage. The show's not on Broadway anymore, and I doubt we're supposed to chase touring productions. The clue has to be hidden someplace where we can get to it. Someplace whoever is setting us up can get to as well."

"So maybe it's backstage at the original *Cats* theater."

"Do you have any idea how tight security is on Broadway

since 9/11? Getting backstage would be damn near impossible."

"I know a ton of people," I said. "We could call someone. Get a tour."

He just stared at me.

"Oh. Right. Never mind." Getting other people involved in my little drama was not a good idea. "Okay, so maybe it is on-stage. Something that happens during the show? A clue made out of one of the songs? The stage direction? Something?"

"I don't think so," he said.

"Me neither," I admitted. For one thing, since the show had closed on Broadway, how could we see the staging? For another, even if it were playing, the curtain would go up at eight, way too late for my personal version of High Noon (or High Ten, anyway). If I had to see the show to save myself, then someone had an even sicker sense of humor than I already thought.

"Let's keep going," Devlin said. "The rest of the message is obviously going to flesh out the first part. That's why it says 'And will be found by following.' Right?"

"I guess . . ."

"By following *One Thing After Another*," he said. "That was on Broadway, you said?"

"Right. I found it on the Internet. Short run in the 1930s."

"Hmmm. Any idea what to do with that tidbit?"

"Nope. Maybe we should focus on *Candide*. At least that's a show I know."

"So who was the patroness of that show?" he asked.

"Ah. Um, well, I don't know the show that well." I made a face. "Actually, I don't even know what a patroness is."

"Maybe the producer was a woman?" he suggested.

"Maybe." Since the answer wasn't going to come to either of

us without divine intervention, I reached for the next best thing. Honestly, how did people survive without the Internet?

"Since *The Love Set* and *When in Rome* were on Broadway, too, maybe there's some connection between all the shows."

"We can check." The browser was open, and I typed "Candide" in the ibdb search box, deciding to start with it because I knew the show a little. The computer did its whirring thing, and then I was rewarded with two hits, both musical versions of the story. I slid the pad of paper we'd been using over to Devlin. "Write down all the women," I said. "Unless you have a better idea where to start."

"None," he said, and then he made a quick list:

Lillian Hellman (book)
Dorothy Parker (lyrics)
Genevieve Pitot (music, second version)

"It's all very clear to me now," he said, staring at what he'd written.

"At least it's only three names," I said.

"But what about them?"

I shook my head. "I don't know. Cross reference them with the other shows, I guess."

"Click here first," he said, tapping the screen. "That should get us more info about the show."

"Yeah. The theater, run dates, list of songs. Pretty much the whole nine yards." I clicked, then looked at him as I waited for the page to come up. "What do you expect to find?" I wasn't challenging him or anything. I just wanted us to be thinking simpatico.

"The songs Parker wrote," he said.

"Why?"

"Because she wrote short and pithy. So unless you know how to pull secret messages from music, or unless you want to read the entire script, then she's our best bet."

"Right," I said. "Cross your fingers."

We both did, and then skimmed the web page. Apparently, that version had been staged three times. Feeling decisive, I clicked on the first one. Revivals are nice and all, but always go with the original if you can.

"Well, hell," Devlin said as the page opened.

I agreed. No list of lyrics. "I could have sworn this database has the lyrics. I guess that's somewhere else."

"See if you can find them," he said, but I was already typing. And as soon as Google came up, I entered: "Dorothy Parker Candide Lyrics."

The list of hits that came up sounded pretty promising, and I clicked on the first one.

Bingo.

The page focused on one of the revival performances, but I didn't care because there, at the bottom of the page, was a section called "Lyric Credits."

"There," Devlin said, pointing to the screen.

" 'The Venice Gavotte,' " I read. "Lyrics by Richard Wilbur and Dorothy Parker." I looked up at Devlin with a frown. "What the hell is a gavotte?"

"No clue. But I'll take an educated guess that it's some sort of dance."

I headed over to Dictionary.com to check out that little theory. Sure enough, a "gavotte" is a French peasant dance. And as soon as I read that, I tossed my arms around Devlin and planted a wet one on his mouth.

"Mmm," he said. "If we keep making such great progress on this clue, we're going to end up rolling around naked by the time ten rolls around."

"So long as we've made sure that my pretty little ass is safe," I countered, "that's perfectly fine with me."

Our eyes met and held, and a wonderful burst of lust tingled up my spine. I remembered the way he'd felt against me in the hotel, not to mention the heat I'd seen in his eyes. *Wow.*

I sighed and made a conscious effort to move two inches away. *So* not the time. "We have to be good," I said. "The clue. Solve the clue and then we'll talk. Or more." I spoke more cavalierly than I felt, but what else could I do? Blush bright red and hide under the table? Not damn likely.

"Such incentive," he said. He shot me one more quick grin, then focused on our notes. I exhaled, relieved to be back to the status quo. At least I knew how to act in my freaky PSW scenario. I mean, how hard is hysteria? But I'm never sure of the role I should play when dealing with men. Especially men I'm hot for. (I know the theoretical answer is that I should just act naturally. Trust me. That one never works.)

"So now we know that the thing we're looking for is at the gathering place of Dorothy Parker," he said.

"That makes no sense whatsoever."

"Agreed. Did she ever do a play at the Winter Garden Theater?" he asked, naming the theater where *Cats* played for years.

I typed a search into Google, then surveyed the hits. "No, but *West Side Story* opened at the Winter Garden, and both it and *Candide* were by Leonard Bernstein."

"I have no idea where that takes us," Devlin said.

"Me either."

We stared at each other, then Devlin shook his head slowly. "Just write it down. We just need to keep going. Something else will jump out at us."

I nodded and made a note. But there was light seeping through the windows now, and ten was barreling down. If something was going to jump out at us, I sure hoped it would do it soon. More, I hoped it was an answer . . . and not an assassin.

Jennifer hunched over the computer, and Devlin felt a pang in his heart. This girl—this flighty woman who'd never faced anything more serious than a run in her pantyhose—was digging in and focusing like a pro.

Even more, as much as she was working to save her own ass, he knew she was also intending to save him, too. Could she? That didn't really matter much. What got him in the gut was that she wanted to try. She didn't even know him, but she was damn sure going to try to save him. And he had a feeling she wanted to save more than just his life. This girl wanted to save the man.

Who else in his life could he say that about?

"Okay," she said, tapping the computer. "I've got two screens open. One with the entry for *The Love Set* and the other with *When in Rome.*"

His earlier musings vanished, and he leaned in closer. "Anything overlap? Cast? Crew? Opening dates? Theater?"

"Working on that." She did some more clicking and dragging, then ran her finger slowly down the screen as he followed along.

Nothing.

Nothing.

Nothing.

And then, "*Wait!*" He stared at the screen, certain that what he was seeing was no coincidence. He leaned over and took over the track pad. "Here," he said, pointing the arrow to "Morgan" in the *One Thing After Another* list. "And here." He manipulated the track pad again, moving the arrow over "Catiline" from *When in Rome.*

"Kenneth Daigneau," she said.

"Somehow he's important."

"Type his name into the search box," she said. "What shows has he been in? *Candide,* maybe?"

Devlin angled the computer toward him so he could type, and in no time at all the search engine spit back a result: *The Love Set, When in Rome,* and *One Thing After Another.*

"No *Candide,*" Devlin said. "But all the others are there."

"Yeah. So what does that mean?"

He wished he knew. More and more, he wished he could just spit out all the answers and make this woman safe. But all he could do was play the game and hope that in the end that was good enough. "If we read the message literally, the place we're looking for is a gathering place. Maybe a restaurant or a hotel or something. And Dorothy Parker went there. So maybe this Kenneth guy went there, too. And that's the connection be-tween *Candide* and these other plays."

"Maybe," she said, though she didn't sound convinced. "But what about *Cats?*"

"No idea," he confessed. "Hopefully we'll figure that out."

"What time is it?"

"Don't think about it," he said. But he couldn't help himself. He looked up at the clock: Approaching six. *Damn.*

"Right." She lifted her chin. "I'm not going to think about it. I'm just going to focus."

"Good girl," he said as she typed "Dorothy Parker Kenneth Daigneau" into the search box.

"Nothing much," she said, scanning the hits that came up.

"Try just entering his name," Devlin said.

"Whoa," she said as the first hits came up. "This has got to be it. *Spamalot!*"

"Holy shit," he said. "You're right." Kenneth Daigneau, as about eight million sites announced, had won a contest back in the thirties to name a processed meat product: Spam.

"*We eat ham and jam and Spam a lot,*" she sang. "The Knights of the Round Table. Arthur, Camelot—"

"And Dorothy Parker," he said. "The famous writers' round table at the Algonquin Hotel."

"That's got to be it. It's a perfect fit." Her brow furrowed, and he knew she was remembering the other piece of the puzzle. "Except for *Cats.* That doesn't fit at all."

"Sure it does. Andrew Lloyd Webber's a knight, and in Camelot there were the knights of the round table, right?"

"True," she admitted.

"And there's more," he said, feeling just a little smug. "About four years ago, I went to a benefit at the Algonquin. Guess who the guest of honor was."

"I have no idea," she said.

"Matilda," he said. "The house cat who lives in the Algonquin Hotel."

Chapter

37

JENNIFER

I don't speak cat, so I had absolutely no clue how a cat was supposed to help us figure this out. Was it a trained cat, who'd respond to my voice, then rush across the lobby, press his paw on a secret button, and open a hidden compartment?

Probably not likely, but as we stepped into the fabulously appointed lobby of the Algonquin Hotel, I tried not to worry about it. After all, we'd figured out the clue. Surely we'd figure out the answer, too.

The place was positively stunning, old-world elegance highlighted by writing desks and other antique furniture in rich, dark colors. Settees and chairs were clustered together in conversation areas, empty now when so many New Yorkers and tourists were still sleeping.

As we moved toward the front desk, I stifled the urge to smooth my clothes and brush back my hair. This was elegance to the max. By comparison, I felt like a street person in my jeans, even if they were designer.

We reached the reception desk, and banged on the little bell. Almost immediately, a petite blonde emerged, her eyes bright and her smile wide despite the early hour. "May I help you?"

"Actually, we need a room," Devlin said, as I looked on in surprise. He caught my glance and shrugged. I didn't protest. I felt scummy and gross, and even though Devlin probably didn't mind—he'd been wallowing in scummy and gross—I was desperate for a shower. And if past experience was any indication, we were going to need some time with the computer even after we found the kitty-cat clue. Assuming, of course, that we were right and Matilda was harboring a clue for us at all.

As the woman took all of our (false) information, Devlin casually mentioned Matilda. "I don't suppose she's up and about?"

"Oh, I bet she's around."

I turned in a circle, visually scouring the lobby. "Um, so where is she?"

I was already having a sinking feeling about this. I had a mental image of me crawling on my hands and knees over every inch of the hotel, shaking a bag of Pounce and trying to urge Miss Kitty out into the open.

Thank God reality turned out to be so much better.

The clerk turned her attention away from Devlin long enough to call out in a stage whisper, "Matilda! Matilda, sweetie, you have admirers!"

And then, just as pretty as you please, this big, beautiful, fluffy grayish-white cat leaped silently onto the top of one of the writing desks. She plumped her rump down and stared at us as if saying, "Well, I'm here now."

I swear, I wanted to kiss her. The cat, not the clerk, although in my giddiness, I would have kissed the clerk, too. Out of a day of horrors, I think this was the one and only thing that had gone smoothly. As soon as this was over, I was *so* getting a kitten.

"Um, can I just go over?" I asked, motioning toward Matilda.

"Oh, sure. She's very used to people."

I guess she'd have to be. So while Devlin finished up the paperwork and gave the woman the cash for our room, I went over to make Matilda's acquaintance.

Sure enough, she was a friendly cat, rubbing her head against the palm of my hand, and then leaping into my lap with little encouragement once I took a seat in the chair by the desk. "What have you got to tell me, sweetie?" I murmured, my nose buried in her fur. "Have you got a message for me on that collar of yours?"

That really would be too easy, so I was completely positive her collar would yield nothing.

Fortunately, I was wrong.

"Anything?" Devlin asked, coming over to join us.

Matilda's purr ratcheted up a notch as I kept my fingers buried in her fur, scratching away at that sweet spot at the back of her neck.

"Oh, yeah," I said. "Matilda's my new best friend. Check it out."

As he leaned in closer, I manipulated the collar so the back side was facing up. It was a stretchy thing, like a woman's bracelet, with links of silver encrusted with diamonds and emeralds (fake, I assumed, but what did I know?). The underside was smooth, though, and on it, someone had engraved a message: WWW.PLAYSURVIVEWIN-CAT.COM

"Thank you, Matilda," I whispered. "If we survive this, I'm sending you kitty treats every week for the rest of your life."

Chapter

38

DEVLIN

Why do you run? What do you wish?
To prevent the Horrors, to shun the fate of a fish.

So scurry, scurry like gaggling geese,
Run to Bishop to make your peace.

The clock is ticking, petals falling,
Not a Beast, but dead . . . and no use stalling.

Devlin stared at the computer screen and decided that the world was one very fucked up place. "This is nuts," he said. "Absolutely fucking nuts."

Beside him, Jenn kept her eyes firmly on the screen, but he caught the way her lower lip quivered. *Hell.*

He slipped his arm around her shoulder. She slumped

against him, and he knew she was losing confidence. And that simple truth was more devastating to him than the day he'd lost his badge.

He turned her slightly so that she'd be facing him if it weren't for the fact that she kept her head aimed toward the desktop. Since he couldn't meet her eyes, he pressed her forehead against his. "Hey. We're going to figure this out."

"It's already six. I've only got until ten. And damned if this game will throw us a straightforward clue. So when? When are we going to figure it out?"

"Right now. We're going to figure it out right now." His voice was firm, determined, and he noticed that when she looked up at him, she was smiling.

"Are you taking care of me?"

"Damn straight." He of all people knew how easy it was to wallow in self-pity. But that kind of thing could kill you. Him, it would just kill his soul. Her, it could kill before the day was out.

"God, I'm pathetic. I'm sitting here letting the asshole win." Her chin jutted out in a way he found both cute and incredibly sexy. "I'm not going to let him win."

"Then get off your ass and do something about it."

She must have taken him literally, because she started to pace, nodding a little as she moved. "Right. Right. Evita, maybe. She's strong. And in the first act especially, she totally gets her way." Her forehead creased in a frown. "Except she dies in the end, so maybe she's not the best choice. . . ."

"What are you talking about?"

Her cheeks bloomed with color. "It's silly."

"I promise to only laugh for ten or fifteen minutes."

"Ha ha." She made a face, but continued. "It's this thing I do when I'm nervous. I pick a character—sometimes I even make up a character—so that I can be someone other than me. It's stupid, but—"

"I don't think it's stupid at all."

"You don't?"

"No," he said simply. "I don't."

"Oh. Well, then. That's cool."

Her smile was sweet and a little shy, and impulsively, he pressed his hands to the sides of her face, tilted her head back, and kissed her. He'd honestly meant it to be a quick kiss. A symbol. A thank-you. Somehow, though, it became more than that. Her mouth opened, not from passion so much as surprise, and he took advantage, exploring her lips with his own, feeling his body burn with a need that had sparked hours earlier and hadn't yet been extinguished

When he finally pulled back, she stared at him, her eyes surprised, shocked, and dreamy. "Wow," she said. She closed her eyes and rubbed her lips with two fingers. "Wow," she said again.

"I'm not going to apologize," he said. "Even though I probably should. Because we don't have time right now. But consider that a promise."

"Keep making promises like that, and you'll find yourself seriously hurting if you don't make good. And soon."

He wasn't sure if he should laugh, so he just nodded gravely. "Absolutely."

"Good. Now quit making passes and get to work."

He scooted his chair closer so he could see the computer screen better. "We'll deal with just the clue now since we're racing the clock. But as soon as we're sure we're safe, I'm going to see what I can find out about this domain name." He also intended to call and see who donated the cat's collar. But he had a feeling that was going to be a dead end.

"You can do that?"

"Sweetheart, I can do anything I put my mind to."

He was expecting a laugh. Instead, she just nodded, all business. "Yeah. I can see that about you." For a second, her face turned serious and he thought she was going to say something else, but she shook it off. Instead, she pointed to the screen. "You can start by solving that piece of shit riddle."

"It's a tricky little bastard."

"So prove to me what a hot shot you are."

"Right." He reached for the phone. "And maybe some food, too." He punched the button for the speed dial, then ordered in a feast of coffee, toast, sausage, and scrambled eggs. Plus a short stack of pancakes thrown in for good measure. To Jenn's wide-eyed stare, he just shrugged. "We need protein. And food. And I think better when I'm not hungry."

"Whatever." She tapped the screen. "It's broken down in chunks—stanzas. I'm betting each stanza is a separate part of the clue."

"I bet you're right. So we start with the first part. Here, pass me your pad."

He took it, then wrote out the first stanza.

Why do you run? What do you wish?

To prevent the Horrors, to shun the fate of a fish.

"I want to live and I wish this game were over. Especially this part right now. And I want to know what the hell is going to happen at ten."

"Actually," Devlin said, "I think that's exactly what those first two phrases refer to."

"Really? They're literally asking me what I want? Why on earth would we be so lucky as to get a straightforward clue in a game as fucked up as this?"

"Because the gamekeeper wants you scared. And the second line is easy. It tells you exactly what's going to happen at ten."

"It does?"

"Ever see *Little Shop of Horrors*?"

"Sure. It's not one of my favorites, but it's fun. I like the movie a lot. I love Rick Moranis."

"The dentist's song. Do you remember it?"

She shook her head. "Sorry."

"The dentist is this total sadist. And he's got this great song, and one of the lines is about how he'd poison guppies."

"Poison," she repeated, her voice toneless.

"Nothing's changed, Jenn," he said, taking her hand. "Ten, remember? Just the same as always."

"Right. You're right. Of course, you're right." She frowned. "Nothing's changed, but . . . I just don't see *how* I could have been poisoned. Or has it happened yet? Is someone going to run by and tackle me and shove a needle in my arm? Force feed me a vial of poison? I don't get it."

"You don't have to get it. You just have to solve it."

"What if there's another message?"

He shook his head, not following.

"On PSW! There's a message center. I pulled up the first one that gave me your profile. But we haven't checked to see if there's anything in *your* message area. Maybe we're supposed to have more information."

"You're right," he said, already pulling up the browser on her laptop. He headed over the the PSW website, navigated to the player login screen, then stopped. "Shit," he said.

"What?"

"I made up a login and password that time. I just wanted to poke around. I wasn't playing the game. Hell, I wasn't even officially investigating."

"So?"

"So I don't know offhand what the login was. Much less the password."

"Oh."

That stumped them both for a few minutes, and he cursed himself for not having used something simple and memorable. He was still berating himself when Jenn bounced back to life. "Wait! Login to my message center and pull up your profile."

"Okay." He started to type. "What's your—"

"I'll do it. It'll be faster."

So while he looked on, she typed in a username, then a password. The screen changed, a message appeared, and Devlin got that sick sense in his gut as he saw what he already knew: That she really had received twenty large. And that he really was marked for death in this fucked up version of *The Amazing Race*.

"Here," she said, pointing at the profile she'd pulled up.

"See? At the bottom is says your username. G-Man. No password, though."

"I've got one I use exclusively," he said, tugging his mind back to the problem. "Let's give it a shot."

She nodded, then went back to the main page for the message center. He typed "G-Man" into the username box, then "TimothyJ5," for his first stage role and age. He hit ENTER and waited for his messages to come up.

"Invalid Password. Please Try Again."

"Fuck. Hold on." He took another shot, trying his birthdate just for the hell of it.

"Invalid Password. Please Try Again."

"Goddammit!" He slammed his hand down, making the desk jump. "Fucking machine!"

"Hang on," she said, her voice soft and soothing. She took his hand, twining her fingers through his. "There's got to be a way in. They wouldn't have given us the username only to screw us over with the password."

His heart was still pounding, but he managed to calm down enough to look at her. Really look at her. "You're a rather amazing woman, Jennifer Crane."

She smirked. "Tell my mother. Better yet, tell me tomorrow, right about now."

"You've got a deal." He pointed to the computer. "Were you just trying to calm me down, or do you have an idea?"

She didn't bother answering, just shifted the laptop so that she could maneuver, moused up to the password slot, and typed. She hit ENTER, the computer did its thing, and suddenly they were in.

"Well, fuck me," Devlin said. "What was the password?"

She smiled, totally triumphant. "PSW. What else?" She

laughed, obviously delighted with herself, then navigated them into the message center.

"You have one new message."

She met his eyes. "Should we?"

"Hell, yes."

She nodded, took a deep, audible breath, then clicked the hyperlink. And as soon as the message came up, David wanted to hit the damn computer again. More, he wanted to hit whoever was behind this bullshit.

Beside him, Jenn didn't look nearly as angry. But her eyes never left the screen as she reached for his hand.

"Fuck," she said.

"I know."

They stared at the message that filled the screen. A message that told them what they already knew, but now had it spelled out in black and white:

>>http://www.playsurvivewin.com<<

PLAY.SURVIVE.WIN

>>>WELCOME TO REPORTING CENTER<<<

ONE NEW MESSAGE
REPORT NO. A-0002
Filed By: Identity Blocked
Subject: Status update.
Report:
- Secondary subject located and encounter successfully orchestrated.
- Time-release toxin delivered.

- Initial message to primary subject in transit.
- Warning and incentive message to secondary subject in transit.
- Game currently proceeding on schedule.

>>>End Report<<

"Time-release toxin," she finally said. "Well, I guess that explains that."

He reached out, turned her until she was facing him. "There's nothing here—*nothing*—that we didn't already know. Something bad is going to happen if we don't solve these clues in time. We knew that. Nothing's changed. We just need to focus on finding the answer."

"Right. Of course." Her brow furrowed and she shivered, then hugged herself.

"You okay?"

"Yeah. Just a chill." She pressed her hand to her forehead. "Do you think I'm getting a fever?"

A wave of fear built in his gut—what if the timing was off? What if they were already too late to find an antidote? —but he kept his expression calm and certain. "You're just scared. You're projecting. Now you're playing the role of the sick victim. *Don't.* Play the role of the survivor."

"I don't—"

"*No.*" He pressed his finger over her lips. "You're the heroine of this story, Jennifer. And the heroine doesn't die. And she doesn't lose focus. Now, is that a role you can play?"

She nodded, a little weak, but definitive.

"Good. Because if you can't, I may have to cast someone else in the part."

She actually smiled at that, and his heart lifted. "Yeah? For the first time in my life, I'm thinking maybe it's time to back out of a role."

"Chance of a lifetime, kid," he said, and squeezed her fingers.

"The show must go on," she retorted.

Since he couldn't think of any more clichés, he tapped the computer. "Back to work," he said, then navigated back to the screen with their clue.

"Right," she said. "Just like the song say."

"All the livelong day," he responded, finishing the line of lyrics from *Working*. They shared a quick grin, then both focused on the screen. "I think I've got the next line," he said, after a few minutes.

"Yeah?" She leaned in close and looked at the pad where he'd written the next bit:

So scurry, scurry like gaggling geese,
Run to Bishop to make your peace.

"*Oklahoma!* 'Chicks and ducks and geese better scurry, when I take you out in my surrey.' From 'Surrey With the Fringe on Top.' Great song," she said. "Except now it's going to be going through my head for the rest of the night."

"There's no production of *Oklahoma!* going on right now. Not that I know of, anyway. Are we supposed to find a surrey? We're in Manhattan for Christ's sake, not out on the prairie. Where are we supposed to—*oh*."

"The park," he said, certain she'd come to the same conclusion he had.

She nodded. "That has to be it. Except what's the Bishop thing?"

"You ever take one of those rides? Talk with the driver?"

"No. And isn't the point of those things to be romantic? What on earth were you doing talking with the driver?"

"Bad date," he said. "And very beside the point."

"Which is?"

"The horses have names. I remember the one pulling our cart was Thibideaux."

"So maybe there's a horse named Bishop."

"Exactly."

"Okay, but what about the rest of the clue? The clock and the petals and the ever-so-encouraging reference to being dead? And what are we supposed to do once we find this horse?"

"I don't know."

"And what about the stalling reference? Are we supposed to go to the horse stalls? Or are we supposed to find the horse with his carriage?"

Devlin frowned. He'd been imagining a scenario where they found the horse, found the carriage, then found the answer. The possibility that the answer might not be there—that they might have to go to the stables—frustrated him. Especially since he had no idea where the stables might be.

"Dev?"

"I don't know," he said. "First we need to find Bishop. After that, everything else will fall into place."

"You're sure?"

"No," he said. "But I believe in positive thinking."

"Me too," she said, then stood up. "Let's go."

He grabbed her tote bag for her, and she headed toward the

door, pulling it open, and then letting out a scream that just about ripped his heart.

He leaped forward, only to have her hold out a hand. "It's okay, it's okay. Oh, shit, he scared me."

Devlin looked around her into the hall and saw the room service cart there, along with a startled-looking waiter in uniform.

"I didn't mean to scare you, ma'am."

"Not your fault," Devlin said. He slipped out, taking Jenn's hand and tugging her along past the cart. Then he took the cover off one plate and grabbed a strip of bacon. "Want some?" he asked her. "Because I think we're getting room service to go."

Chapter
39
JENNIFER

"We're never going to find a specific horse," I said. "We don't even know that this is where he's working from, especially now that the Plaza is essentially shut down."

The taxi had dropped us off catty-corner to the Plaza Hotel, soon to be the Plaza condominiums, with just a few hotel rooms thrown in for good measure and to appease the locals who'd gone ballistic at the thought of the landmark hotel being transformed into a truly exclusive domain. A compromise had been reached (amazing, really, when you realize both politicians and real estate developers were involved in the squabble) and now the place was undergoing massive renovations.

All of which would be of no interest to me whatsoever, except for the fact that the most popular location from which to hire a carriage and driver for a ride through Central Park was the little area by the statue of General Sherman just across from the Plaza. And now that there were fewer tourists in the area, there were also fewer carriages.

"We start here," Devlin said. "We ask all the drivers if they know a horse named Bishop, and if they don't, we get the name of the company they work out of. I'll keep asking drivers and you call the companies and do the same. That's my plan. Direct, to the point, and hopefully brilliant."

I didn't have a better plan. Plus, I agreed that his was pretty good. So we headed past General Sherman to the line of carriages. There were only five lined up, and I felt a little twinge of pessimism. It must have shown on my face, too, because Devlin said, "It's only eight. Still early. There are probably more carriages coming."

"Evening is the time for romantic rides," I said. "And I don't have until tonight. Hell, I don't even have until lunch. For all we know, the clue's just going to lead us somewhere else. Probably all the way down to Battery Park. *If* we even find the clue in the first place."

"We'll find it," he said.

I wanted to be as confident as he was, but I wasn't doing a very good job. Still, my pessimism wasn't going to stop me from doing my damnedest to find Bishop. So while Devlin started at one end of the line, I started at the other.

"Hi," I said, to a twenty-something driver with a dark brown horse. "That wouldn't happen to be Bishop, would it?"

"Nah," he said. "That's Roger. Twenty bucks gets you the short tour around. Great way to see the park. Head back home and tell all your friends."

"Home's Midtown," I said, "but thanks anyway."

"No prob. Bring a date some night," he added, but I'd already moved on to the next horse in the carriage line. This one wasn't Bishop, either, but he did give me good news. So good, in fact, that I almost kissed the driver *and* horse. I managed to restrain myself, though I did yell for Devlin at the top of my lungs, causing every tourist and driver in the area to turn and stare.

Devlin raced over. "Bishop?" he said with a glance toward the horse.

"Not this one, but he says Bishop works this corner."

"They should be along anytime. He's usually here before me. Probably already in the park," the other driver said. I didn't know his name, but I decided he was my new best friend.

"Should we wait?" Devlin asked. "Do you know for sure he's here today?"

The driver shook his head, and I felt the fear well up again. "Sorry. He hardly ever misses a day, so I'd lay odds he's here. Of course, he coulda gotten an all-day job. Wedding. Someone gettin' engaged, that kinda thing."

I met Devlin's eyes.

"We'll hope not," he said.

"We can't just wait around," I said. "Tick tick, remember?"

"I know. How long's the ride through the park?" he asked the driver.

" 'Bout twenty minutes."

"We'll wait fifteen. He's not back, we'll call his boss. Guy must have a cell phone."

"Sure thing," the driver said. "He's with Central Park Carriages. Not my outfit, but a good place. Owner's solid. He'll track Sean down if he can."

"Sean?"

"Bishop's driver."

"Right," I said. To Devlin, "So, we wait?"

"We wait."

And so we did. Neither one of us really spoke, but we both hopped to our feet like little electrified bunny rabbits every time a carriage arrived. Six new ones in the next ten minutes, and none of them Sean or Bishop.

I was sitting there fretting again, when another carriage pulled up, this one with a ruddy-faced driver and a thin, brown horse. Not the hefty workhorses we'd seen pass by already.

Considering the way our luck was going, I was slow to get up, letting Devlin take this one. He did, waiting as a young couple climbed out, patted the horse, then headed to the crosswalk. As they walked away, Devlin approached the driver and said something. The driver answered, they chatted some more, and then Devlin turned to me with an expression I recognized but wasn't expecting to see: success.

I was on my feet in about three seconds, shoving my way through the crowd as I trotted toward the blue carriage.

"This is Sean," Devlin said, introducing me to the driver. "And that's Bishop."

"Hello, Bishop," I said, rubbing my hand down the horse's nose. "Hiya, Sean. We're very glad to see you."

"Always glad to have a fare," Sean said, with an Irish accent. "But why are you so interested in this rig?"

"We're interested in the horse," Devlin said as he held out a hand for me, then helped me up into the carriage.

As Sean looked on, Devlin followed. "All right," Sean finally said, climbing back up onto the driver's bench. "I can take a hint. No questions."

"Thanks. Just the short ride, okay?"

"You got it." Sean turned around long enough to make sure we were settled in, then urged Bishop on. And suddenly, there I was, taking a romantic carriage ride through Central Park in decidedly unromantic circumstances. I glanced over at Devlin and smiled. What a pity . . .

I reined myself in and managed to focus, half-listening as Sean described the sights, and half-watching as Devlin slid his hand in between the padded seat and the padded back of the bench.

So I wouldn't be sitting there like a dolt, I scooted over to the facing seat and started doing the same thing. Nothing there.

"Maybe there's a storage container somewhere?"

Devlin looked around, but didn't see anything. He half-leaned out of the carriage, but, still, nothing.

"I know I should just keep on with my tour—there's the ice-skating rink, by the way—but you got my curiosity brewing. You lose something back there?"

"Just looking around," I said.

"And what's all this about you two waiting for my carriage specifically? I'm flattered, but I'm the inquisitive sort."

Devlin and I exchanged a glance, and after a second, Devlin drew in a breath. "We're on a scavenger hunt. Follow clues through the city kind of thing."

"And a clue led you to me?"

"Your horse. And your carriage," I said.

"Actually, that raises a good point. Is this the carriage that Bishop usually pulls?"

"Yup. Cornelius—that's my boss—he's good about keeping us with the same horse and carriage."

"And this would be called a surrey?" I asked, looking around the blue buggy.

"I call it a vis-à-vis. You know, 'cause four folks can sit looking at each other. The real name? You got me there."

"Anyone take a ride recently and hide anything?"

"Nothing I'm aware of."

"Shit," I said, but mostly to myself.

"We're coming up on the dairy," Sean said, pointing out a building to the right. "Folks come there now to play chess, stuff like that. You want me to keep up with this?"

"Go right ahead," Devlin said. To me, he crooked a finger.

As Sean continued to describe the surroundings—the large rocks that lined the carriage path were typical of the island's topography—Devlin and I stared at the notebook where he'd copied the clue.

"This part," I said, pointing to the bit about the Beast. "Maybe it refers to Bishop. Maybe the clue's hidden in Bishop's saddle."

"She's pulling a carriage," Devlin said. "She doesn't have a saddle."

"The thingamajig, then," I said, pointing vaguely toward the horse and the big strap of leather around her chest. "The thing attached to the carriage."

"Not a Beast, but dead, and no use stalling," Devlin said, his voice thoughtful.

"And the clock ticking line, too. Don't forget that." *I* certainly couldn't forget it.

"Don't worry. That's definitely at the forefront."

"Damn rollerbladers!" That from Sean, and both Devlin and I whipped forward to face him. His already red face col-

ored more. "Sorry. But that girl just cut right in front of
Bishop. Almost spooked the old girl. Bad enough she was on
the lane in the first place." He looked like he had more to say,
but he kept his temper in check. "Never you mind. It's no
problem now." But he turned, looking down the lane in the
direction the girl had gone, and I could almost see the angry
vibes rising off of him. In the distance, I could just make out a
blond ponytail swinging rhythmically over tight black biker
shorts and a black Lycra top. One of those typical Manhattan
pretty girls who was convinced the normal rules didn't apply
to her.

I tried to focus back on the clue, but something about the
girl's cockiness nagged at me. And then, in one quick burst of
inspiration, I had it. I was right! I *had* to be right. "Devlin," I
said, grabbing his hand. "I've got a pretty big ego and all, but
what if the ticking clock thing doesn't really refer to me?"

Devlin shook his head, clearly not following.

"Broadway reference, right?" I looked wildly around, then
found what I was looking for: a chrome bud vase with a single
tulip inside. "The Beast. What if it means *Beauty and the Beast*?
He'll stay a beast if he doesn't find love by the time the last petal
falls. But not me. I don't stay anything at all. I end up dead," I
said, lowering my voice so Sean couldn't hear.

"Not a beast, but dead," Devlin said, clearly picking up on
my groove. "I think you've got something."

I scooted over to the far seat and tried to tug the vase out of
its holder, but it wouldn't budge.

"Inside," Devlin said, moving to sit next to me.

I nodded, then yanked out the tulip. And then, even though
I really didn't want to, I stuck my finger down inside and

found . . . nothing. I looked at Devlin, panic really building in me now. "It's almost nine. I'm running out of time!"

"You're sure there's nothing in there?"

"Positive!"

"You think your next clue's in the vase?" Sean asked, looking over his shoulder.

"It's our best guess," Devlin said. "But it doesn't look like there's anything in there. Mind if I unhook the vase, just to make sure?"

"If you can get it off, be my guest."

As Sean went back to steering us down the path, Devlin opened his pocket knife to the screwdriver, then went to work on the metal band that kept the vase secured to the side of the carriage. "Damn, this thing's tight," he said, grunting with effort. "Okay, I think I got it loose. See if you can tug out the vase."

I balanced on the front seat, grabbed the top of the vase, and pulled. It didn't come free, but it did wiggle, and that gave me enough confidence to keep at it. A few more turns from Devlin's screwdriver and a few more tugs from me, and the vase slipped free.

Devlin grabbed it from me immediately, then turned it upside down and smacked it sharply against his thigh. I stared, at first baffled, and then incredibly relieved as something cylindrical and wrapped in duct tape finally came dislodged.

"Holy shit," I said. "Gimme."

He did, and I put my manicured fingernails to good use, destroying the polish, but managing to get the tape loose. Slowly, I realized that what I was revealing was a shot glass from the Jekyll & Hyde Club, a kitschy restaurant a few blocks away.

And there, nestled at the bottom under a large cotton ball, was a pink and white capsule filled with tiny little granules.

I shook the capsule out into my hand, then looked up at Devlin. "That looks like an antihistamine. Don't tell me all this time we've been freaking out over the possibility of me getting a rash."

"I know you're nervous," he said. Smart man. "Take it."

Our voices were still low, and I don't think Sean heard. More, I didn't want him to hear, which meant that I had to restrain myself from screaming in frustration, fear, and a whole bunch of other indefinable emotions. The truth is, I have a phobia about pharmaceuticals, and the thought of now taking some pill of unknown origin was enough to make me more than a little queasy. Too queasy, and I might throw the whole thing up. And how counterproductive would that be?

"Just take the damn thing," Devlin said.

Right. Sure. No problem.

I'd just about convinced myself to do that when I realized we were back where we started. "Home again, home again," Sean said, pulling Bishop to a stop.

I caught Devlin's eyes and he nodded. I understood what he meant—*let's get down and away, and then you can take it.* Despite the freaky circumstances, I felt a rush of warmth. I'd never really communicated this well with anyone before. So well that we didn't even need words. Was it Devlin? I wondered. Or was it just the circumstances?

At any rate, Sean climbed down from the driver's bench. I half-stood, then reached out to take Sean's offered hand. As I did, I automatically scanned the crowd behind him, tourists and locals come to either take a ride or ogle the horse. As Sean's fingers closed around mine, I saw a flash of blond hair in the nearby crowd. The people shifted, and I saw the biker shorts, black Lycra top, and rollerblades of the girl from the path.

She looked up, I saw her face, and the world turned red. *Bird Girl!*

And, goddamn it, she was holding a gun!

"Devlin!" I screamed, kicking out and catching Sean in the chest. He went sprawling on the concrete just as a shot rang out, barely missing Devlin, who'd thrown himself down inside the carriage.

I yelped and stumbled backwards as the crowd scattered, clearing a path for Bird Girl's next shot.

Not that we were waiting around.

I scrambled up and onto the driver's seat, taking the reins and screaming, "Go!" Not horse-speak, but Bishop knew what I meant, and she bolted onto the street.

I heard the crack of wood as a bullet stuck in the side of the carriage.

I gasped, bouncing as the carriage lurched over curbs, Bishop going as fast as she could toward Fifth Avenue.

Devlin scrambled up next to me. "She's back there," he said. "On those damn rollerblades."

"She's going to catch us," I yelled. "There's no place for us to go. Bishop's just not maneuverable enough."

He took the reins and pulled Bishop to a stop. "Come on," he said, yanking me down to the ground. He grabbed a passerby and handed him the reins. "This horse belongs to Sean. He'll be along any second." To me, he yelled, "Run!"

I didn't argue. I ran, Devlin right beside me. Fifth Avenue was wall-to-wall people, and even though she'd fired at Devlin back by the horses, I didn't think she'd fire into the crowd. Back there, she'd had a clear shot. Here, though, well, she'd likely hit a tourist. More, she'd likely get caught by a civilian looking to play hero. Whoever Bird Girl was, she wasn't dumb. I already knew that much.

And that, I hoped, gave us an advantage.

Only one block, and I had a stitch in my side and my lungs were burning. "Not . . . a . . . runner . . ." I managed.

"Just keep going," Devlin said, and, damn the man, he didn't even sound tired.

I sucked in air, slowing as I looked back. About a block away I saw a flash of blond, moving fast in our direction. *Shit!*

"Down here," I yelled, tugging him onto 54th Street and down just a bit until we were right in front of the Manolo Blahnik boutique. "In," I said, not waiting for a response. "There's a back door," I said, under my breath. "We need to get back into the employees' area."

I'd discovered the back door when a friend of Brian's had worked here. She'd indulged my passion for a grand tour, and showed me every nook and cranny. Great stuff. Unfortunately, she'd moved to Los Angeles before I'd been able to hit her up for use of her employee discount.

The Manolo boutique is very modern, very clean, and very shiny. That early, it was also pretty empty. To say that we—sweating, panting, and more than a little rumpled—were out of place would be a hideous understatement.

The salesgirl, though, didn't even blink. She just approached, smiled, and asked if she could help us.

I was about to ask for the use of the restroom—that was the only ploy I could think of to get us back there—when Devlin stepped forward. He pointed to three different pairs of shoes. "Her size," he said. "If you could have them wrapped and ready to go by tomorrow."

The salesgirl blinked, but didn't argue. She looked at me.

"Size eight," I said.

"Here." Devlin opened his wallet and peeled off a huge wad of bills. "Now, if you don't mind, my ex-wife has a bit of a grudge against my fiancée." He hooked his arm around my shoulder and hugged. "Maybe we could go out your back door? And if you see her, if you'd not mention that we were here, I'd be very grateful. *Very* grateful," he added meaningfully, sliding his wallet back into his pocket.

"Of course, sir. Right through there, sir." She pointed to the back door, and away we went. As the employees' door closed behind us, I heard the electronic ding that announced a new customer entering the store. I had no way of knowing if it was Bird Girl, but I was still certain it was.

We picked up the pace, emerged onto an alley, then trotted over to Avenue of the Americas. Devlin caught us a cab and, with one final glance around, I climbed inside.

Bird Girl, thank God, was nowhere to be seen.

Chapter

40

BIRDIE

I stop, out of breath and sweating, as the Fifth Avenue tourists give me a wide berth, their gazes wary.

My gun is pressed tight against my thigh, but now I open my backpack and slip it inside. At the moment, I have no more use for it.

I've lost my quarry.

I'm disappointed by the loss, and furious with myself for yet another failure. But also, curiously, I am excited as well. My foes have a few tricks of their own. And that, I have to admit, ratchets my excitement up a notch.

Of course, I must once again accept a certain level of fault. I hadn't expected the little bitch to recognize me. After all, it had been days since I'd seen her, and for just a moment, I regret buying the shoes that she'd so coveted. Nothing sticks in a woman's mind like another girl's victory in the shopping arena.

Also, I must be practical and acknowledge that this is the first assignment I've had in which my subject is aware that I'm coming. That shifts the dynamic and, perhaps, I have not adjusted my methods sufficiently.

But never mind. This game is still young, and I'll find my quarry easily enough.

Since the police will surely come to investigate, I move even farther away, crossing over to Madison. I take off my rollerblades and put on the pair of sneakers I've tucked into my backpack. Only then do I pull my PDA from my pack and power it on. I open the tracking software and wait for it to load. It does, but there's no image. No blip. No little ping showing me Devlin's location.

My temper spikes. *Damn.*

A muscle twitches in my cheek, and I tell myself that I'm not irritated. After all, I like a challenge.

But as I walk down Madison, my rollerblades in my hand and my gun tucked close in my fanny pack, I have to admit that's not entirely accurate.

The truth is I don't like being inconvenienced.

I don't like anything, frankly, that gets in my way of winning.

JENNIFER

"She bugged me," Devlin said, catching my eye as the cab maneuvered through the busy streets toward Times Square.

"She bugged me, too," I said. "But, honestly, I'm tempted to use a little bit harsher language."

"Not annoyed. *Bugged*. Tagged. Electronically booby-trapped."

I sat up. "What? What are you talking about?"

But Devlin wasn't answering. Instead, he was emptying his wallet into his lap. He kept the cash and his driver's license. Then he rolled down his window and tossed the rest into the street.

"Devlin!"

"Have you taken the pill?"

"I . . . no. Not yet."

"It's nine-thirty. Take the thing. Leave yourself some wiggle room."

"You really think I should take it? I don't even know what's in it. And I don't feel bad. What if there's nothing wrong with me, and *this* fucks me up?"

"I don't think that's the way the game works. Mel took the antidote, right? And she was fine."

"You're right. I know. I'm just nervous." Even as I said that, I was remembering Bergdorf's. The way Bird Girl was always there. The way she seemed to follow me, even taunt me by buying and then tossing my shoes.

And the way she fell against me.

"Devlin," I said, turning so that my right side faced him. "Look at this."

He ran his finger over the red mark, about a quarter of an inch square on the back of my arm, just above my elbow. "What is it?"

"She bumped into me on Sunday. I didn't think anything of it. Her ring scraped me, though. Do you think—"

"Yeah, I do."

"And she timed it. When she met me, she timed it so that the poison would kick in at ten today."

"Take the damn pill," he said.

And, so help me, I did.

Chapter

42

DEVLIN

Devlin watched, his breath held tight in his chest, as Jenn closed her eyes, then dry-swallowed the pill. She stayed perfectly still, and Devlin was certain that his heart had stopped beating. He reached out, grabbed her hand. "Jenn! Dammit, Jenn, say something!"

"Mmmm," she said. "Cherry-flavored." And then she opened her eyes and grinned at him, her expression light and full of mischief.

"Dammit all! I thought—" He reached out and grabbed her, then pulled her close.

She wrapped her arms around him, too, and he let himself get lost in the moment, this one tiny slice of time where his life felt good. And real. Finally, he pulled back, holding her by the arms so he could get a good look at her. "You're okay?" he asked. "You're really okay?"

"I think so. I suppose the capsule could be some sort of freaky time-release. But I think I'm fine."

He couldn't help it. He grabbed her and pulled her close again.

"Gee, Devlin. I didn't know you cared." Her voice was light, teasing, but there was a question hiding under the levity. A question he felt obligated to answer.

"I do care," he said. "I really do."

This time, she pulled back on her own. Her green eyes searched his face. Whatever she saw there must have satisfied her, because she nodded curtly. "She almost had a bullet in your head."

"I know," he said. "Thank you."

"Just doing my job."

"You're a hell of a protector," he said.

"I thought you didn't need one."

With that, he couldn't quite look at her. When she'd burst into his life yesterday, he really did believe he'd be just as well off if he caught an assassin's bullet. Now, though . . .

Well, now things had changed. Somewhere along the way he'd started to come alive again. Jenn may have saved him from a bullet, but she'd also brought him back from the dead. He may have started out only wanting to help the girl, but now he wanted to help himself. Now he wanted life. His life, and hers. More, he wanted retribution. Revenge against the s.o.b. who was pulling their chain.

He didn't quite know how to tell her all that, though. So instead, he just said simply, "I changed my mind."

He was still looking out the window, but he could feel her watching him. She scooted close so that their hips were touching, then took his hand in hers. "Good," she said. "Uh, Devlin? We'll go back and get those shoes, right?"

"Hell yes," he said. "At those prices, I figure we'd better."

"Good." She sounded so relieved he had to fight back a chuckle.

"Then again," he began, teasing her. "It's not like you picked them out. You probably don't even like them. Maybe we should just blow it off."

She shifted on the seat to face him dead-on. "Watch your mouth! They're Manolos, Devlin. Of course I like them."

"All of them."

"Every single glorious pair."

"That is such a girl thing."

"Well, I *am* a girl."

He took his time looking her over, enjoying the way her cheeks flushed as he did. "Yeah," he finally said. "I'd noticed."

If she had a clever or flirty response, though, he didn't get to hear it because they'd reached Times Square.

"Where to?" the driver asked.

"Empire State Building," Devlin said.

"Come on, buddy! You just told me to drag you here."

"What are you complaining for? I'm the one paying."

"Shit," the driver mumbled, but he kept on driving.

"Where are we going?" Jenn asked.

"Right now, we're just moving. We need to think. And if we move, she can't find us."

"What did you mean when you said she bugged you?"

"She must have put something on me. In my wallet, maybe. Or my shoes. Probably not my clothes, because how would she know what I'd wear?"

"What are you talking about?" Jenn asked. "And how? How on earth would she get to your stuff to leave a bug, anyway?"

He didn't answer. Couldn't bring himself to say it out loud. Not wanting to admit the truth. Not to himself and especially not to Jenn.

"Devlin?" she prodded.

When he finally answered, his voice was thick with self-loathing. "Because a few nights before I met you, I picked her up at a bar. And I slept with her."

Chapter

43

JENNIFER

"You slept with her," I repeated, letting the statement roll around on my tongue. "You slept with the woman who is now trying to kill us?"

"Looks that way, yeah."

"Well, fuck." What was I supposed to do with that information? I wasn't entirely sure. Rationally, I could see how he might pick up some gal in a bar and screw her. Not politically correct, but everyone has their moments. I mean, the guy had been depressed, right? I once went home with a guy I met in a bar after I flubbed my first New York audition. Not something I'm proud of, but it happened.

So maybe I understood. But understanding didn't matter. I was pissed. More, I think I was jealous. "Why did you do that?"

"Because I'm an idiot, that's why." He ran a hand through his hair, and I caught a glimpse of how distraught he was.

This was a man used to keeping his emotions under control. He'd been knocked off-kilter—hard. Oddly, that made me feel better.

"Devlin . . . " I reached out, took his hand in mine, and for just an instant I held on. Then he snatched his hand back.

"Don't. Okay? Just don't."

Well, hell. I leaned forward and tapped the Plexiglas divider. "Pull up there, will you?"

The driver did, and as Devlin gaped, I grabbed his phone, then tossed it into the nearest trash can. Then I went into the store and bought one of those pay-as-you-go cell phones. When I got back in the car, Devlin was staring at me, the tiniest hint of a smile playing around his mouth. "You handling me?"

"More or less. That's my job, right?"

"Thank you."

"For what? For the cell phone?"

"For saving my ass back there. If you hadn't seen her when you did, I'd be dead meat."

"You two still heading for the Empire State?"

I shook my head. "You know what? We'll get out here." I tugged on Devlin's sleeve. "Come on. I'm sick of riding around. Let's find a Starbucks and regroup."

Because this is New York, it took all of about three point seven seconds to find one of the coffee shops. I swear, the things multiply faster than bunnies. We went in, ordered, and then grabbed a table near the window, but off to the side. A view, but sheltered from the prying eyes of passersby.

"So what do we do now?" I asked, once we were both sipping our drinks (mine a latte, his a Frappuccino).

"Interpret the next clue," he said. "Play the game." He nodded at the cell phone I'd left on the table. "And call Brian again and give him the number so he can find us."

He didn't say the rest, but I heard it anyway: If he's still alive.

I decided not to think about that. "You think she's still interested in him?"

"I think it's not worth the risk."

"Right," I said, then voiced the question that had been on my mind ever since we found the pill. "And you?"

He didn't even pretend to misunderstand. "I already told you. I'm not giving in to the little bitch," he said. Then he smiled. "And I've got you to help me out."

"Lucky you."

He reached out, took a strand of my hair, and curled it around his finger. I swear, I almost melted. "Don't discount yourself."

"You would have seen the girl," I said.

"Maybe. But that's not what I meant."

"Oh." I felt my cheeks flush, and I looked down, finding sudden fascination with the lid on my latte. If my guess was right, he'd tried to self-medicate by sleeping with our assassin. But it hadn't worked. I mean, he'd been a wreck when I'd found him in his dark apartment. So was he saying that I *had* helped? And if he was saying that, then what did that mean? For me? Or, I guess, for us?

"Jenn?"

"Sorry." I forced myself to get it together. "I'm, uh, just a little distracted. You know. My life is safe and all that. Except it's not really vacation time, is it?"

"Nope. She's after us. And if we don't stay on top of the clues and solve this game before she catches us, I'm going to be one very unhappy camper."

"So why'd you sleep with her?" I blurted out the question before I could stop it, managing to completely mortify myself in the process. I shouldn't care. I shouldn't be jealous. But I did, and I was. So there.

From Devlin's expression, I think he knew how I felt. More, I think he kind of liked it. Well, yay for him, but that didn't change the fact that I felt like a twit. "Devlin," I said. "Maybe it's important. She was obviously using you."

"She was using me." He ran his palms over his face. "But I guess that was fair since I was using her."

I squinted at him. "To forget."

"To forget," he acknowledged. He turned to look at me, and I swear his eyes burned right through me. "Kind of like what you wanted. Only it didn't help. Doesn't help. All it did was leave me more hollow." He bit out a snort of derisive laughter. "Not to mention marked for death."

"There's a lesson in there about one-night stands," I quipped.

"No shit," he said, then shrugged. "It's not important. All that matters now is the outcome. I've ditched my wallet and I'm not carrying my phone. Whatever she planted on me to track is most likely gone."

"We should get you new clothes, too," I said. "New shoes. Nothing as fancy as Manolos . . ."

"Next place we pass," he said. "So long as they fit, I'll be fine."

"Men."

"I could scour the town for the perfect running shoe, but right now, we need to focus on figuring out the next clue."

That raised an interesting little dilemma. "*What* next clue?"

"I don't have any idea."

But I did. All of a sudden, I knew exactly what the clue was. Worse, I knew that it was gone.

Chapter

44

JENNIFER

"I had it," I said. "It was right in my hand with the pill. In all the commotion, I must have dropped it."

We were back near General Sherman, hunched over as we scoured the ground. We'd been at it for over fifteen minutes, and my eyes were about to fall out.

"We'll find it," Devlin said. "And it's not your fault."

"Of course it's my fault." I stood up, straightening and rubbing my back. Nothing. Not even shards of glass from where it had gotten run over by a carriage wheel. The thing was simply gone.

"Somebody probably picked it up," I said. "Some tourist is putting back shots of tequila with it right this very second."

Devlin straightened too, and looked around the crowd. "You might be right, and we probably shouldn't stay here any longer in any case. Who knows when our friend will be back."

"She's your friend," I said, with a devious tone.

He grinned at me, but this time it was real, with none of the self-loathing I'd seen earlier. "Not hardly." He held out a hand. "Come on."

"Where?"

"I've got an idea," he said.

We walked past the row of horses and carriages to the street, and Devlin stepped off the curb, arm stretched out to hail a cab. I looked wistfully back at the carriages. We'd thoroughly scoured Bishop's carriage again—Sean, thankfully, hadn't held our little stunt against us. Especially after we'd handed him a load of cash to repair the bullet hole. We hadn't found the glass, though, and I could only stand there wishing we could do it all over again.

I didn't understand how I lost the thing, but lost it I had. Some protector. One fucking clue comes into my hands, and I'm so busy watching my own ass that I can't even keep a hold of it.

"Quit beating yourself up," Devlin said, as he ushered me into a cab.

"I can't help it."

"Try. We found the antidote. You're alive. I'm alive. Those are the important things."

"You may be alive, but for how long? If we can't find that glass, we're stuck. You're a walking target with no way to win the game. No way to end it. The game turns into a race, Devlin. A race that you can't win. You can only lose."

"I don't intend to lose."

I leaned back in the seat and exhaled through my nose. "Yesterday, you probably would have done cartwheels at the idea of some freak with a pistol waiting to take you out. Now you're an optimist?"

"I've got a new perspective," he said with a wicked grin that for some reason had me blushing.

"Yeah? Well, I'm glad." I twined my fingers through his. "Why don't you just leave?" I asked, leaning forward with sudden inspiration. "Go away. Leave town. Move to Mexico."

He lifted an eyebrow. "Are you suggesting a romantic retreat?"

"Damn it, Devlin, be serious."

"I am," he said, "because that's the only thing that would get me out of this city right now. I didn't ask for this, but I'm damn sure going to see it through." He turned away from me, looking out the window at the passing street.

"All right," I finally said. "But does that go for everything?"

"What do you mean?"

I swallowed, wondering if I should really go there. Then I decided what the hell. One thing I was learning: life's short. "I mean that you didn't ask for them to take your badge. Are you going to see that through, too? Work to get reinstated?"

"Jenn . . ."

There was a warning in his voice, but I didn't care. "See it through, Devlin. I may not be able to imagine leaving the theater, but this cop stuff is in your blood. Even in your funk, you stepped up to the plate to help me. So how come you didn't do the same for yourself?"

"You're pretty wise, Jennifer Crane."

"Don't tease me, Devlin. I'm serious."

"So am I. But right now, the only thing I'm worried about

seeing through is this game. Not my career. Just my ass. And yours, too."

"My ass appreciates it."

"And I appreciate your ass," he said with an exaggerated leer that had me laughing. It also had me ending the subject. I know how to take a hint.

I held out my hand. "Pass me the phone." He did, and I dialed, determined to follow the only clue we had left. The shotglass I'd lost was from the Jekyll & Hyde Club, and the way I saw it, that was the only lead we had. I called information first, then got put through to the club. One ring, two, then a recorded message with the restaurant's hours. I checked my watch, then cursed.

"Not open yet," I said, snapping the cell phone closed and passing it to Devlin. "Damn."

"Doesn't matter," he said. He leaned forward and gave the driver an address on 42nd Street.

"Where are we going?"

"To see the one person who might be able to help us."

"But what about involving outside people? Doesn't that put them at risk?"

Devlin's face shifted, his jaw cutting a firm line. "It might," he said. "But with this son-of-a-bitch, I frankly don't care."

Chapter

45

DEVLIN

Jenn didn't ask any questions as Devlin led her up into the skyscraper. He was glad of that. Right now, he wanted to think. Needed to organize his thoughts. And he wanted to mentally play out—in every painful, bloody detail—exactly what he intended to do when he saw the man.

He'd just been finishing up a scenario where he beat the cretin to a bloody pulp when they arrived in front of the reception desk. "We're here to see Thomas Reardon," Devlin announced, when the pert twenty-something greeted him. Beside him, Jenn shifted and he heard her barely audible gasp of surprise.

He didn't bother to look; he was concentrating on the receptionist, keeping his eyes locked on hers. He might not have his badge, but he knew how to be persuasive when he wanted to. And he wasn't leaving this building without first chatting with Reardon.

In front of him, the girl squirmed, her expression shifting from polite welcome to something else entirely. Confused horror? No, that made no sense. The whole firm couldn't be in on the scheme, and even if a few higher-ups were involved with bringing Grimaldi's computer game out into the real world, there was no way this barely legal receptionist had been drawn into the scheme. Devlin had to be reading her wrong.

"I'm . . . I'm sorry," the girl finally stammered. "Do you have an appointment?"

"No, but it's imperative we see him. We'll only take a few minutes of his time."

"I . . . Well, I . . . just a moment." She picked up the phone, dialed an extension, waited, and then spoke. "Yes, hi, it's Gillian. Um, there's a gentleman here who wants to speak to Mr. Reardon. He says it's urgent. Of course, sir. Certainly. Thank you."

She hung up the phone, her expression now one of relief. And about *that,* Devlin was certain.

"Mr. Jackson is on his way," she said. "Can I get you anything to drink?"

"What about Mr. Reardon?"

"Ah, you'll have to talk to Mr. Jackson."

He considered protesting some more, just for form, but it wouldn't do any good. "A couple of coffees would be great," he said, figuring they could both use the caffeine. And while she headed around a corner to what had to be a refreshment center, Devlin settled on the leather sofa next to Jennifer.

Immediately, she pounced. "Thomas Reardon!" she whispered. "I thought you said he was clean."

"Not clean," Devlin explained. "Just no dirt we could see."

"You mean he might be behind all this? Placing the clues? The collar on the cat? All that kind of stuff?"

"It's possible."

"Shit."

He nodded, knowing exactly how she felt. Thomas Reardon had been mixed up in Mel's ordeal, but the FBI had never been able to pin anything on him. For all intents and purposes, Reardon was Grimaldi's attorney, nothing more. And there was nothing illegal about representing a dead computer genius. Even if that genius's online game had suddenly gone live in the real world.

"So you think he might know where we need to go next?"

"Exactly," Devlin said. "Even better, he might be able to shut this whole thing down."

"But if the FBI never managed to nail anything on him, what are you going to bargain with? He's just going to say he's clueless, and that will be that."

She was right, of course, but since Devlin was all out of ideas, they were going to see this through. He was about to tell her that when the receptionist came back with their coffee, followed almost immediately by a tall, thin man with salt and pepper hair topping a dour expression.

"I'm Alistair Jackson," he said. "How can I help you?"

"We'd like to speak to Mr. Reardon," Devlin said.

"Are you a current client?"

"No, actually, I'm with the FBI."

"Identification?"

"I'm not here officially," he said, sideswiping the request. "But it is important to me personally that I see Mr. Reardon."

"And the young lady?"

"Jennifer Crane," she said, holding out her hand. Jackson took it, then released it, his expression never softening.

"I'm sorry but we won't be able to help you."

Devlin started to open his mouth, not sure what he intended to say. Probably some bluster about cooperation and official inquiries and bullshit like that. Didn't matter. Mr. Jackson's next words shut him up real fast.

"I'm afraid Thomas Reardon is dead."

Chapter

46

JENNIFER

I waited until we'd gone back down the elevator, crossed through the lobby, and exited the building before I said a word. But as soon as we were outside, I couldn't hold it in any longer. "She did it. She *must* have done it."

"I don't know," he said. "But I'd be willing to make book on it."

"So what now?"

He took my hand and tugged me across the street, jaywalking, of course, in the fine tradition of New York natives.

"Where are we going?"

"We need to sit. And we need to think." And with that, he led us to the Bryant Park Café, nestled behind the library and conveniently located just across the street from the recently deceased Mr. Reardon's offices.

We sat outside, and when the waiter delivered our water, I

actually felt human. I was in a restaurant, with a guy, enjoying an unseasonably warm afternoon in New York City. If it weren't for the whole psycho-trying-to-kill-us thing, the afternoon would be perfect.

It wasn't, though, and I sobered up pretty quickly. "What now?" I asked.

"How good a look did you get at that shot glass?"

"It was from the Jekyll & Hyde Club," I said. "That's all I noticed."

"But there could have been something etched in the glass on the bottom," he said. "Something important."

"I know." I sank down a bit in my seat and fiddled with my silverware.

"I wasn't criticizing," he said. "Just stating a fact."

"A bad fact," I said. "Got any good news to go with that little reminder of my ineptitude?"

He chuckled. "No, but I have an idea that might turn out to be good. Fair enough?"

"At this point, anything."

"Jekyll and Hyde played as a musical, didn't it?"

"So it's definitely part of our theme."

"So we check the theater. Maybe something was left for us at the box office."

"And we still need to check the Club. Maybe someone left a message with the manager or put something in the lost and found."

"Right. As soon as they open."

I checked my watch. "Actually, it's right at 11:30. They should be open by now. Should I call?"

He shook his head. "No, we should go there. Since we don't

know what we need, better to show up in person. Less likely someone will brush us off if we're standing right in front of them."

"Fine." I was pushing my chair back when the phone rang. I checked caller ID, then snatched it up. "Brian! Thank God! Where are you?"

"Jesus, Jenn, I just found out! I've been at Larry's going over some last minute lyric changes, and I just checked my messages. What the fuck is going on?" His voice was thick, and I could tell he'd been crying. Probably got word from the cops, then thought to check his voice mails and found the message from me.

"You can't go home," I said. "Stay where you are and don't go home."

"I have to give a statement to the cops."

"Make them come to you," I said.

"They are." He made a strangling noise. "What's happening?"

"It's PSW, Brian, but don't tell the cops that. It could only make it worse. Just say you don't know."

"PSW? But how? Why?" Now there was terror in his voice in addition to the grief. He'd heard all about Mel's escapades, but I know he'd never expected one of his own. I sure as hell hadn't.

"It's my fault," I said, even as Devlin laid a firm hand over mine. "I got sucked into this fucking game, and I didn't realize—" I choked back a sob. "I didn't realize when I asked your help on that stupid puzzle . . ."

"Oh, shit," Brian said. "They wanted to kill me. Oh my God. Fifi's dead because of me."

"It's not your fault," I said firmly. From across the table, Devlin squeezed my hand, as if saying *it's not your fault, either.* But I knew that it was. At least a little bit, Fifi's blood was on my hands. And, unless I was careful, Brian's would be, too.

"You have to stay hidden," I said. "She might still be looking for you."

"She?"

"The killer's a woman, Bri. That freaky bitch we saw at Bergdorf's. The one who tossed the Manolos."

"Holy shit. Tell the cops. Get them looking for her."

"I can't," I said. I took a deep breath. "But maybe you can."

"What?"

I looked up at Devlin, saw that his face was tight. I mouthed a question: *Okay?*

For a second, he didn't do anything, but then he nodded.

I exhaled and spoke into the phone. "When you talk to the police tell them about the girl in Bergdorf's." Describing her to the police probably wouldn't do any good. But maybe we'd get lucky. We certainly hadn't with the shot glass. And since we were now operating without complete clues, I figured we needed whatever advantage we could grab. "Tell them about how she was acting strange. About, I don't know, about whatever you want. Just don't say it came from me. I call the cops, I'm in trouble. *More* trouble," I amended. "But you saw her, too. She was acting suspicious. Following us, even. But that's *all* you know, Brian. You can't know anything about the game."

"I don't know anything," Brian said flatly, "except that my cousin is dead."

"I'm so sorry."

"I know, Jenn. I—" His voice broke.

"You have to stay hidden," I said. "You understand that?"

"I've got a show, Jenn. I've got rehearsals. I've got opening night. I've got—"

"A life, Brian. And if you want to keep it, you need to do what I say."

"Jenn . . ."

"At least for a day or so. Make up an excuse. Give me time here. We're going to end this thing, Devlin and I. I promise we are. So please, just lay low for a little bit. Please. For me. I don't think I could stand it if something happened to you."

Silence, and then, "You're going to get the bitch who killed him, right?"

"I promise." I didn't know how I'd make good on that promise, but when I said it, I meant it.

"I want to help."

"I know you do," I said. But about that, I wasn't promising anything. I'd already dragged him into this. I really didn't want to pull him in any further. "I have to go," I said. "Be careful."

"You, too."

We hung up, and Devlin passed me a napkin. I must have looked confused, because he reached out and brushed his thumb across my cheek. I'd been crying, and I didn't even realize it.

"You okay?" he asked.

"No." I stood up. "Let's get out of here."

Since we were already near the Plymouth Theater, we decided to check there first to see if anybody had left something for us at the box office. If we got lucky, great. If not, we'd hoof it back up Sixth to the Jekyll & Hyde Club. Mostly, I just needed to move. To feel like we were making progress. Because once we stopped making progress, the game was all over. Once that happened, we were really and truly fucked.

"She's going to find us," I continued. "We're going to be running around town trying to figure out some missing clue, and that bird bitch is going to find us."

Devlin went as still as stone beside me. Alarmed, I turned to him. "What did you call her?" he asked.

"Bird Bitch," I said, a little cautiously. "It's stupid, but that was the nickname I gave her."

"Why?" he asked, his fingers just a little too tight on my arm.

"Um, Devlin, I'm not—"

"Why did you give her that nickname? You only saw her the one time before this morning, didn't you? In Bergdorf's?"

"Right. But she was wearing a halter. And she had this huge—"

"Tattoo," he finished, closing his eyes, and then letting go of my arm so that he could rub his temple. "Birdie," he whispered, and when he turned to me, his eyes were lit with excitement. And also, I thought, with fear. "I know her," he said. "I know who our assassin is."

DEVLIN

Rage burned through Devlin as his long strides ate up the sidewalk. They'd left the café and were heading toward Broadway. Ostensibly to cut up from there to 45th Street and check in at the Plymouth's box office. But Devlin wasn't thinking about any of that. Not about the possibility that the Plymouth house manager could be holding a clue, not about the Jekyll & Hyde Club, not even about the woman trotting along beside him, trying desperately to match his pace.

No, all he was thinking about was that he'd been had. He'd been taken for a fool, and he'd been used.

That was beginning to be a goddamn habit. He thought about Randall, his partner, now cold in his grave. Randall had turned on Devlin, had gone so far as to try to take him out once Devlin got wind that he was on the take. But Devlin had won. It had cost him everything, but he'd won.

He'd won against Birdie once before, too. But could he do it again?

"Devlin. *Devlin!*" Jenn reached out and grabbed his arm, yanking him to a stop. "What is going on?"

"I helped put her away," he said. They'd stopped in a storefront, a kind of open space where various vendors set up shop. He stepped further inside, moving away from the street. "About five years ago. She was on the fringes of an organization we were taking down. I was doing grunt work. Paper pushing. But I ran across some anomalies, and they tracked back to this woman. This hard-as-nails woman who'd do just about anything if the price was right."

"You caught her," Jenn said.

"Not me. The FBI. But, yeah. She wouldn't have gone down if it weren't for me."

He watched Jenn's face as she processed that information. "So this is personal. She's got a personal vendetta against you." Her brow furrowed. "We were right. It isn't coincidence that we're involved. Someone's hand-picking the players."

"Looks that way."

"There's one thing I don't get, though." She cleared her throat, her cheeks flushing as she focused on the ground rather than on him. "If you . . . I mean, if you and Birdie, you know, then why—"

"Didn't I realize who she was while we were doing the nasty?"

She grimaced. "I wouldn't have put it that way, but yeah."

"I never saw her, those years ago. I read her file. I followed her trail. But I never actually saw her."

"Not even a picture?"

He shook his head. "She was good. We didn't have any pictures. Once she was in custody, there were mug shots, but by
then, I was on to other things. I'd been low man on the totem
pole, but the work I did got me noticed. By the time she was
actually captured, I'd been shifted to other assignments."

"But you knew about the tattoo?"

"That I knew. Witness statements. It's pretty distinctive."

"And yet the other night . . ."

"Let's just say that I thought she was so enthused by the moment that she never managed to completely disrobe. Now it
makes sense. She kept the tattoo covered on purpose."

"Oh."

He reached out and took her hand. "Jenn, it didn't mean—I
was lost. Or I was trying to get lost."

She turned moving backwards into the racks of purses that
lined the little cubicle they'd entered. "You don't owe me an ex-
planation."

"No," he said. "I don't owe you one. But that doesn't mean I
don't want to explain anyway."

"Devlin, I—oh, *shit!*" He reached out, grabbing the metal
grate from which the purses hung, and shoving it, hard, so that
it started to tumble. Then she grabbed his arm and pulled him
toward her. "Run!"

He ran, following on her heels as the purse rack clattered to
the ground behind them. A sharp *whiz* sounded by his ear, a little too close for comfort, and he hit the ground, pulling Jenn
down with him. Together, they crawled behind a glass case filled
with jewelry.

"Stay down!"

"No shit," she said.

He pulled out his clutch piece, then lifted his head just enough to see a woman with dark glasses, a platinum blond wig, and a long black trench coat picking her way over the purse rack. She was partially hidden behind other racks and cases, but he could see clearly enough that her weapon had a laser sight. State of the art, and far outmatching the piece he'd hidden at his ankle.

Still, if he could just get a good shot . . .

He looked around, assessing the area. The place hadn't been too busy. Most of the customers bought things from the vendors at the front door; fewer ventured into the back. An Asian woman was prone on the floor, and Devlin marked her as one of the vendors. A twenty-something redhead with spandex shorts, a fanny pack, and a *Lion King* t-shirt—a tourist—huddled in a corner. Devlin couldn't see any more civilians, but he figured they were out there. He assumed at least one of them had called 911.

Birdie probably assumed as much as well, which meant she wasn't going to try to wait them out. She'd leave soon, probably taking a hostage just in case.

And she'd try for them again at the next opportunity.

As if to prove his point, she reached down and hauled the redhead to her feet. She jabbed the gun into her side, looked around, and then headed back out the way she'd come in. Less then three minutes, Devlin knew, and she'd gopher into the subway tunnels. He wasn't worried about the tourist. Birdie wanted him. And she wanted her freedom. She wasn't going to increase her exposure by killing a civilian.

As soon as she stepped out onto the street, Devlin took Jenn's arm. He led her in a crouch to the back of the space, then pushed out through the emergency exit. He still had his gun out, and he covered the area, but it was clear.

"Come on," he said, heading up the alley and away from Times Square.

"Where are we going?"

"Away. As far away as we can get, and as fast as we can get there."

Chapter
48
BIRDIE

Twice now. The little bitch has foiled me twice now, and it's really beginning to piss me off.

I keep my gun pressed to the redhead's side, hidden from view, as we march down into the subway. I keep her close, myself at the alert, as we wait for the train to pull in. I wait, watching as the subway belches out its load of passengers, then hang behind as those of us waiting struggle on. And then, as the doors begin to shut, I shove the girl to the ground, catch the door, and hustle inside.

The train pulls away, and I aim an air kiss toward the girl. Why not? In a way, she just saved my ass.

I don't bother to take a seat, as I'm getting off at the next stop anyway. And as I hang onto the bar, I consider my next move. First, of course, I'll lose this outfit. It was, I realize, a mistake, but I'd still been in the biker shorts and top when the tracker had kicked back on. I'd been in a brutal hurry, and I'd wanted something to hide the outfit and my hair. So I'd gone for the quick fix, making purchases I normally would never have considered. I hadn't expected Jennifer to notice me, but she did.

I give her credit for that. Like me, she's tuned to notice those little fashion faux pas.

I try to think what's nearby, and remember a row of clothing stores on Avenue of the Americas. I can pick up something suitable and then head to my next destination.

As the subway pulls into the station, I pull the shot glass out of my pocket. The Jekyll & Hyde Club, it says. And that's all it says.

It must be a clue, this glass that I watched tumble from Jennifer's fingers.

I don't know if she held on to it long enough to see the logo, but I hope so. Because I intend to go there next. And my hope is that Jennifer and Devlin will join me there.

Not for lunch, but definitely for some entertainment.

Chapter
49

JENNIFER

Holy *shit.*

The whole time we were running, that phrase was whipping through my head. And if I hadn't noticed her loitering by a jewelry case, Devlin might be dead.

Oh, God.

I stopped, bent over, and put my head down between my legs. In a second, Devlin was at my side. "Are you okay? Are you hurt?"

"You could have been killed," I said, still sucking in air. I think I was hyperventilating. I told myself this was an audition. I had to play calm, cool, and collected. The unruffled Lady of the Manor. Two more breaths and I stood up straight and faced him. "I'm okay. I'm okay now."

"You're sure?"

Instead of answering, I turned in a circle. "Where are we?"

"A few blocks from the library. Come on." He took my hand and walked me to the corner bus stop. He checked traffic, then pulled me back against a building. Beside us, a fruit stand beckoned, and people bought apples, bananas, and bundles of flowers. Normal stuff.

"You hungry?"

I realized I was staring and shook my head. "Just thinking. Jesus, Devlin."

"I know." He frowned. "I wouldn't have thought it possible, but maybe she put some sort of device in my tennis shoes. Or maybe someone else is tailing us and relaying our position to her."

"I don't know what to do about the tail, but let's find a Foot Locker or something and get you some new shoes."

He didn't argue, and after we got our bearings, we realized there was a shoe store just a few blocks over. We were lucky and managed to get a salesclerk's attention right off the bat. As the guy went off for Devlin's shoes, we sat waiting, eyeing everyone who walked by. I don't know about Devlin, but I was on pins and needles, expecting the bird bitch to pop out from around corners, maybe even drop from the ceiling brandishing an Uzi.

"I'm glad you paid attention," Devlin said. "That's how you noticed her."

I had no idea what he was talking about, and told him so.

"Watching faces. What we talked about earlier. You paid attention and it saved my life."

"Ah," I said. I wasn't quite sure how to tell him that his safety tip hadn't been the key. "That wasn't exactly what happened."

"Don't tell me you just got lucky?"

"No. Well, sort of." I cleared my throat. "She was wearing an Armani trench coat," I said. "And low-heeled boots. It's March, but it's been warm. And so I noticed the outfit. Then I noticed the face and, well, you know what happened next."

"In other words, I was saved by your fashion sense."

"Pretty much. If she'd been Levi's and a denim jacket I doubt I would have paid her a second glance. That's tourist clothes."

"A dress?"

"Depends on the designer, but probably. After all, I'd have to check out her shoes."

"The wonders of the female mind," he said, but he said it with a smile, so I didn't have to hit him.

The clerk came back with Devlin's size, and he switched shoes, asking the clerk to toss the old ones. We paid cash, then headed back out, watching our back the whole way.

"Do you think that did it?" I asked.

"I don't know," he said. "But I hope so. Because if the tracker wasn't in my shoes, then I'm fresh out of ideas."

We walked up Avenue of the Americas to the Jekyll & Hyde Club, watching faces as we did. Fashion sense can only take you so far.

It was a bit of a hike, but we were pumped up on adrenaline. Also, we'd decided to forego the Plymouth Theater, at least for the time being. Times Square was just too hot.

As we walked, I looked sideways at Devlin. "If you'd had a clear shot, you'd have taken her out. Wouldn't you?"

"Bet your ass."

"Self-defense, right?"

He stopped, turning to look at me, his forehead furrowed. "Damn straight."

"Would you feel guilty? Remorse?"

His face hardened. "Not even a little bit. The bitch knew what she was getting into when she came after us. Hell, when she got into that life."

"She made her decisions, then."

"Exactly."

"Randall made his decisions, too," I said, then started walking again, hoping I made my point.

A few seconds later, Devlin fell into step beside me again. We walked the rest of the way in silence, and after a few minutes, the Jekyll & Hyde Club loomed in front of us. I paused just long enough to admire the kitschy, overblown entrance, with stone columns, skeletons decked out in suits guarding the entrance, Romanesque statuary, and dozens of other haunted-mansiony-type details.

Devlin looked them up and down before turning to me. "Cute," he said. "Come here often?"

"Out of town visitors get a kick out of the place," I said. "An old boyfriend brought me here once. That's how I found it in the first place." I cleared my throat. "Actually, there's another place in Greenwich Village, but it's the Jekyll & Hyde *Pub*. So this should be the right one."

"Lucky for us you knew it was here. I've never heard of it."

"Really? It's a total tourist magnet."

"Exactly," he said, in the tone of a native New Yorker who eschewed the kitschy tourist stuff. Ah well. What can I say? I love my transplanted-ness. How else would I have an excuse to come to places like this?

We headed to the entrance and told the livery-clad cast member that we'd like to go in for lunch. Everyone on staff tended to be aspiring actor. For a while, I'd even considered working there myself.

"You're lucky, miss," he said in a cockney accent. "The mistress herself is giving tours today. You wait here, and she'll be along shortly."

Devlin raised his eyebrows, but didn't argue as we waited in a roped off queue. Come the evening, I knew, the area would be filled with excited teenagers, tourists, and couples out for a different kind of bar experience. Right now, thankfully, we'd have the place pretty much to ourselves.

We didn't have long to wait, and after only a few minutes, the heavy doors opened and a diminutive woman with granny glasses stepped out, costumed in period garb that I didn't quite recognize. A cross between a nineteenth-century lady and a scullery maid, maybe. She held a cocktail in one hand, pressed the other against her mouth, and belched.

"Oh, dearies, dearies, do excuse me. One tends to take a few too many nips after spending too much time in the master's laboratory. A sad truth, sad," she said, with a little shake of her head. "But come, come," she said, gesturing us inside. "Let us see if the master is willing to let you in. He's very particular, you know. His work is so important. So . . . ground-breaking."

As she spoke, she led us into a dark passage, mirrored on one side and with a closed door on the other. The door closed behind us, leaving us trapped in the alcove. Devlin shot a quick glance my way, but I just shrugged. It was silly and designed for kids, but I loved the place. And even though it was supposed to be scary, considering what real life was like at the moment, the foolishness was really quite refreshing.

"I'm Prunella Pippet," our guide said. "I've been working

with the good doctor, helping him organize his collection of . . . curiosities." She peered at us closely. "You know the story of Dr. Jekyll?"

"Sure," I said.

"And of Mr. Hyde?"

"Absolutely."

Prunella nodded, ostensibly satisfied. "You've been here before, I see. Well, we'll have to see if you're still deemed worthy of entrance. If you have the strength of character to withstand the horrors you'll find inside."

As she spoke, the lights dimmed and the mirrored wall changed to show a mummified man—who looked remarkably like television's Crypt Keeper—stumbling toward us, cackling. As he did, the ceiling began to collapse, protrusions bearing down toward us. "Be strong, dear guests!" Prunella cried. "You must prove you're worthy of entering."

I shot a quick glance toward Devlin, sure he was probably rolling his eyes, but to my surprise, he was actually grinning.

Suddenly, the ceiling halted. Prunella sighed with apparent relief. "Thank goodness you've been deemed worthy!" The wall behind her opened and she escorted us to a traditional-looking restaurant entrance, complete with a hostess at a podium. Traditional, that is, except for the glass elevator shaft now revealed beside us, showing the mummified bodies of two lost travelers wasting away on top of the elevator car. Pretty cool stuff, all in all.

"Two?" the girl asked.

"Actually, we just need—"

"Sure," I said, cutting Devlin off.

He cocked a brow in question.

"We don't know it's at the lost and found. We might as well sit. The clue could be anywhere here."

He nodded, and we followed the hostess past a long bar on our right, mostly empty now, but it would likely be full to overflowing that evening. On our left, the walls were lined with creepy portraits over tables filled with tired adults and rapturous children.

The eyes in the paintings moved, keeping track of us as we followed the hostess to a table nestled under a huge bronze statue of Zeus. "Be careful not to anger the god," the girl said, then left the menus and headed back to the front.

"This place is . . . interesting," Devlin said.

"I think it's a hoot."

"I'd rather we didn't have all those eyes staring at us," he added, nodding to the portraits. "Who knows who might be behind those pictures."

I started to laugh, but caught myself. Under the circumstances, he had a point. The place was a literal house of horrors. "Maybe it was a mistake to come here," I said, looking around. Dark and spooky, with at least four floors of restaurant space, the place overflowed with places to hide.

I looked around again, this time searching the place for Birdie hiding in the dark. I didn't see her, and that was good, but she could be anywhere. The place had nooks and crannies, as well as over-the-top attractions, like the Frankenstein-inspired platform that rose from our level all the way up to the "attic" where lightning would bring the creature to life. Or the talking gargoyle. Or the animated, mummified rock band.

All in all, the place was a feast of sight and sound. That made it fabulous as an attraction, but terrible for us.

As if to prove my point, a group of teenagers bustled in, their raucous laughter battling the ambient din of the place. A girl in the center of the crowd wore a bright pink shirt with SWEET 16 emblazoned on it. From the noise of the group, I had a feeling it was going to be a heck of a party.

"We should get out of here," I said.

"Wait." Devlin put a hand on mine. "We're here. Let's see what we can learn. Just keep your eyes open."

"Believe me, I will," I said, then screamed at the top of my lungs when a hand closed on the top of my head.

"My, my, you are a live one," said a doctor in a white lab coat. "Perhaps I could have the use of your brains for a little experiment?"

"Um, no," I said, not really into the spirit of the thing at the moment.

He was going to argue—after all, that was his job—but our waiter came up then and the doctor disappeared into the dark.

"You look like two weary travelers come for a little excitement at the hand of the good doctor. Can I provide you some refreshment after your long journey?"

"Actually, we're looking for information."

"Ah, a man of learning you are."

"Something like that," Devlin said with a bemused look in my direction.

"It's a scavenger hunt," I said. "We think the last clue led us here, but we don't know what we're looking for. We're thinking maybe someone left the next clue for us in the lost and found."

"Ah, I'm afraid you're out of luck, dear lady. All that's in there is a pair of glasses and a pink sweater."

"Oh." I frowned. "What about a message. Maybe for someone named Devlin? Or Jennifer? Or Paul Winslow?"

"A message, huh? That one, I don't know. You want me to go check?" he asked, sliding out of character. I almost chastised him. This place was like a training ground for actors. He shouldn't slip like that.

"That would be great," Devlin said, but as the guy turned, Devlin stopped him with a curt, "Wait. Do you always memorize the contents of your lost and founds?"

"Not hardly. But the girl was asking just a few minutes ago. You both playing the same game?"

I swear my blood turned to ice when he said that. "Is she still here?" I whispered. "Where is she?"

"The library," he said, pointing up a floor. Devlin and I both turned and looked that direction, but we didn't see a thing. "You want me to tell her you're here?"

"No!" we said in unison, then Devlin added, "Just see about those messages, would you?"

"Sure thing," the waiter said.

As soon as he was out of earshot, Devlin met my eyes, his hard and cold.

"She got here first," I said. "How? She couldn't be tracking us if she got here first."

"The shot glass," Devlin said. "She probably saw you drop it."

I closed my eyes, cursing myself.

"It's just as well she's here," he said, leaning over and reaching his arm under the table. When he came back up, I saw the flash of metal in his hand before he concealed the gun. "It's time to end this thing."

"Devlin, no!"

He could hear the terror in her voice, but he wasn't about to give in to it. "We have an advantage here, Jenn. I'm going to take it."

"Damn it, Devlin, she might already know we're here. What if she nails you?"

"Unless we can follow the clues to the end of this thing and stop the game, she's going to nail me eventually. I've got a chance now. I'm taking it."

"You're right. You're right. I'm just—God, what if she gets you first?"

"She won't." He slid out of the booth, then did a double-take when she followed him. "Stay here."

"Like hell. I don't have a gun. I'm sticking with you."

He wanted to argue, but she was right. "Fine. But you do *exactly* what I say."

"You're the director."

He headed across the aisle to the booth next to the Frankenstein lift. The birthday group had sat there, and now they egged on an actor clad in a lab coat, who had started fiddling with knobs between them and the lift. Another actor in a ratty coat with a hunchback was hobbling over to help. Probably time for a show to start, Devlin thought. Good. Maybe the distraction would give him some cover.

He kept the gun close at his side, out of view, and then started up the metal spiral staircase to the next level. Jenn was right at his heels, and they emerged into the shadows. He peered cautiously around, taking in the haunted-house decorations, complete with open coffins and tables topped with all variety of séance paraphernalia.

Jenn tapped lightly on his shoulder, and when he turned she pointed. He followed the line of her finger and his heart skipped a beat. *Birdie.* Right there, sipping on a drink, her hand resting lightly on a purse, and her eyes scanning the room.

He pushed Jennifer back into the shadows, essentially hiding them behind a vertical coffin with an animatronic corpse inside.

"Did she see us?" Jenn whispered.

"I don't know. She's waiting for something, though. She's probably flirted with a waiter or the bartender. If she doesn't already know we're here, I bet someone's going to be telling her soon."

"So what do we do?"

"Follow me."

He eased along the wall, getting a few stares from the patrons on that level. The design of the level kept them pretty well shielded from the side of the room Birdie was on, and he said a little prayer, thanking God for small favors. They emerged from behind the centerpiece near an elevator, then froze when the doors slid open. A waiter got out, and Devlin watched as he marched to Birdie, then bent to tell her something. She immediately stiffened and stood, then headed for the iron railing at the edge of the level. She peered down, obviously looking for someone on the lower level. Them, of course. She eased along the railing toward the spiral staircase, peering over, searching for the two people she wasn't going to find. Below her, lights flashed as the Frankenstein show began, and the deep throaty laugh of the mad doctor drifted up toward them. Somehow, Devlin thought, that was fitting.

He tightened his grip on the gun, stepped out from behind the pillar, and—

"Oh, there you are! I checked on the messages, and there wasn't anything. Do you want—"

"Get down!" Jenn screamed, dragging the waiter to the ground with her as Birdie reached for her gun and turned.

But Devlin was faster. His was already up and aimed. "Freeze!" Devlin said. "FBI. Put the gun down, Birdie. Game over." Birdie just grinned, and Devlin got a sick feeling in his stomach. "Do it," he said. "Don't make it worse than it already is."

And then, to his surprise, she slowly bent down, laid her gun on the ground, and kicked it toward him.

Every person on the level was staring at him, Devlin knew that, but he'd tuned them out. Right now, it was just him and the bitch as he walked toward her, the gun aimed at her chest. "Hands on your head," he said.

"Now, now, Agent Brady. You can't really be planning on shooting me. After the fun we had."

"Hands on your head," he repeated.

"You don't have a badge, Agent. Shoot me, and there'll be a whole new investigation. You'll be back hoofing on the Great White Way, because with two dirty shootings, the Feds won't be returning your gun."

"Now," he said, taking another step forward.

"I see that you're a very determined man." And then, in a move of such acrobatic grace that he was impressed despite himself, she reached behind her, grabbed the railing, and vaulted over.

"No!" he yelled, racing in that direction, then looking over, expecting to find her battered on the salon-level floor. Instead, he saw her sprawled on the lifeless body on the platform, which had been ascending right as Birdie had jumped. Now she scrambled to her knees and started to leap the shorter distance from the platform to the ground as the mad doctor and the hunchback stood frozen in disbelief.

Devlin raised his gun, but he couldn't get a clear shot. Not with all the kids and actors in the way.

Dammit!

He pulled the gun back just as Birdie shot him a triumphant look. And then, without looking back again, she raced toward the exit.

Devlin reached the spiral staircase in two long strides, descended in no time, and was back in front of the bar with his gun and sweeping the place before five seconds had passed. But even that short amount of time was too long. She was gone.

Dammit all to hell, she was gone.

Chapter

51

JENNIFER

Since Devlin was in a particularly crappy mood after losing Birdie, I tried to take charge. While he retrieved Birdie's gun and laid a load of bullshit on the manager, I again asked about the lost and found. About messages. About anything in the place that might have the initials PSW. Nothing.

Just in case I'd read the shot glass wrong, the hostess offered to call the Jekyll & Hyde Pub in Greenwich Village for me. I let her, but I wasn't expecting anything. The glass had clearly said the Club. And that's where we were.

Dead end.

We headed in silence to the Plymouth, but that was another dead end. Great.

"What now?" I asked as we loitered in front of the box office. I had my back against the side of the building and was scanning the streets. I didn't think we'd run into Birdie again, but I wasn't inclined to take chances.

"Rest," Devlin said. "And regroup." His voice was still hard, his features tight. Missing Birdie at the Club had gotten to him, I knew. What I didn't know was how to draw him out of the funk. Since I didn't have a better idea, I decided to use the direct approach.

"Snap out of it, already," I said as we headed into Times Square. "This isn't over, and we're alive. Under the circumstances, that seems like a pretty good outcome."

He turned, a little too sharply, to face me. I could practically read the response on his face—Birdie was still out there; ergo the outcome was bad.

I stared him down.

"Fine," he finally said. "You're right. Just because she slipped past me once doesn't mean she'll do it again."

"Exactly."

"Except we still don't know what the next clue is. So we still don't have any way to shut down this game."

"Yeah," I said. "That's definitely a downside."

He cursed softly, his shoulders dropping a bit. "Come on," he said after a moment. We hurried up Seventh and this time we chose a Doubletree. At this rate, I was going to be intimately familiar with each and every hotel chain in the city.

As soon as we were in the room—locked, double-bolted—I flopped onto the couch. The room was a suite, and that was nice. The place was bigger than my apartment, in fact, so in the midst of the horror, I got to enjoy a bit of luxury. Sort of.

While I flopped, Devlin went to the window.

"Are we safe here?"

His shoulders lifted just slightly. "I think so. She's probably going to lay low for a while, and I'm guessing we got rid of the tracker when we ditched my shoes."

"Right," I said, but not entirely confident. "Where else could it be?"

"Exactly," he said, though he didn't sound any more confident than I felt. Then again, who could blame us? The woman kept popping up. Like a bad penny, as my dad would say.

I frowned as he pulled out the cell phone. "Who are you calling?"

"Reinforcements," he said, his features hard.

I blinked at him. "You're kidding me, right? You're going to pull somebody else into this?"

"Not just anyone," he said. "The FBI."

"Devlin!"

He held up a hand. "We're out of options. We don't know what the next clue is. But we do know who the assassin is. We call in the FBI. Not the agency, just one guy. A friend. I think he'll help us."

From his expression, I didn't think he was entirely convinced, but I nodded anyway. "Go on."

"We don't ask his help with the game. But we get him searching for Birdie. She's obviously been released from prison. She's obviously in the city. And if she's running around killing Reardon and firing at us, then she's leaving a trail. She's good, but there's always a trail. And five years have made her a little sloppy, I think. We've got a good chance of taking her down if we work that angle."

"But bringing someone else in . . ."

"I know," he said, his jaw firm. "But I still think we should do it. We don't know the next clue, Jenn. And I don't want to sit around with a target painted on my ass." He drew in a breath. "I sat in my apartment acting like a victim long enough. It's time to be proactive."

I studied his face, but I could see that he meant it. More, that he needed it. And since I didn't have a better idea, I agreed. "That settles it, then," I said. "Proactive, baby," I added, with a laugh as Devlin wrapped an arm around me and pulled me close for a quick kiss before he dialed the phone.

I curled up beside him on the bed as he dialed then asked for Agent Mark Bullard. As soon as they started talking specifics—pulling security camera information from Reardon's office, trying to locate witnesses near the carriage shooting, and a bunch of other cop-sounding things—I knew that Agent Devlin Brady was really and truly back. He'd been there for me, of course, but now he was back for *him*. I still couldn't fathom leaving a career in the theater, but I understood that Devlin had left it for something he loved better. And then he'd gotten burned by what he'd loved best. Now the wounds were healing.

Feeling a little sappy, I gave him a quick kiss on the cheek, then slid off the bed. I didn't need to listen to Agent-speak. I'd much rather look and feel like a girl. So I headed off to the bathroom.

I stripped down, turned on the water, then stepped in under the blast.

Heaven.

I indulged for about three minutes, then stepped back out, dripping, and plodded to the door. I checked—discreetly—and made sure I hadn't locked it. Not that I was going to overtly suggest a shower tryst. But if Devlin got the idea, well, I wouldn't kick him out.

Once full access to the bathroom had been established, I got back in the shower and let the water sluice over my body. I thought about Devlin and got all tingly and enjoyed that for a little while. But tingly's not as fun by yourself, so I tried to shift my thoughts to a less gooey area. Considering the circumstances, that wasn't hard.

Except, of course, that I really didn't want to think about clues and assassins and targets and racing for my life.

Which meant that I had nothing to think about except my career.

Proactive.

The word kept going through my mind. Devlin had called Agent Bullard because he was being proactive. And wasn't that what he'd told me I needed to be? What Brian had told me, too?

The thing is, I knew they were right. I'd been in Manhattan for years now with no big break. No small breaks, for that matter. And I knew why. I probably had always known why, but getting up close and personal with an assassin had brought the truth right to the forefront: I wasn't really trying. Believe me, after trying to survive, I know the difference.

Although I thought that my name on a billboard sounded like a fabulous thing, what if I had a fear of success? Of not living up to my own hype? Or the hype I'd built up in my head?

These last few days had been an object lesson in reality, though. And I knew it wasn't the hype that mattered. It was the living that counted. And if I wanted to really live, I was going to have to start making the same kind of effort in my career that I'd made to save my ass.

I'd been going along in the theater, but I wasn't busting ass. I wasn't doing anything and everything to make my own luck. I was waiting for it to fall in my lap.

That's the kind of thing that will get a girl killed. Or at least kill her career.

Right there in the shower I made a solemn oath. As soon as this ordeal was over, I was hiring Brian's coach Nicolae. And signing up for acting classes. And finding an agent. And making it a point to hit at least ten auditions a week. I was giving myself an ultimatum. Put up, get serious, or get the hell out of New York.

Since I had no intention of moving back to California, I figured I'd have a part by Christmas.

As I turned off the water and wrapped myself in a towel, I couldn't help but think about the irony. For years, I'd been telling my family that I was killing myself to get on Broadway. I hadn't been, though. Not even close. And who would have thought that it'd take a real life-and-death drama to make me realize it?

I rubbed at the fog on the mirror, then finger-combed my hair. I wore no makeup, but I was clean and smelled fresh, and considering how Devlin was used to seeing me, I figured I was batting a thousand.

Except that I had no Devlin.

Okay, whiney girl alert, but where the heck was he? I mean, I was *naked* in here.

"Dev? You still on the phone?"

"I'm off," he said. "Just thinking."

What was I supposed to say to that?

"I feel fabulous," I said. "All nice and clean again."

"Great."

I waited. Nothing.

Shit.

Okay, fine. We'd had a connection earlier. Lots of little connections, actually. And I wasn't on the verge of dying from a toxin, and he wasn't about to be shot. We didn't even have any place to be since we had no idea where to go next.

So why weren't we in bed? Why wasn't he doing wild and wonderful things to my body?

Why, why, why wasn't he keeping that promise?

I toyed with the idea of just getting dressed, going out there, and pretending I didn't care. But I did care. And proactive was my new motto.

So . . .

I very bravely snugged the towel around me, took a deep breath, opened the door—and stepped right into Devlin's arms.

"There you are," he said, his voice deliciously husky. "I thought you were going to stay in there all night."

"Oh. I . . . um . . ." So much for sexy repartee.

He trailed a finger along my shoulder and I shivered, the simple towel suddenly seeming like *way* too much clothing. "I made you a promise earlier," he said, closing his fingers over where I'd knotted the towel. "I was thinking now was a good time to make good."

With that, he dropped my towel and pulled me close to him. And then—oh my *God*—Devlin Brady proceeded to show me just how very well he kept his promises.

Chapter

52

JENNIFER

Wow.

Oh. Wow.

And, just so you know: *Wow*.

I don't think there was an inch of my body that Devlin didn't explore, and with each exploration he somehow made my body sing.

Who knew that the area between your big toe and the next was all that erotic? I certainly hadn't. But now, as I slowly woke up in his arms, the room dark around us, I wiggled my toes and thought that I'd never look at thong sandals the same again.

"Hey," he whispered, stroking my hair. "You awake?"

"Mmphblg," was about all I could manage. But I did roll over, snuggling against him and just breathing deep. He smelled really, really good, and I would have been very, very happy to just stay there forever. I snuggled closer, liking that idea. "You know," I said, dreamily, "maybe this isn't so bad. Maybe we can just stay in this hotel room forever. Stay in this bed forever. Just like this."

He made a noise that suggested he was pretty keen on that, too. And since I was on a roll, I continued to spin my scenario. "We'll just live in this room. Nothing but us and room service and sex."

"I can live with that," he said. "At least when I die, I know I'll die happy."

"And we can haunt this room. Better," I said, rolling over and staring at the ceiling. "We can haunt that bird bitch."

"Absolutely," Devlin said. "We can—"

"Devlin!" I sat up, grabbing his arm and cutting him off. "Oh my God!"

He was up immediately, his expression alarmed, and rolled out of bed. He came up, his gun in his hand, his face tense and alert.

"No, no," I said, "it's okay." I reached over and pulled him back into bed. "I'm sorry. But that's it. I figured it out!"

He looked at me, his expression dubious. "Figured what out?"

"The clue. Devlin, I know where we're supposed to go next."

"The clue," he repeated, his brain still fuzzy from sex. "The clue that we lost? The shot glass?"

"Yes! Only we didn't really lose it. Or, we did, but it doesn't matter because the only thing that's important is the Jekyll & Hyde Club."

He shifted, propping himself up on one arm as he stared at her. "Explain."

"The Jekyll & Hyde Club is supposed to be a haunted restaurant, right?"

"That's the schtick."

"Well, that's also the clue." She leaned back, the sheet pulled up around her chest and her expression as smug as he'd ever seen it.

He lunged for her, pulled her squealing to him. "Okay," he said, nibbling on her neck. "Tell me."

"Can't. You've gone and got me all distracted."

He came in for another attack, nimble fingers racing over her skin, tickling her until she surrendered amid peals of laugher. "Okay! Okay! I'll tell, I'll tell."

Smug, he leaned back against the headboard. "Come on, babe. Spill it."

"The shot glass sent us to a haunted place."

"Right."

"And what sent us to the shot glass?"

Probably a trick question, but he answered anyway. "The horse clue."

"Right. And . . ." She rolled her hand, egging him on.

He might have gotten the answer right, but he still didn't see the big picture. "And . . . I have no idea where you're going with this."

"Bishop," she said. "That's the name of the horse."

"Right. So?"

"The clue could have said Sean. Or it could have been hidden in any other horse's buggy. So why there?"

"Because that was the horse our tormentor took a ride in," he said, just to get a rise out of her. It worked, and she aimed a sternly arched brow his direction. "Or," he amended, "maybe it's because the name of the horse is important."

"Bishop," she said again, this time overly emphasizing the word. Then, "Haunted," with that same emphasis. "Get it?"

"No," he said, feeling a bit grumbly now. "Come on, Jenn. Don't torture me."

"Well, I could make you beg . . ."

"You could," he admitted. "But I can think of other things that would be much more fun to beg for."

"Good point," she said, her grin wide. "The Bishop of Broadway."

As soon as she said it, he got it. In fact, it was so painfully obvious he was embarrassed they hadn't seen it before. "David Belasco," he said. "Of course!" A pioneer of Broadway, and American theater for that matter, Belasco had a bizarre tendency to wear a cleric's collar. Not that bizarre considering he was schooled in a monastery, but some of the rumors about the man—including that he ran a high-end bordello—suggested a demeanor that was less than saint-like.

Not that any of that mattered for their purposes, Devlin thought. But one rumor was all important: The Belasco Theater was widely rumored to be haunted.

"You're amazing," he said. "For a woman who said she didn't know how to play this game, I'd have to say you're acing it." Not that he was surprised. He'd been able to tell from the first moment she'd barreled her way into his apartment that this was a woman who got whatever she put her mind to. If she ever truly decided to apply herself to the theater, he figured, Broadway would never be the same.

In front of him, the woman who would one day be a diva blushed an appealing shade of crimson. "I'm giving it my best shot. That's for damn sure. It's amazing what a little motivation will do for you."

"That," he said, "I believe. So what now?"

"Now," she said, "we get into the theater. And I know just the way to do that."

Chapter

54

JENNIFER

"I have to come in with you," Brian said.

I'd called him to meet us, and he'd arrived in record speed. Now Brian, Devlin, and I were standing on 44th Street outside the Belasco Theater, dawn's light just beginning to break. A street sweeper hummed along. Around us, the city was beginning to stir, just like it did every day. Ordinary. Typical.

And yet there wasn't anything ordinary or typical about it.

I sucked in a breath and shook my head. "No. Just sneak us in somehow. If we're lucky, it'll slide by under the radar. I don't think we're watched all the time. That wouldn't make any sense. And I don't want you getting dragged into this any more than you have to. I wouldn't have even called you except I didn't know what else to do. We have to get into that theater."

"Because the next clue's in there," Brian said, his face pale and his eyes more tired than I'd ever seen. "And you can end this thing. Get safe. And after that, you can find the asshole who killed my cousin."

"That's right," Devlin said.

"Well, you need me for that."

"Brian, just get us in. Make up some excuse. You don't—"

"No." He held up a hand. "Look, I get that you're worried about me. I'm worried about me, too. But my cousin is dead because of this game and I've missed rehearsal because of it. Miss again, and I'll be out of the show. This assassin's already messed up my life, I'm not letting her mess it up more."

He took a deep breath. "I *am* going to help you. You want in that theater, I'm going in with you. It's damn near impossible to get backstage at a theater these days. You sure as hell aren't sneaking in. Who else are you going to call?"

I met Devlin's eyes. I'd gone through exactly that train of thought. We could probably fake it, pretend to be reporters, something. But that would take time. Time we really didn't want to waste.

"Jenn, dammit. Let me help you end this. Let me do this for Fifi."

I nodded because I really didn't have a choice. We needed Brian, he knew it, and we weren't getting in that theater without him.

"It may not even be inside," I said. "We don't know what we're looking for. Maybe a message with the house manager or the guard or left at the box office."

"That's a point," Devlin said. "If we have trouble getting into the theater to *look* for a clue, our gamemaster would have a problem getting inside to *leave* a clue."

"Maybe," Brian said. "We'll ask."

We would, of course. But I already knew the answer would be no. That just wasn't clever enough. Somehow, the clue got inside the theater. Considering everything our tormentor had pulled off so far, I really was going to sweat the details of how he'd managed that.

The nondescript stage door was just a few yards down from the pristine set of dual double doors that opened into the Belasco's lobby. Since the box office wasn't open yet, that's the door Brian took us in. He pulled open the metal door and we stepped into a plain, white-painted area with a hall leading off to the left. In front of us was a little office with a cluttered desk, a television, and a wizened man sitting there in a security guard uniform. The man looked up, his eyes owlish behind glasses. "Hey, buddy. What you doing here so early?"

Brian hooked a thumb toward me and Devlin. "Friends from out of town. I promised them the grand tour, but they're catching an early flight. So they dragged my sorry ass out of bed."

"Tourists," the guy said, with a shake of his head and a friendly grin. "Go ahead on in."

"Thanks, Marvin."

We followed Brian to the left, entering a labyrinth of narrow corridors. "Stage and green room are that way," he said, pointing. "Wardrobe and some principals' dressing rooms are downstairs. Chorus upstairs, along with some old dressing rooms being used to store extra props, promo stuff, other assorted junk." He frowned. "Any ideas what we're looking for?"

"Not a one," I said.

"Are there lockers? Like for the chorus?" Devlin asked.

"Sure. For that, we go down."

We followed him down the narrow corridor, took a quick left, and ended up in a quick change area created in the wings out of a few pipes and a curtain. We maneuvered around that and then, before I knew it, we were on the stage.

"Wow," I said.

I'd been on a stage before, of course. But I'd never actually been on a Broadway stage when it was dressed for a show, though of course I've been in tons of Broadway theaters, sitting in the audience like everybody else.

Theaters on Broadway are surprisingly small. Most people expect them to be huge, like the concert halls touring productions are often staged in. But the beauty of Broadway is in its intimacy, and this theater was no exception. A good size, sure. But not overwhelming.

And elegant . . . my gosh, this place was amazing.

I knew that it had been restored, and the job that had been done was superb. As I stood there on stage, I looked up and saw ornate glass fixtures that looked like they'd come from Tiffany, and an intricate mural of naked nymphs over the box seats and extending over the proscenium.

I stood, imagining myself kicking it up and belting it out. Someday . . .

"Jenn." Devlin's voice was soft, but firm.

"Sorry." I felt my cheeks heat, and turned away from my fantasies. Once I survived my reality, though, I'd be back. Someday, I thought, I'd be back for real.

We continued across the stage, but I paused. "Could it be something on stage? There's no guarantee that we could get back here. So maybe it's something out in the open. A clue in the set or the scenery or something."

Devlin and Brian looked at each other and shrugged. "It's worth looking around," Brian said, "but I don't know what it could be. I've been living with this set for weeks now, and nothing odd has popped out at me."

I turned in a slow circle, trying to think. "You're probably right," I said. I wandered upstage, inspecting the little wooden shack erected there in a cluster of fiberglass trees strung with plastic and silk vines.

"Puck's cabin," Brian said before I could ask. "This is the opening set piece. I'm actually in the first scene, you know."

"Yeah?"

He nodded, then crossed the stage toward me, his arms out. "I come over like this—I'm a pain-in-the-ass who spends the show harassing Puck—and when he comes out of his cabin, I fly up out of the way before he can catch me."

"You told me about the flying," I said. "How do you—"

He pointed to a prop in one of the trees; an ornate bird with a long, flowing tailfeather crafted out of some sort of metal. "There's a handle under there. I do a twirl and a leap and I catch the handle. When I tug down, that activates the mechanism and it pulls me up and over to that catwalk." He pointed and Devlin and I both looked at the catwalk. Long and dark, it would make a pretty good hiding place for just about anything. Or anybody.

I shivered, and smiled at Brian, hoping he didn't notice my reaction. "Sounds unnerving," I said, scrambling to make conversation. "Can you show me now?"

I was kidding, but he must've thought I was serious because he shook his head. "The mechanism's not turned on." He nodded toward the wings. "The union guys would have my head if

I touched the board. I'm thinking you'll just have to wait until opening night."

I laughed, then hugged him. "I am so proud of you. Your first Broadway show and you're already flying."

He rolled his eyes. "Let's just find the clue so I don't get fired."

"Good plan." But while he and Devlin started to inspect the stage props, I looked back up at that catwalk again. Something about it just seemed creepy.

"Hey." Devlin's hand came down on my shoulder and I yelped. He laughed. "Sorry."

I shook my head. "It's okay. I'm just jumpy. Probably expecting the ghost of David Belasco around every corner."

"That's better than the alternative," Devlin said, and I agreed it was.

We finished inspecting the stage, finding absolutely nothing that seemed weird, out of place, or that hinted at being a clue. Defeated, we moved on to the stairs, then headed down into a basement. The electrical equipment was off in one room, and across a cramped hall was a cavernous room filled with lockers.

"Wardrobe," Brian said. "I've got about five changes down here, three up in the quick change area. It's a madhouse in here during a show."

"So what are we looking for?" I asked.

"Check the names on the lockers. This show's got a big cast, doesn't it? Maybe there's a dummy locker. Someone with the initials PSW."

We split up and started checking the rows of lockers, but we didn't find anything.

"A message board?" I suggested. "Someplace you guys leave notes for each other?"

"Sure," Brian said. We trotted back out into the hallway. Down at the end was a corkboard. A few dirty cartoons were pinned up, but nothing out of the ordinary.

"This isn't working," I said, moving to my right and taking a seat on a step. "There's too much down here, and we don't know where to look."

"We have all the information," Devlin said. "We just have to interpret it."

"Bishop and a haunted club," Brian said. "That's what you told me."

"The Bishop reference has to be Belasco himself," Devlin said.

"And the theater is haunted," I added, unable to keep the frustration out of my voice. "We know that. That's why we're here. But it's a big place. A clue could be anywhere."

"Clubs are private, aren't they? Exclusive?" Devlin asked, more or less rhetorically. "So what's private in a theater?"

"Dressing rooms," I said. "Bathrooms." I met Brian's eyes, trying to see if he'd thought of something I'd missed. "Um, I guess that's it."

"Apartments are private," Brian said, and right away, I knew he'd nailed it.

"David Belasco kept an apartment here," I said. "Of course!"

"And it's supposed to be the most haunted part of the theater. That and the elevator, I think."

"So how do we get to this apartment?" Devlin asked.

"The elevator still goes up there," Brian said.

I lifted an eyebrow. "The *haunted* elevator?"

He stared me down. "You've been running for your life for days now. You're going to let an elevator weird you out?"

I shrugged. The man had a point.

His brow furrowed. "Actually, now that I've mentioned it, I'm not sure it's really our best bet. The place has been totally cleaned out. I think there are air-conditioning shafts running through it now. It's a mess."

"It's still the best idea we have," Devlin said. "Let's go."

We followed Brian to the elevator, an ancient metal thing covered in peeling gray paint. A long lever took the place of buttons, and a tattered stool remained for the elevator operator. Above, a single lightbulb sputtered and hummed.

I looked at it dubiously, but soldiered on. The box seemed sized for a single passenger, but we all three squeezed in. Fine with me. This wasn't a place where I wanted to be alone.

Devlin took a look at the elevator, shrugged, and shifted. The elevator lurched, then moved.

"So far, so good," he said.

I was certain the cable was going to break and we'd plummet to our death, but it creaked slowly and steadily upward. When it stopped, Devlin pulled open the metal door, and we emerged into the gutted remains of the once grand apartment of the Bishop of Broadway.

"Man," I whispered, "it really has been cleaned out."

"It used to be amazing," Brian said. "I've seen pictures. Built-in bookcases, ornate columns. Lots of furniture that would fetch a bundle at Sotheby's these days."

"It's a mess now," I said. The walls had been stripped of any coverings, revealing bare plaster with numerous nail holes. The floors were battered, and not a stick of furniture remained in the cavernous space. Like Brian had thought, a large air-conditioning shaft ran across the far side of the main room.

About the only thing intact, in fact, was the fireplace and hearth. Brian and I wandered that direction while Devlin stayed behind, inspecting each nook and cranny with more patience than I had.

"These tiles were stolen by slaves in Spain and brought here," Brian said, fingering one of the beautifully glazed tiles.

I ran my finger over one, leaving a trail in the dust, as I looked at him. "How the hell do you know that?"

"One of the guys in the show put together a website about the theater and the ghost. After I got cast, I read it." He shrugged. "No big deal."

"Did the site mention anything else? Like where someone might hide a clue in this mess?"

"Not really," Brian said, but he was frowning, like maybe he did have someplace in mind. "But maybe the fireplace? It's definitely a permanent fixture."

"A secret compartment," Devlin said, calling from the far side of the room. "David Belasco was famous for having secret compartments all over his apartment. There were even rumors some of the compartments were compact beds for his liaisons with various women."

Since hidden compartments sounded appropriately mysterious, I figured Devlin had to be right. The only question was, *where* was the compartment we needed?

"I still say the fireplace," Brian said. "Nobody would plaster over it, or put furniture in front of it, or dismantle it."

"Ideas?" I said, pacing in front of the fireplace.

"Inside," Devlin said. "A loose brick, maybe?"

"You look," I said.

He shot me a grin, then got down on his hands and knees and poked his head into the fireplace. "Why do men always have to do the dirty work?" he asked, his voice echoing in the hollow space.

"Ha ha," I said. And then, because he'd made me feel guilty, I got down there with him and started poking at the bricks myself.

"Cozy," he said.

"Mind on the job," I retorted.

While we poked in there, Brian started to tug at the tiles, just in case one of them came loose and revealed a secret hiding place. Nada. And by the time I emerged, I think I could have played a chimney sweep in *Mary Poppins*. It wasn't soot (at least, I don't think it was) but the dust was pretty dang thick.

"What's the new plan?" Devlin asked, standing next to me, and looking about as ratty as I did.

Instead of an answer, I sneezed, then stamped my feet as I tried to de-dust myself. Honestly, it didn't seem to do much good.

"Do that again," Devlin said.

"Devlin," I whined. "The dust is clinging. All the stomping and slapping in the world isn't going to change that. I need a washing machine."

He made a face and then stomped himself. Instead of the dull smacking noise I'd expected, I heard a hollow thud. I met his eyes and then, without another word, we both dropped to the floor. Twelve large tiles ran the length of the floor, protecting the hard wood from flying soot and ash. I grabbed at the one Devlin had stomped on and tried to pry it up with my fingers. No luck.

Devlin snatched his knife from his pocket and bent down, then slid the blade into the cracked grout. I held my breath as he levered the knife and then, sure enough, the tile popped off revealing a hollow space under the floor.

"What's down there?" I asked.

Devlin shook his head. "Nothing."

I swear I wanted to just collapse right then. I'd been so sure . . .

And then he said, "Hang on. It looks like this goes back under the floorboards." He laid down, then pulled out a copy of *Playbill*, February 2006 issue, with *Spamalot* on the cover.

"Well, hell," I said. "I was so sure we finally had it right."

"I think we do," Devlin said, sitting back. He waved the magazine. "Last month's issue. Published back when someone had to be planning this thing. So there was plenty of time to write something in here or slip a note inside." He held it up by the corner and shook it, but no mysterious pieces of parchment fell out.

Brian had settled onto the floor next to Devlin, and now he was leaning over, scouring the pages as Devlin flipped through. I settled in and joined them, trying to read upside down.

Playbill is the theater magazine that is handed out at every Broadway production. Each magazine is the same, except for the middle part and the cover, and those are customized for a particular show. So the magazine has the list of scenes, cast list, all that kind of stuff. Most folks keep them as souvenirs. Personally, I have a whole drawer full of them.

Each month, it changes, updating the cast (if it's changed)

and running new ads and articles in the part that's uniform across all productions.

Since it's a printed magazine, I expected our clue to be something written in Magic Marker across a page, or printed on a Post-it note and stuck inside.

What I wasn't expecting was what we eventually found: An advertisement, very clearly directed toward us.

"He's Not Dead Yet," Devlin said, reading the ad's headline. "Paul S. Winslow salutes all the players. www.survivethe game.com." He looked up at me and shrugged. "That's all it says."

"Guess we surf the 'Net," I said. I'd dropped my tote by the fireplace, and now I pulled out my laptop, fired it up, then typed in the web address. Then the three of us held our breath until the page came up.

TO WIN THE GAME, TYPE THE PASSWORD HERE:

THE PASSWORD IS ON DISPLAY BESIDE THE PATRIOT
WHO WATCHES OVER THEM ALL

I looked at Brian. "You're the puzzle guy. Any brilliant ideas?"

He shook his head slowly. "This is the kind of thing you two have been dealing with?"

"'Fraid so."

"Shit."

"That about sums it up," I agreed. "But this is it. 'To win the game,' it says. We have to figure this out. If we figure this out, it's *over.*" And wouldn't that just be a slice of heaven.?

"We'll get it," Devlin said, and he reached out and squeezed my hand.

I squeezed back, and I swear I felt the earth move. I blinked, then put my hand on the floor. "Oh, shit," I said. "Do you feel that? For that matter, do you hear that?" A decidedly mechanical hum, along with a kind of thrumming that shook the floor ever so slightly. I looked at Devlin, and then we both looked toward the elevator.

"Get behind me," he said, pulling out his gun.

Neither Brian nor I argued, and we all stayed still, waiting for the elevator to open. It didn't. And then, as quickly as it had come, the creaking stopped and the floor quit shaking. We all looked at each other, not quite sure what to make of all that.

"Birdie?" I whispered.

"I don't know," Devlin said, still holding his gun at the ready.

"I'm not sure which would be worse," I admitted. "Birdie or Belasco's ghost."

"*I* know," Devlin said, and, honestly, so did I. "But how could she have found us? I can't believe she planted anything on you, and I've switched out everything. Nothing I'm carrying was in my apartment when she was there."

"The gun," I said.

He frowned, but nodded. "It was locked up and hidden. It's possible. But unlikely."

"If anyone got into this theater," Brian said, "Marvin would know. Let's call him and ask."

Since we all thought that idea was dandy, he did just that. I couldn't hear Marvin, but from Brian's side of the conversation it sounded like all was well.

"Nobody in or out," Brian reported. "So I guess we're safe. At least," he added, "we're safe for right now."

"**Y**ou did good, old man," I say, with a wide smile.

He looks at me, relief shining in those watery eyes.

My smile widens, and I cold-cock him with the butt of my gun. He falls to the floor, his expression never changing.

I find tape and bind him, then drag him back into the hallway and, finally, into one of the dressing rooms. He'll be out for at least half an hour, I expect. And that should be plenty of time.

After disposing of the man, I head back into the theater and continue our little tour alone. Before, I'd politely requested his assistance in showing me around. Now, I peek through the sets and props, getting a feel for the place. I've already left a few hints for Agent Brady, suggesting to him that I'm here. If he's too stupid to interpret my clues, that certainly isn't my fault.

The best little hint, of course, was running the elevator. A silly trick, but so apropos considering the rumors about this theater. Ghosts! Why should Agent Brady be afraid of a ghost when there's something much more sinister prowling in the wings—me?

I don't know exactly where he is, of course, because the tracking software isn't specific enough to have pinpointed his exact location. From my own observation, I can assume that he's in the apartment of which the old man spoke, most likely with the woman. I don't know what they're looking for, and I admit I'm curious. They must have interpreted the next clue. For that, I give them points since the shot glass is still in my suite at the Waldorf. But what, I wonder, do they expect to find here? More, I'm afraid that they are drawing close to the final culmination, and that means that I don't have long to toy with Agent Brady.

I tilt my head up, looking roughly in the direction of the apartment, imagining that I can see the two of them up there.

Surprise, I think, as I work out the details of my oh-so-perfect plan.

And it *will* work.

After all, who doesn't like a surprise?

"**S**hould we take the clue and get out of here?" I ask, feeling antsy.

"If we're safe," Devlin said, "we should stay. At least for a bit. See if we can't figure out this clue and end this thing."

Made sense to me, and so we went to work, pacing through a dusty, abandoned apartment as we tried to figure out an obscure clue. And tried to ignore the creaking and groaning of the resident ghost. (That might be a slight exaggeration, but now that we'd heard the ghost once, every creak of a floorboard caused my pulse to race. The only benefit was that it kept my adrenaline high. If Birdie or Belasco showed up, I'd be out of there like a shot.)

"On display," I said, quoting the clue. "So like on a sign?"

"Probably," Devlin said. "It says it's *beside* the patriot, so that

would make sense. We should probably figure out who the patriot is and work backwards."

"Right. So who's a patriot?"

"A Broadway patriot," Devlin clarified.

"Irving Berlin," Brian suggested.

"Good," Devlin said. "So what would be beside Irving
Berlin?"

"Is there an Irving Berlin Theater?" I asked. "I can't think of
one, but maybe . . ."

Devlin shook his head. "I don't know of one. Not here, anyway."

"Me neither," Brian said.

"A statue," Devlin said. "Surely there's a statue of Irving
Berlin somewhere in this city."

"Right. Right. Sure," I said. "There has to be."

We all looked at each other. Finally, I shrugged and
checked the computer. "Nothing," I said. "I'm not finding
anything."

"Try 'patriotic statue,'" Devlin said. "Actually, try 'patriotic
statue Broadway.'"

I did and—well, what do you know? "You're brilliant," I
said, smiling. Because three hits down on the list was a reference
to George M. Cohan, who wrote a whole slew of patriotic musicals, and has his statute right in the middle of Times Square,
where he can watch over them all.

But that still didn't answer the more important question.
What the hell was the password that was on display beside good
old George?

"Let's go look," Brian said. "Probably something on the
statue plaque, right?"

"I don't know," I said. "I mean, it says 'beside.' The plaque would sort of be underneath George."

"Duffy Square's not too big," Devlin said. "We'll spread out and each walk the area. Hopefully one of us will figure out what the password is."

"And if we don't?" I asked.

"We will," he said, with a firm look in my direction.

I nodded. He was right. We would because we had to.

Brian checked his watch. "It's still early, so hopefully the line at TKTS won't be too long. I'd hate for them to be standing on some brick or something with the clue etched on it."

"Good point," I said. "Maybe we should start at that end of the square and work our way down to George. This might take awhile, after all." TKTS is the discount ticket booth that's set up at one end of Duffy Square, and pretty early in the day, tourists flood the area, all trying to snag cheap seats to a hot show. It's madness, but a controlled-queue madness, and one I've been a part of on more than one occasion. I mean, why pay full price if you don't have to?

I started to pack up the laptop again so we could get out of the theater and head over to the square. I was just about to close the browser and shut the thing down when I had a little flash of inspiration. "You guys," I said, "what if . . ." But I never finished. My fingers were already way ahead of me, and as I'd been talking, I'd typed "TKTS" into the little box on the screen.

My finger paused over the ENTER key, startled by the low drone of the elevator, once again moving the ghost of David Belasco up and down.

"Devlin?" In front of me, Devlin had pulled his gun, had aimed it at the still-closed doors.

"I don't believe in ghosts," he said firmly. "But I do believe in Birdie."

Oh, hell.

My first reaction was to run, but then I remembered. I had the key to ending this whole thing right in front of me. If I was right, we could end this right now.

My finger didn't even wait for me to finish gathering those thoughts. I pushed the ENTER key, and as Devlin kept steady aim on the door, I kept a close watch on the screen. The hourglass whirred and the computer purred. The elevator creaked to a stop. And then, just as the doors started to slide open, the computer beeped and a message appeared.

GAME OVER
THE ASSASSIN'S ASSIGNMENT HAS BEEN TERMINATED
OFFSHORE BANKING INFORMATION FORWARDED
TO YOUR MESSAGE CENTER

CONGRATULATIONS.
AND HAVE A NICE DAY

"It's over!" I shouted. "You bitch, it's over!"

But I didn't trust Birdie to have gotten the message . . . or to comply even if she had. The doors squeaked, Devlin braced himself, and I ducked.

The elevator was empty.

I started to breathe once again.

Behind me, I heard Brian exhale, too.

"She's not here," I said. "God, maybe this place is haunted."

"I don't believe that," Devlin said, his jaw tight, his body tense. He stalked to the elevator, making sure it really was clear, then turned back to me. "Something's going on, Jenn. Why is this elevator moving?"

"It moves by itself all the time," Brian said. "That's why the place has the rep for being haunted. Personally, I think it's a short in the system."

"It's over, anyway," I said. I turned the laptop so he could see. "We won. Birdie's been pulled off. The game's done."

He scowled at the screen, but didn't do anything.

I put my hand on his arm. "Devlin," I said. "It's *over*. She's not here. How would she have even found the place? We tossed the tracking device."

He still didn't look convinced, but after a moment he nodded. "Even so. Let's get the hell out of here. Haunted or not, this place gives me the willies."

I had no argument with that, and I moved to shut down the laptop again.

"Hang on," he said. He nodded at the machine. "May as well check the message center."

I nodded, and we navigated over to the PSW site. Sure enough, there was a message for Devlin, complete with all the information about how to access a Cayman Island account with a balance "in excess of twenty million U.S. dollars." Nice.

We were just about to head over to my message center (I wasn't expecting nearly as big a reward from my role as protector) when another message came in for Devlin.

I stared at the screen, my entire body going cold. "That's got to be from her," I said. My finger hovered over the key. "Should I?"

Devlin nodded, and I clicked. And sure enough . . .

>>http://www.playsurvivewin.com<<

PLAY.SURVIVE.WIN

>>>WELCOME TO REPORTING CENTER<<<

You have one unread message.

New Message:

To: G-Man

From: Birdie

Subject: Playing by the Rules

Congratulations. I just received the news of your success on my PDA, and considering our close, personal relationship, I thought I would personally alleviate any concerns you might have regarding your continued safety.

I play by the rules, Agent Brady.

I had my chance at you during the course of this game, a game at which I'm sorry I failed. I would have liked watching your brains splatter on the wall.

But I keep my commitments. It's a point of honor with me. If you've read my file, as I know you have, you already know that's true.

Just one other thing: You're safe now, because you won the game. But come after me, seek me out, try to find me again so you can put me back in a cage, and it's no longer about the game. Then it becomes personal. And then, I will kill you.

XXOO

Birdie

Chapter
57
DEVLIN

They rode down the elevator in a silence, but this time it wasn't the morose silence of people trying to figure a way out of the mousetrap. This was a happy, contented silence. In fact, beside him, Jenn was doing a little jig.

She caught him looking at her, then reached over and squeezed his hand. "We did it," she said, then pulled herself up onto her tiptoes and kissed him.

He returned the kiss with enthusiasm, then stroked her face. "It's over. For you, anyway. You can concentrate on getting famous."

One eyebrow arched. "For me," she repeated. "You mean that you're—"

"Going after her," he said, but he was watching Brian, not Jenn.

"Fifi," Brian said in a whisper. "Thank you."

"You don't have to thank me. It's what I do," Devlin said. "Or at least I will, as soon as I get my badge and gun back." He shifted as he spoke, feeling the comfortable heft of his clutch piece back at his ankle. Oh yeah, once he had a badge and a gun, he was going to make sure the bitch went down.

"Good," Jenn said simply, and then she kissed him again. "I'll worry, of course. But this time you'll be the one chasing her. And you'll have the FBI to back you up."

"Exactly."

The elevator groaned to a halt and they stepped out, then maneuvered the short distance to the stage. They'd just stepped on and were heading across when Jenn stopped, then turned and stared out into the house. "Wow." She drew in a breath, then started in on "Always Look on the Bright Side of Life" from *Spamalot*, bouncing around the stage as she did until she finally goaded him into joining in the silly song with her. She had a wonderful voice, clean and pure and big. So big it seemed to fill the theater. It sure as hell surrounded him, and as they blew through the last lines of the song, he swung her around, then gathered her in his arms and pulled her close for a kiss.

"Wow," she said as she came up for air. "You've got a great voice to go along with great kissing."

"I would say get a room," Brian said, "but maybe you guys should stay and I should go."

Jenn pulled back and rolled her eyes. "Mind out of the gutter," she said.

"On the contrary," Devlin said. "I think it sounds like a fabulous idea."

She stamped on the stage, the sole of her sneaker making a dull *thwack, thwack*! "Nah. Floor's too hard."

He couldn't stand not touching her, so he pulled her close again. "We'll find someplace with a Serta."

"Just not your apartment. Not until it's fumigated."

"I think I can afford a hotel now. How does the penthouse at the Waldorf sound?"

She made a skeptical face, then nodded. "Yeah, well, if that's the best you can do . . ."

He laughed, then kissed the top of her head. She'd been brightening his world since the first moment she'd pulled open his drapes. "Come on," he said, and they started across the stage once more.

After a few steps, she pulled him to a halt. "Wait. I can't just leave." And then, while Devlin looked at her curiously, she made puppy-dog eyes at Brian.

He shook his head. "Come on, kid. I'll get in trouble."

She dropped to her knees, her hands clasped. "Please? Pleasepleasepleasepleasepleeeeeeeeze?"

Apparently Brian found her as irresistible as Devlin did because he crossed his arms, put on a stern face, but nodded anyway. "Okay. Fine. Let me go turn it on and get the harness." He moved off into the wings, Jenn's delighted squeal echoing behind him.

As Jenn got up and started jumping around the stage making happy noises, Devlin watched, amused. She really was alive on stage, and he wondered how much more energy a full house would pump into her. From what he could tell, so far, she hadn't tried nearly hard enough to get her theater career off the ground. But if she focused, if she really put that wonderful mind to it, he was certain she could manage anything. It was just a question of how she wanted to look at her life.

He moved upstage and leaned against one of the fiberglass trees, watching her from several yards away. At first, Devlin had been clueless about what she'd wanted so much to do here on stage. But as soon as she'd headed for Puck's house, he'd realized. Jenn wanted to fly.

Well, he couldn't fault her for that. Hell, if Brian got the gadget working, he just might take flight up to the catwalk, too. After all, it had been a while since he'd had fun on a stage. The theater used to be his playground. Now it was the streets and courthouses of New York. Big change, that.

A few days ago, he'd been so lost in guilt and grief that he hadn't had the energy to push through the administrative muck and get his badge back. He wanted it now, though. Hell, he needed it. Because how else was he going to take Birdie down?

She may have said that he was off the hook, but she wasn't. Not after killing Fifi. Not after poisoning Jenn.

And, frankly, he didn't believe her claim that she was through with him. Why should she let him go? Birdie wasn't the type to lose gracefully, although he did have to admit that she always played by her own personal code of conduct, her own set of rules. So her declaration that she was playing by the rules now shouldn't surprise him.

Still, something about her message to him bothered Devlin. Not so much in what she said, but in what she didn't say.

He was missing something.

He reached a hand back and stroked his sore neck. Damn, his muscles were tight. He needed a long, hot shower, preferably with Jenn right there with him. An image of them together whipped through his head, and he fought the urge to tell her to screw fun and games with Brian's prop. He had some other fun and games in mind.

But they could spare some time. Now that the game was over and they weren't worried about Birdie finding them, they could lounge in bed for days if they wanted. And he definitely wanted. Wanted to purge this game from his system. Wanted her warm and naked under him. Wanted to forget the horror their lives had been and remember just the good part, the part where they'd found each other.

Most of all, he wanted to forget the depression he'd been in before Jenn had walked through his door. And he *really* wanted to forget that he'd actually slept with Birdie.

The bitch had been bold, he'd have to give her credit for that. She'd had no way of knowing that he'd never seen her. He could have seen pictures from the file, the trial. Hell, he could have watched through one-way glass at various interviews prior to her prosecution so many years ago. He hadn't, of course. But how had Birdie been sure? Or, if she *wasn't* sure, why had she taken the risk? Why get that close? Why needlessly put herself in a position where he might recognize her?

Unless it wasn't needless at all . . .

If she needed to get close to him in order to —

Oh, shit!

He started to lunge down to retrieve his gun, was halted by the cold, controlled voice.

"Don't move another muscle, Ace. Not if you want the girl to live."

He froze. On the stage, just inches away from Brian's bird, Jenn froze too, her eyes wide. Terrified.

"Now stand up, slowly, and put your hands behind your head."

He did as she said, and as he did, Birdie circled around, appearing first in his peripheral vision, leading with her gun. She turned her head just enough to smile at him, then activated the laser sight. A pinpoint of red suddenly stained Jenn's shirt, right above her heart.

Jenn looked at him, her hands above her head in the classic pose of a victim. Her eyes, however, were bold and fearless. *Good girl,* he thought. *Don't let the bitch see she's gotten to you.*

"Now grab your pants leg above the knee and pull up the material. I want to see the gun."

He did as he was told, calculating whether he could grab it and fire. He could, but the odds of Birdie emptying a round into Jenn's chest were too high.

"Little finger. Pull the gun out. Drop it on the floor."

He hesitated, frozen, calculating all his options, and running through all scenarios. All of them bad.

"*Do it!*"

He did.

"Good man. Now kick it aside."

He kicked, anger burning away the raw edges. He was sharp. He was primed. And he was waiting for an opportunity that wasn't there yet.

Bluff and stall. It was the best he could do right then, and it was damn little at that.

"Clever," he said. "The tracking device, I mean. The one you implanted in the back of my neck."

The pinpoint of red never wavered from Jenn's heart. "You knew? I'm so disappointed."

He rubbed at his neck. "I figured it out."

"Well, aren't you the clever one . . ."

He shifted his weight, planning on taking a step forward, but—

"I really wouldn't do that if I were you."

He stopped, dead in his tracks, and wondered if she could hear the beating of his heart. If she could see the hate in his eyes. He cast a quick glance toward Jenn, saw her stony expression and the rapid rise and fall of her chest. She was terrified, but she was holding it together. Playing the stoic victim. The survivor. *Good girl. Stick with that part.*

He wondered where Brian was. Had he encountered Birdie? Had he called for help? There wasn't any way to find out, and Devlin had to assume that no help was coming. It was him and Birdie—and her with a bullet aimed right at Jenn's chest.

"I thought you said you were playing by the rules. The game's over, Birdie. Time to fly away home."

She smiled, slow and thin. "Aren't you witty? But not very bright. *You* were the target in the game. You won fair and square, which means that for the time being at least, you won your life. I meant what I said, though. Come after me and I will kill you."

"I'm not coming after you. I don't even have a badge."

"I know. So sad. Poor you. Killed your partner and now this. Not even able to protect this poor innocent girl." She smiled then, and despite himself, Devlin realized that her already beautiful face now glowed in an almost ethereal manner. Lit from within by the fire of murder.

And any second now, she was going to pull the trigger.

Chapter

58

JENNIFER

It's a miracle that I didn't pee my pants. Terrified doesn't even begin to describe it. I was floating on fear, high on adrenaline, and at the same time totally and completely confident that Devlin would figure something out.

I just wasn't sure how.

And since his gun was about three yards from his foot, and I had a red patch of light aimed at my chest, I figured that now was as good a time as any to be self-sufficient. That oath I'd taken to be proactive? Time to kick that plan into high gear.

But how?

I kept my eyes on Devlin, who had his eyes on Birdie.

"Dammit, Birdie," he said, "just go. We don't have a thing on you. I'll lay odds there's nothing tying you to Brian's death."

She lifted her brows, then looked meaningfully toward the wings. "You mean Cousin Felix's death?"

A wave of nausea crashed over me, and it took every ounce of strength in my body not to scream and run into the wings to search for Brian. Devlin shifted, just long enough for his eyes to meet mine, and I swear I could hear his thoughts: *Don't panic, stay still, somehow we'll get out of this.*

I trembled a little—I couldn't help it—and as I did, I looked up. I was still standing underneath Brian's bird. Underneath, and a tiny bit to the left.

And that's when I had the idea.

A terrible, scary, potentially disastrous idea. But an idea nonetheless.

I turned my head, just slightly, and looked back at the catwalk.

"Look at me, you bitch!"

I looked at her, licked my lips, and prayed I hadn't just shortened my time here on earth. But I had learned what I'd aimed for. The catwalk was as high as I remembered. The angle of ascent was steep, and shifted upstage. If the thing was operational—a big if, since I had no idea if Brian had managed to flip the switch—and if I could grab hold before she managed to kill me, then maybe, just maybe, I could get away. She might expect me to try to dive out of the way, but I doubted she expected me to fly.

She was a smart girl, though. And she'd figure out pretty quickly that I hadn't moved the direction she'd expected. So unless Devlin was clued in to my plan—unless he managed to get to his gun the split second I needed him to—then I was only buying myself a few more moments of a bullet-free lifestyle.

Under the circumstances, I decided it was worth the risk.

Now I just had to hope that Devlin and I had bonded over

these last few days. At least enough so that he could read my mind.

I stared at him, willing him to understand, but he was still trying to talk her down. "I'm the one you have the grudge against," Devlin said.

She had her eyes on me, so he was pretty much talking to the side of her head. I didn't care. My concentration was entirely on Devlin. I kept rolling my eyes kind of backward and up, toward the catwalk. I hoped I looked terrified and spasmodic (to Birdie) and brilliantly cunning (to Devlin).

In my head I was screaming. *I'll jump! You go for the gun! Please, please, please understand me!*

But the trouble with meaningful looks is that they really only seem to work in the movies. I might be casting meaningful looks back toward the catwalk, but Devlin didn't seem to be getting it.

"You want revenge?" he said. "Take me down."

"No!" I screamed. "She's not going to win. She's going to crash and burn and we're going to fly out of here. Not you, Birdie. *Us.* We're the ones who're going to fly away home." As coded messages went, that one was pretty crappy, but considering the stress factor, I figured it wasn't a half-bad improv. And if Devlin caught on, well, then I'd deserve a standing ovation.

"Shut up, you bitch," Birdie said, without even raising her voice. I swear, I think that scared me the most of all.

She turned her head just slightly, giving Devlin a tiny bit more attention. "I'm not going to kill you, Devlin. Not here, anyway. I told you. I play by the rules."

"Birdie," he said, his voice tight. "She's nothing to you."

At that, she shook her head. "Oh no," she said. "As a matter of fact, she's everything to me. And do you want to know why, Agent Devlin Brady?"

He just shook his head.

Her thin smile chilled me. "Because she's important to you," she said, then lifted her gun.

"Jump!" Devlin yelled at the same time.

But I'd already jumped even as he said it, throwing myself backwards and to the side and—thank God—managing to catch the handle hidden in the bird. In the split second it took, I prayed that Brian had turned the power on, because if he hadn't, I was dead.

I heard the sharp crack of a gun exploding, then screamed as I felt a bullet rip through my thigh. I almost slipped, but I hung on, biting my lower lip against the pain in my leg as the device whisked me up and away toward the catwalk, my view of Devlin now blocked by the black drapes that hung in the wings. It was just me and Birdie and the hope that he was there. That he'd gotten his gun. That he'd save me.

I clung to that hope as tightly as I was hanging on to the tailfeathers. But even so, it was a tenuous grip. Birdie was already repositioning her gun, and I saw the red dot bounce over the black drapes. Only milliseconds until that dot found my chest, and I knew there was only one way out. Straight down. I had to let go and fall, probably breaking my legs—or more—in the process. Definitely passing out from the pain. The bullet in my leg already had me woozy, the adrenaline the only thing keeping me conscious. Add another layer, and I'd be out.

The red dot moved. Shaky, then steady. And then there it was. Right on my chest. I loosened my grip. I was out of time.

"Hang on!" Devlin called, and even as his voice cried out,

the crack of a gun echoed through the empty theater, along with a scream that I was pretty sure belonged to me.

I sucked in air and glanced down. The red dot was gone and so was Birdie.

Fear poured out of me, replaced by a wash of relief so powerful it sapped my strength. I couldn't hold on, and I let go, crying out Devlin's name as I fell, bracing myself for the harsh pain of impact, then landing—far too quickly—with a *whompf* as the wind got knocked out of me.

The catwalk. The bird had delivered me to the catwalk.

With a groan, I rolled over onto my side. The world had turned a funny shade of gray, kind of like it was inside-out, and I blinked, trying to make colors come back. Nothing.

Below me, I could make out a gray Devlin blob. He stood over another blob that I assumed was Birdie.

"Jenn, don't move," he was saying. The words crested over me like warm water.

"Okay," I sang. "Okay." I scrunched up my forehead, thinking that there was something important I wanted to ask. Oh yeah. "She's dead, right?"

"She's dead," Devlin confirmed.

And on that happy note, I let the gray take me away.

Epilogue

JENNIFER

When the gray disappeared, I found myself groggy and achy and cast in a slightly greenish light. I moaned and shifted, and felt a tug on my right arm. I looked down, saw an IV stuck in my forearm, and felt a fresh wave of nausea. I hate needles.

I shifted to the left, making a point not to look at the thing stuck in my arm, and was treated to a wonderful view: Devlin, sound asleep in what looked to be the world's most uncomfortable chair. Beside me, a host of monitors hummed and beeped, the green LED display boosting the ambient light that slipped in through a venetian-blind-covered window.

"Devlin," I whispered. "Devlin."

His eyes opened, and the smile that followed warmed me to my toes. "Welcome back, sleeping beauty."

"How long have I been out?"

"About sixteen hours. You had surgery." He nodded toward the end of the bed, and I realized dully that I couldn't feel my leg. I jumped, suddenly alarmed, and Devlin was right there, holding my hand and making reassuring noises. "It's fine. You're fine. You came through great."

"Brian?" I held my breath, fearing the worst.

"He's fine. Even better off than you. She cold-cocked him. He was out by the electrical panel. Mild concussion. They admitted him for observation, but he'll be released in the morning. I'll bring him up to see you."

I swallowed, so relieved I could only smile my thanks.

"Mel's here, too," he said. "And Matthew. She did get special dispensation and busted tail getting here. She's pretty impressed with you."

"Yeah? I'm impressed with me, too. Where is she now?"

"Outside Brian's room, talking with Mark."

"Mark?"

"Agent Bullard. He's on the case. Birdie's dead, but she left a trail. And with any luck, these new leads will pan out, but at least we've got something to work with. We're going to find out who's behind this. And we're going to shut them down."

"We?" I asked, looking at him pointedly.

"I'm not back on active status yet, but I've got my advocate working on pulling together my case. I'm going in tomorrow for a rescheduled admin hearing. If what we're hearing is true, the tide's shifted, and only a few naysayers still think I threw in with Randall."

"So you should get your badge back."

"That's my plan."

"I'm glad," I said, which sounded really inadequate, but was totally heartfelt. "Of course," I added in a teasing voice, "you could just blow off the agency and come back to Broadway."

"Maybe I will. And you can leave the theater and become a

cop. You kicked some pretty serious butt these last few days."

"I think I'll stick with the theater," I said, rubbing my thigh. "Reality's too damn painful."

Devlin squeezed my hand. "Probably a good plan. But I meant what I said. You did great. Better than great, actually. Especially at the end. You and Brian were both brilliant."

"Not exactly what I had in mind for my Broadway debut."

"Then you'll have to work on making your second debut even more spectacular."

"Yeah," I said, fiddling with the sheet.

He stroked my face. "You can do it. And I'll be there in the front row, cheering you on come opening night."

"You will?"

"Absolutely."

I pressed my lips together, wanting to ask the next question, but certain it was way too forward. Was he being polite and encouraging? Or romantic and encouraging. Did he like me? Or did he *like* me?

"By the way, I have a little present for you."

"Yeah?" I tried to push myself up on one elbow, but fell back against the pillows. I was just too tired. "What?"

He reached down and grabbed a large box, topped with a big red bow. He slid it onto the bed next to me, a self-satisfied grin spreading across his face.

I hesitated only a second, then tugged the lid off, squealing with delight when I saw what was nestled among the crumpled-up tissue paper: three pairs of Manolo Blahnik shoes. The three pairs, as a matter of fact, that he'd bought on the spur of the moment during our race down Fifth Avenue.

"Wow," I whispered. "This is so . . . wow."

"You can exchange them if you want a different style or something. We didn't exactly have time to examine all the stock."

"No, no," I said. "These are great." Though, actually, he had a point. I mean, my little aquamarine kitten heels weren't in the box . . .

I frowned then, and almost told him to take the shoes back. That it was too much for me to accept. But then I remembered the obscene amount of money he'd won in the game, and what we'd been through together and . . . well, everything.

It wasn't like charity. Instead, the Manolos were a token of Devlin's affection. And that was something I wanted as close to my heart as possible. And since I love shoes with a passion, I figured these Manolos were about as close to my heart as they could get.

I looked up at him, then, hoping I wasn't reading too much into the gift.

A tiny grin played around his mouth, and the corners of his eyes crinkled with amusement, as if he knew exactly what I was thinking. He leaned in closer, then captured my mouth with his, and kissed me. Not a chaste kiss. Not a get-well kiss. But a kiss with promise.

And Agent Devlin Brady, I already knew, was a man who kept his promises.

I sighed, overcome by the sheer perfection of it all. My Manolos, my man. My life.

And a whole bunch of dreams that, someday, were going to come true.

Up Close and Personal
with the Author

I'm always a little nervous during an interview, but this time, when I sat down to talk with myself about *The Manolo Matrix*, I wasn't nearly as apprehensive. I mean, I'd already interviewed myself for *The Givenchy Code*, and I knew that—despite taking all those journalism classes in high school—I'm really kind of a wimp in the investigative reporting arena. So this new interview would be a piece of cake.

ME: Okay. I'm ready for my interview, Mr. DeMille.

ME: Cocky much? I mean, I tried to do you a favor last time, tossing you some softball questions, and now you're throwing that back in my face?

ME: (holding up hands, figuring softball questions maybe aren't so bad) Hey, hey! I'm not complaining. Coffee?

ME: Thanks. Okay, let's get started. *The Manolo Matrix* is the follow-up to *The Givenchy Code*, right?

ME: Um, you wrote it. Don't you know the answer to that?

ME: (piercing glare)

ME: (clears throat) Yes. *Manolo* is the second book in a trilogy.

ME: Did that make it easier or harder to write?

ME: A little of both, actually. The parameters of the game had been worked out in *Givenchy*, so that part was easier. But the nature of the clues in *Manolo* were actually harder, believe it or not.

ME: What do you mean?

ME: The clues relate to the target. In *Givenchy*, Mel's an expert in codes, so in the context of working out the plot, when there was someplace for the characters to go, I could work backward and create a clue (it wasn't that simple, believe me, but that pretty much sums it up!). For *Manolo*, though, the clues all relate to Broadway shows. So if the characters need to go someplace, I had to come up with a clue that had some Broadway connotation to get them there. It made the parameters tighter, and that made the execution more difficult.

ME: Wow. That sounds really analytical when you put it that way.

ME: It does, doesn't it? Yeah, well, that's me. Miss Analytical Writer. (Not.)

ME: Why Broadway?

ME: Honestly? I love musical theater, and this was an opportunity to work musicals into a book in a fun and different way. Plus, the series is set in New York. How could I do a Manhattan series that never touched on the theater district?

ME: What research did you do?

ME: Lots of reading, and I was also fortunate enough to get a backstage tour of the Broadhurst and the Shubert. I got to walk on the *Spamalot* stage! And the really cool thing was that I'd just seen the show the night before. Very fun! (Unfortunately, because of the nature of clue juggling and my imagination, I wasn't able to work those actual theaters into the story. I used the Belasco instead, which is another cool theater.)

ME: Brian mentions that a cast member had created a website about the Belasco. Is that true?

ME: The cast member part isn't, since the show is a figment of my imagination. But I did find a wonderful website about the Belasco theater created by an actor. Visit my website at www.juliekenner.com and you can link to it!

ME: Speaking of Brian, isn't he a cliché? A gay male friend for the heroine?

ME: Hello?? It's musical theater. 'Nuff said.

ME: So what's up next?

ME: *The Prada Paradox,* coming in 2007! It's the final book of the trilogy and (cue crescendoing music) the ultimate question—who's behind the game—will be answered! I have some great twists and turns planned for *Prada*; I think readers will have a blast!

ME: Great! I think that about sums it up. Thanks for doing this interview!

ME: That's it? You're really gonna have to work on that hard-hitting thing.

ME: Next time, girlfriend. Next time . . .

Never buy off the rack again—buy off the shelf...
the book shelf!

Don't miss any of these fashionable reads from Downtown Press!

Imaginary Men
Anjali Banerjee
If you can't find Mr. Right,
you can always make him up.

2cool2btrue
Simon Brooke
If something's too cool to
be true, it usually is...

Vamped
David Sosnowski
SINGLE MALE VAMPIRE ISO
more than just another
one night stand...

Loaded
Shari Shattuck
She's got it all: Beauty.
Brains. Money.
And a really big gun...

Turning Thirty
Mike Gayle
27...28...29...29...29...
Let the countdown begin.

Just Between Us
Cathy Kelly
The fabulous Miller
girls have it all.
Or do they?

Lust for Life
Adele Parks
Love for sale.
Strings sold separately.

Fashionably Late
Beth Kendrick
Being on time is so
five minutes ago.

Great storytelling just got a new address.

DOWNTOWN PRESS
A Division of Simon & Schuster
A VIACOM COMPANY

Available wherever books are sold or at www.downtownpress.com

13459

Good girls go to heaven...

Naughty Girls go Downtown.